D1737944

The Well

A Mystery/Thriller

Book One of the
Arizona Thriller Trilogy

Sharon Sterling

This is a work of fiction. Names, characters and incidents either are the product of the author's imagination or are used fictitiously. Any resemblance to actual persons living or dead is entirely coincidental.

Acknowledgement

To members of the Native American tribes and their sacred sites that are mentioned herein, I sincerely hope I have conveyed my deep respect and appreciation for you, your culture and your traditions.

Chapter 1

The second he walked in she was going to kill him. He would be an easy target, standing backlit in the wide-open doors of the garage. When he pulled the filthy string of a single overhead light bulb he would be a silhouette like a paper target on a shooting range. She was a good enough shot from this distance to put a hole in his heart.

The snub-nosed 32-caliber pistol felt solid, cool against her jeans-clad thigh. She placed her hand over it, rubbed its smooth metallic skin then picked it up and with arms straight she sighted down the barrel and mentally rehearsed it again. He usually came home around seven or eight o'clock but she could wait, here in the dark at the back wall where he couldn't see her but she could see him.

The wood-frame garage stood fifteen feet square, the doorway made of two five foot wide panels that swung outward on rusty hinges. The dirt floor where she sat had been smoothed and hardened by time, tires and oil. The exterior was decorated by a few remaining streaks of weathered white paint. In here the planks were grey and rotted at the bottom. They gave a little against her back. The garage had been built in the 1950's for the boat-like cars with fins typical of that era. It was deep enough for his bullet-shaped 1978 Datsun 280-Z, and bare of anything except the tool cabinet that served as her hiding place.

The minutes ticked by slowly, filaments of time she spun in silence. An hour passed with no sound of life, save for the far-away bark of a dog, the whispered scurry of a rodent and the hushed susurration of her own breath.

Suddenly, as if through someone else's eyes, she saw herself crouched in this dirty place with only spiders and field mice for company, waiting for a dirty man to come and die. With an inward shrinking the word *coward* came to her. No. She was no coward. It had taken every courageous fiber of her body and every cell of mind to dare the thought of killing a man she had believed was invulnerable. Only days before, the truth had crashed in followed by a wave of hatred. The man's only true shield was an invisible crust of evil.

But was this the justice she craved? Should the final minutes of his accursed life pass so easily? It would be like squashing a cockroach rather than delivering a fitting end to a man she loathed for *his* cowardice, the least of his flaws.

She put the gun down on the dirt floor. Hugging her legs toward her, she lowered her forehead to her knees. *No,* she thought. *It should be more...fair, more...fitting. But how?*

Out of the dank silence an idea materialized, penetrated her mind, coalesced there. *A better way...a much better way.* She rose to leave, picking up the gun and reminding herself to clean and oil it before she gave it back.

***

Psychotherapist Alexandra Davis, better known as Allie, opened her office door and looked down the corridor toward the waiting room for a glimpse of her new client. The girl sat in profile, staring at the wall. She cradled her left hand in her right and the left wrist was wrapped in bloody gauze and a Halloween trick or treat bag.

Allie drew a deep breath and retreated to stand motionless in her doorway. Doctor VanDeusen, the psychiatrist who had referred the woman, hinted that accepting this client would be more a favor to him than to Allie. Now she understood why.

She pushed away the image of the orange and black bag wrapped around its pathetic, bloody 'treat', and asked herself, *What else did I see?*

The woman's slender figure draped in dark sweat pants and a shapeless t-shirt, long, wispy brown hair falling like a veil around a thin, pale face. The woman sat as if in a trance, motionless on the edge of the waiting room chair.

The client was fifteen minutes early for her appointment but Allie's instincts told her she couldn't let this client wait. She strode down the corridor then slowed to compose herself before she entered the waiting room. She stepped in front of the girl.

"Hello, you must be Crystal," she said, smiling.

The girl nodded but didn't get up.

"I'm Allie Davis. Pleased to meet you Crystal. Um…I won't offer you my hand because I see you have a problem there."

No reply.

"Is that something that needs to be seen to right away?"

The girl shrugged.

"May I look?"

The girl obediently held out her arm, removed the wrapping and revealed a blue veined wrist scored by thin, red marks that appeared clean and dry. Finally she spoke. "I did it this morning, after I saw Doctor VanDeusen. Then I poured peroxide on it. I don't think it needs stitches or anything." She re-wrapped her wrist.

3

"Well, I'm glad you took care of yourself, Crystal. Are you ready to talk now?" The girl nodded. "My office is down this way," Allie said, and indicated the east corridor. Her client obediently got up to follow her.

In the small, ten-office professional building the receptionist's area was located strategically against the back wall of the waiting room, directly across from the frosted glass entry doors. The opaque doors provided privacy for clients while admitting natural light. The receptionist had a full view of the entire waiting room from her desk, as well as the entry to the east and west corridors. Swinging half doors in a low wall on either side of her cubby gave it a semblance of definition and privacy.

Wanda, the receptionist, was a heavy set woman in her fifties who had dyed her close-cropped hair a defiant black. Allie never saw Wanda smile, not even at clients who might desperately need reassurance. Now she crossed her arms over her ample chest and inspected Allie and the client as they walked by. Her glance went meaningfully to the girl's wrist then to Allie. She shook her head and rolled her eyes upward in a clear expression of contempt.

Allie's teeth clenched but she said nothing. Instead, she touched Crystal's shoulder lightly to guide her down the hall.

Crystal stopped just over the threshold of the office. "Where do you want me to sit?"

"Where ever you feel most comfortable." She indicated both the chair and sofa. Crystal chose the chair. She, lowered herself slowly and sat rigidly upright on the edge of the cushion.

Allie opted to sit in her desk chair, directly across from Crystal, rather than take a more casual positioning on the sofa. With this client she would not ignore the so called elephant in the room by beginning

4

the session as she usually did, with friendly platitudes about the weather.

"I'm glad you came in today, Crystal. You must have been pretty upset to hurt yourself like that. Is that something you do often?"

Tears began to well in Crystal's eyes. She blinked, obviously willing them back.

"Can you tell me what happened?"

"Do I have to talk about it?"

"In here, Crystal, you don't have to do anything you don't want to do." Crystal nodded and curved her colorless lips in a polite smile.

Allie continued, "Eventually you will want to talk about it because that's the way I'll be able to help you."

Crystal nodded. A new client orientation should come next but Allie was aware that her client was in no condition to process detailed information, so she related, as briefly as she could, the confidentiality rules and conditions of therapy that would guide the sessions.

Crystal finally eased back a little into the seat. Allie said, "Doctor VanDeusen sent me a little information about you this morning but I haven't had a chance to look at it. Would you mind if I glance at it? Then we can talk some more?"

"Okay."

Allie reached for her reading glasses with impatience. Her "over forties" pigeonholed her by age, but more important, they were simply a nuisance. She had never before had to wear glasses. Now she told herself, *it is what it is. Get over it.* In less than a minute she skimmed the first page of Doctor VanDeusen's notes, the outline for a complete psychiatric assessment The demographic section said said Crystal was thirty-two years old, rather than Allie's guess of early twenties. She was married, had two young children and described herself as a stay-at-home mom.

Doctor VanDeusen had scribbled 'histrionic' and 'borderline' in the diagnosis block on his assessment, and underlined in the margin, 'uncommunicative'. The first two words were provisional diagnoses that Allie took with a grain of salt but she couldn't argue with 'uncommunicative' A client who wouldn't talk did present a special challenge.

When she looked up Crystal was nervously twisting a strand of lank brown hair as she stared at the floor. Allie hesitated. The woman's fragile emotional state made her wary of asking the usual first appointment questions but she had to begin somewhere.

"Why don't you tell me more about your children?" she suggested.

Crystal shrugged.

"What are their names? How old are they?"

"Well, Kaylee is four and Toby just turned two."

Allie leaned forward to hear the soft, mumbled, replies.

"They call it the terrible twos, but he's still precious."

Allie said, "They are adorable at that age but they can be a handful, can't they? Kaylee and Toby. Cute names. Are they much alike?"

"Different as cactus from roses. For Halloween, Kaylee is going as a princess. Toby...my neighbor--she has kids--gave me an adorable pumpkin costume for him, but he won't wear it. I'm just going to paint his face like a cat, and pin on a tail, you know?"

As she talked about her daughter and son Crystal's face gradually softened and at last she smiled, revealing a chipped upper front tooth and crooked lower teeth.

Allie knew it was a mouth innocent of orthodontics and may have lacked even basic dentistry. She was relieved to see no signs of rampant decay because a client with a mouth full of rotted teeth would have raised the possibility of amphetamine dependence. The drug known as crystal meth had arrived in the area as a fad more than three decades ago but had soon become a staple in the drug culture, the drug of choice for many in the area. Lately its use was challenged by a new demon, heroin.

Crystal talked about her daughter's pre-school. She took pictures from her wallet to show Allie. Now the session was going well.

Allie took the photos and saw two round-faced, smiling children. They looked robust and happy, in contrast to their wan and fragile mother. Allie waited for the opportunity to ask Crystal about her husband, speculating that an issue with the husband or maybe even a boyfriend might have provoked Crystal's emotional storm.

"So, Crystal, what happened before you got so upset you cut yourself? Did you have an argument with your husband--maybe your mother?"

"My husband and I almost never argue and I get along fine with my mom. She lives in Maine. We don't talk on the phone very often. Occasionally we e-mail."

"How about other relationships, then? You know, what you tell me in here is completely confidential, other than the few exceptions I mentioned earlier."

Crystal shook her head with a thoughtful look. Her negative answer came out more as a question. Who else could she have relationship problems with?

Her client's innocent unknowing indicated to Allie that there was no boyfriend to complicate Crystal's life or add another level of complexity to future counseling sessions. She drew a deep breath. "We're going to have to stop soon, Crystal. Do you feel comfortable enough with me to come back next week?"

Crystal smiled and nodded.

"I've asked you a lot of questions today. Is there anything I should have asked but didn't, or anything else you want to ask me, or tell me?"

"No."

"Okay, then." Allie entered the date and time of their next appointment in both the computer and her spiral-bound appointment book then filled out an appointment card which she handed to her client. But the session wasn't over yet.

"Before you go, Crystal, I'd like to go over a few things you might do if you get real stressed again, instead of hurting yourself."

Crystal's eyebrows lowered and she reached for a strand of hair. Allie noted the flicker of defensiveness. She said, "Reaching out might seem like the last thing you want to do, but you did it today, and now that you've taken the first step, I have confidence that you can do it again if you need to." She handed Crystal a card printed with the telephone number for the local crisis line. Crystal stared at the card and made no comment.

"One thing I've learned about you today, Crystal, is that you love your husband and your children. You seem to be an honest person. I get the idea you prefer to be silent rather than say something you don't mean or something that's not true."

Crystal nodded again.

"Now I want you to promise me that you love your family enough to stick around for them, even if that means you'll face and talk about some painful memories. Will you do that?"

Her client looked up and met Allie's eyes with confidence. "Okay."

Allie smiled at her. "Good." She noted that in the last fifteen minutes of the session, Crystal's posture and facial expression had undergone a subtle transformation. The young woman now sat back in her chair and looked directly at Allie when she spoke. The compulsive hair twisting had ceased and her brow was smooth. Allie watched while Crystal absentmindedly unwound the plastic bag and gauze from her wrist, wadded them up and stuffed them in her purse.

A surge of relief came over Allie. She felt the muscles in her stomach loosen, her shoulders drop in relaxation. She said, "If nothing you try seems to work and you still feel like physical pain is the only recourse, hold a piece of ice in your hand until you feel better."

"A piece of ice? " Then Crystal smiled again as she understood the concept of mild pain without injury. "Okay."

Allie's gut told her the client meant it. Crystal would be all right, at least for the near future. Allie walked down the hall with her to see her out the front door.

Back in her office, she sank into the easy chair, exhausted by the intense focus she had exerted in the past hour. She had learned a lot about Crystal, but not enough. She needed to know the root of the woman's distress so she could do more than supply her with a few coping techniques. She picked up the telephone to call Doctor Ralph VanDeusen, the local psychiatrist who had referred Crystal.

He answered and said, "I'm guessing you called to tell me how it went with little Crystal Navin,"

"Yes, I have her signed permission for us to talk."

"Just like you to dot the i's and cross the t's. You're a veritable slave to the Privacy Act."

Allie skipped over his reference to the federal confidentiality law. "You know, she cut herself today, between the time she saw you and when she got to me."

He laughed. "What's one more borderline for your budding practice?"

Allie said, "I'm not so sure she does have borderline personality disorder."

"So if that's not her problem, what do you get? Is she using?"

It was a fair question, even in this small rural town. Illegal drugs had spread north from Phoenix and east from Las Vegas and other urban areas like a contagious disease, creeping over the Mogollon Rim into Cottonwood and the whole Verde Valley to add another misery to the common scourge of rural poverty.

"I don't think she's using. She says not. She's certainly depressed and very anxious. She said the cutting was a first time thing for her. She gave me a verbal contract not to do it again between now and our next appointment. I told her it's a bad habit she doesn't have to fall into. She seemed to understand that."

"Good!"

"I'm concerned about two issues. One is that she may need to be on an antidepressant or anxiety medication. The other is that although she gave me a pretty good personal history and she seems straightforward, she wouldn't tell me what triggered the crisis."

Doctor VanDeusen's voice sounded relaxed. His answer conveyed the same casual attitude. "She gave me the gist of it. It seems she started to feel anxious when an uncle she hadn't seen in years came back to town and she saw him on the street. She couldn't--or wouldn't--tell me why she hates the man. Or maybe she's afraid of him. She said she started to think about suicide after she saw him. That scared her enough to bring her in to see me."

"I did the suicide scale with her and she scored very low."

"Most women with young children don't suicide. I think you know that."

"Don't be so certain of what I know, Doctor V. You might think to look at me that I've been at this work for twenty years, but I'm still a newbie. Of course Crystal doesn't fit the profile for suicide. Maybe this uncle of hers is an abuser of some sort. She has that learned helplessness look, the victim affect, doesn't she?"

"I questioned her about a history of sexual or physical abuse but she said her husband would never lay a hand on her and she doesn't remember much from her childhood. I told her abuse victims often think of suicide but they're thinking of killing the wrong person."

Allie's head jerked back. *Killing the wrong....? Oh!* "She seems like a gentle person to me, Doctor V. She doesn't seem capable of violence."

"Don't be misled by first impressions. She came across like an angel with me too, initially. When I offered to put her on an antidepressant she refused. When I pressed the point a little, she got agitated. I couldn't calm her down. She started to yell."

"I can't imagine her yelling."

"You do have a lot to learn." His voice changed as he imitated the client in a whiney falsetto. "She said, 'What, you just want to throw the bitch a pill and shut her up? I won't shut up!' She looked like a harpy. I thought she was going to come across the coffee table at me. Don't underestimate her, Allie."

"It did occur to me that I might have to Title Thirty-Six her some day for danger-to-self, but I didn't think we'd ever have to consider danger-to-others."

"Think about it. We not only have to protect our own reputations, our licenses, our assets, we have to worry about every celebrity, politician, or abuser that a motivated and deranged patient might harm."

Allie remembered, aside from senseless terrorist slaughters, an assassination attempt in Tucson and other killings that had made the national news years ago. She said, "Like the Congresswoman, the school and theater killings."

"Right. And since she won't take medications there's no use in her coming back to see me. She's all yours."

Allie couldn't say she felt gratitude that Doctor V had gifted her with this client but she was determined to be polite. "It will be a challenge but I do appreciate the referral, Doctor V."

Next, Allie glanced at her notes, placed them in a folder with other new-client paperwork and locked it in her desk drawer. *Out of sight but probably not out of mind*, she told herself, and wondered if this would be another keep-me-awake-until-all-hours case.

She leaned back and looked around her office. During moments of doubt, it gave her a reassuring sense of her own professionalism and competence. In addition to her desk and task chair, the office was furnished with a sofa and easy chair upholstered in muted tones of grey and peach that coordinated with the charcoal grey rug.

Between the sofa and chair an end table held a candy dish filled with hard candies and a box of tissues within easy reach. Another candy dish on her desk held a collection of small sea shells and tumbled stones in a variety of colors, shapes and markings. She gave these small tokens to clients as transitional objects when she had to be away from the office, when clients had to miss consecutive appointments, or when they just needed some tangible symbol of her caring between sessions.

The office walls held her framed Master's Degree from Tulane University in the place of honor directly above her desk, flanked by the Arizona Board of Behavioral Health Examiner's license on the right and her under-graduate diploma on the left.

Allie hardly noticed them any more. When she did they neither boosted her confidence nor inflated her ego. They were there for the benefit and reassurance of her clients. They validated her, authorized her to ask the questions, "What brings you here today…how well do you sleep at night…what about your relationship with your mother…what are these tears for…are you having thoughts of harming someone else…how dangerous are you to yourself?"

They were mundane questions, impertinent questions, intimate questions. The answers often shocked or surprised her. Following colleagues' advice, she had placed the sofa and chair at the far end of the office where they wouldn't block her speedy exit through the door if a client attacked or threatened her.

On her first day as a tenant here, the office manager had told her that in case she ever felt threatened by a client and needed help, she should call the receptionist to ask for a cup of coffee. That was the receptionist's signal to send help, preferably in the form of someone large and muscle-bound, followed by a call to nine-one-one. In the three years Allie had done this demanding work she had been lucky. None of her clients had ever threatened or tried to hurt her.

Now she considered the framed drawing on the far wall over the sofa and wondered if she should take it down. The exquisitely detailed, realistic pencil sketch depicted a Navajo girl in buckskin skirt and cotton blouse who held a bowl containing small ears of corn.

Recently a client had looked at it in surprise and asked Allie why she had a drawing of an elf in her office. Curious, Allie asked two other clients what they thought of the figure. One thought it must be a Hindu goddess and inquired if Allie herself was Hindu. The other client believed it depicted a homeless old woman. Intrigued, Allie asked coworkers and colleagues, none of whom had any trouble identifying the drawing as that of a pre-adolescent Native American girl.

Such is the power of projection, she thought. As with one of those Rorschach ink blot tests, people fill in gaps of detail from their imaginations, from deep wells of emotions, associations, images and ideas. Ideas from their unconscious minds, if she wanted to psychologize about it.

She glanced at the clock. Almost time for her next appointment. The next client, like Crystal, was new to Allie. She was intrigued that the woman was a member of the nearby Yavapai-Apache Indian tribe. Allie was proud of her own one-eighth Cherokee blood, although she had no feeling of belonging to that tribe or any detailed knowledge of her heredity.

In fact, Allie had what one colleague called 'a fixation' about Native Americans. It may have started in grad school when she watched a video about the Hopi Tribe, whose young women wore their hair in two wing like arrangements on the sides of their faces, meant as a likeness to butterflies. The Navajos' intense appreciation of beauty expressed in their poetic chants and songs resonated with her as well. She told herself if she wasn't careful she could become an Indian groupie.

The first glimpse of her next client, Kim Altaha, almost stunned her. *Graceful, powerful!* she thought. Kim was obviously not burdened with the internalized shame afflicting some Indians as a result of centuries of White prejudice.

Kim carried herself with the dignity of a beauty queen. She stood almost six feet tall, with slender limbs, long, silky black hair, and a lovely face. Her forehead was high and broad, her jaw line square. Her high bridged nose was strong rather than beaked or prominent. Her dark eyes were large and deep set. She wore little or no makeup and had dressed simply in a white blouse and knee length cotton skirt that set off her smooth, sun burnished skin.

Walking down the hall with her client, Allie thought that here was the beautiful Indian princess pictured in paint-on-velvet and described in lurid western novels. Beauty like this had inspired foolish romantic dreams and steamy sexual fantasies in both men and women since the days of Columbus himself, from Pilgrim John Smith to the kid down the block reading a graphic novel. She reminded herself sternly to contain her awe. *None of that counter-transference. No hero worship.*

When they reached the office Kim appeared composed and confident as she took a seat on the sofa and waited for Allie to speak. Allie hesitated for only a second before she began the session as she usually did, with small talk, pleasantries, then an orientation to counseling. Finally she got down to business.

"What brings you here today, Kim?"

"I'm here because I got arrested."

"Oh, are you court ordered for treatment?"

"My sentencing isn't until November fifteen, but I figure I'll be ordered for anger management counseling, so here I am. The judge might be satisfied that I'm here on my own and let it go at that. I don't want to go to jail, and I'd rather do individual than group."

"You were involved in a fight or an argument? With your husband?"

"Not married. It was my neighbors who were fighting. The jerk was beating her up. I went over and helped him stop."

"Helped him stop?"

"I beat the crap out of him."

Allie could picture this obviously healthy and fit young woman flattening a male opponent who would be no match for a goddess incarnate. She was careful not to show her amusement. Instead, she moved easily to history taking, an integral part of every first session. She learned that Kim was single, lived alone in a small house in the nearby town of Camp Verde and worked at a hardware store. She had no history of arrest or mental health treatment.

Allie wondered, *is she really here to change things about herself, or just to avoid going to jail? And why me? There are therapists closer to where she lives. For that matter, why doesn't she get counseling through the Tribe? She could probably get it for free instead of using her employee insurance. With me she has a copay.*

She said, "Kim, I'm glad you came today, and I hope I'll be able to help you although I really don't know how much effect I can have on your legal problems."

"That's fine. I'll take my chances." Kim looked away from Allie, then reached over and selected one of the hard candies from the dish on the end table. After she unwrapped it and tucked it into her cheek, she said, as if she had read Allie's mind, "The reason I didn't get counseling in Camp Verde or through the Tribe is because it's a small town and a small tribe. Everyone knows everyone else's business. They don't need to know any more of mine."

"I can understand that. I'm curious about the woman you helped, your neighbor. Are you and she very close? I guess I'm wondering what prompted you to take such decisive action."

"I'm an instrument of Karma."

Momentarily speechless, Allie leaned back in her chair.

Kim's face hardened. "What? You think Apaches don't know about karma? We're all just ignorant savages to you?"

"No, of course not! I would never...I respect... . It's just that I've never heard anyone say that before." She silently told herself to regroup. "So if you believe in karma, don't you believe that we're all instruments of karma as well as recipients of karma?"

"Maybe. But some of us have more of a...duty, I guess you'd call it, a direction." Allie remained silent.

"I don't know how to explain it but sometimes I have an urge to do something that's more than an urge, it's a mandate. I know it's the right thing to do even if it's against the law--White law or Indian law. That's what I call karma."

Allie nodded. "Of course. But now it's gotten you in trouble. I'm curious. Do these urges or mandates come in the form of voices talking to you?"

Kim's chin tilted upward, the line of her mouth hardening. "I don't hear voices. I'm not crazy."

"I wasn't suggesting you're crazy, or psychotic as we call it. People who are psychotic seldom question their unreal ideas or beliefs. They think they're sane and the rest of the world is crazy. From what you've said to me so far, it sounds like you're well grounded in reality."

"Then you know what I'm talking about, knowing you have to do something even though it doesn't make sense to other people?"

"Most therapists understand there are things in this world that can't be explained by psychology *or* science and that aren't crazy. An inner guidance, inner knowing, is one of them."

Kim tilted her head to the side, as if to question. "Sometimes I feel like I'm the only one who gets these…instructions. How can I explain it to people?"

"Do you have to explain it to anyone, if you're sure it's right?"

Kim put her hand to her cheek and stared into space, appearing to ponder the question.

Allie didn't interrupt her train of thought. She wondered if she should speak about herself at this point. She asked herself the therapist's duty question, *If I self disclose now, is it truly for her benefit, or for some benefit of my own*?

Finally she said, "I'm going to share a personal story with you, which I don't often do with clients." She searched Kim's face for a sense that Kim felt comfortable enough to hear personal information about her therapist.

Reassured, she continued. "During my last month of grad school in New Orleans I came down with a killer virus that put me in bed for a few days. Unfortunately it gave me time to wonder where I would end up when I finally owned my Master's degree. I had never planned to stay in Louisiana, but other than that, I just hadn't planned.

"The second day in bed was horrible. Fever, misery and worry. Toward afternoon I drifted off to sleep when a voice, like my own inner voice, said, 'Up and over the Mogollon Rim'. That's all, just that one phrase, not like a command so much as encouragement. It sounded so clear it woke me up, but since I had no idea what or where the Mogollon Rim was, I wondered about it for a few minutes, then went back to sleep."

Kim said, "But you must not have forgotten it. Isn't that why you came to Cottonwood?"

"Not consciously, anyway. I thought about the--the dream, I guess you could call it, a few times but I didn't know the Mogollon Rim was in Arizona. After I got here I saw the name on maps and in magazines but I didn't recognize it until I heard someone say it. Then I remembered. The word is pronounced so differently--'Mo-gee-on,'--from the way it's spelled. I only recognized it by the sound, not by the written word."

"Hum."

Allie shrugged, ready to refocus attention on Kim. "Anyway, Kim, I appreciate the trust in me you showed by telling me about yourself. I want you to know you're not alone. Lots of people who see therapists struggle with some hard to understand experiences. People can have a spiritual crisis just as they can have an emotional crisis. In your situation, it's healthy to question yourself about those mandates or instructions you get. Check it out with me or someone else you trust. It's called 'reality testing'. We all need to do it now and then."

At the end of the session Kim stood then paused in the doorway. Looking at the framed drawing on the wall she said, "I like your picture of the Navajo girl. Did you do that?"

Allie managed a calm reply that didn't convey her surprise. "It was done by a talented artist up in Flagstaff."

***

She left the office after five o'clock. The sun was settling behind Mingus Mountain, shedding a golden afterglow across the valley. She drove south on Main Street past Cottonwood Kids Park, and turned west onto Highway 89A, known locally as Cottonwood

Street here. On its northern stretch its name changed to Main Street. If she had continued on past the intersection she would have been headed east-northeast, toward Sedona. Of course she couldn't afford to live in Sedona, she thought, somewhat wistfully. She had found an apartment less than a mile away on a quiet side street.

As she drove she noticed again and loved the fact that the local streets honored their western identity with names like Mesquite Drive, Ocotillo Circle, and occasional wild cards like Marauder Road and Dancing Apache Lane.

Gradually her focus turned back toward the day's events. When Kim came to mind, the uneasiness inside her defied her own analysis. She felt a real mental connection with Kim. She also felt that Kim was not trusting yet. There was much Kim did not want to share with her.

Then, thoughts of Crystal, sweet, pale, mommy Crystal, with a trick or treat bag around her bloody wrist. Allie didn't know if she felt more compassion or more anxiety about this client. Would she be able to help the troubled woman before she really hurt herself--or someone else?

She glanced out of her side window toward the sun-bathed mountain top nearby and shook off her preoccupation. *Be here now,* she told herself, a mantra from Gestalt therapy.

The air flowing against her skin from the open car window felt just a few degrees below balmy, thin and bracing like mountain air, for heaven's sake, while Halloween was approaching and November was just around the corner. Back East it would be cold, if not freezing, by now.

When new in the Valley, she had made it her goal to explore the area in any weather, so every weekend she visited a nearby town or tourist attraction and on Sundays she hiked with a local group led by a wiry, deeply tanned and apparently indomitable woman in her seventies.

Cottonwood, in the Verde Valley, is on the southwestern edge of the Colorado Plateau, not far from the escarpment called the Mogollon Rim. The Rim, like a scar across the midsection of the state, extends two hundred miles from western Arizona almost to the border with New Mexico. Thousands of square acres around it are considered 'Rim Country'. but the Rim itself is a distinct feature that appears as an extended two thousand foot cliff marking an abrupt change in elevation from six thousand feet to four thousand feet.

Cottonwood is just one of three towns in the Verde Valley with a population of over ten thousand. The others are Sedona and Camp Verde. Although 'Verde' means 'green' in Spanish, Allie thought it was a misnomer. Viewed from a higher elevation, only a narrow strip of green appeared in the valley, along a meandering north-to-south trail cut by the Verde River. Stands of the water-loving cottonwood trees that gave the town its name marked the river's path.

So many sights in Arizona were unique, she thought. On one sight seeing trip, she was startled to see the western character of the little town of Jerome suddenly morph into a glimpse of Tuscany, with villas capped by orange tile roofs set on sloping hillsides with long, winding access roads gracefully demarked by dark green spires of Italian cypress.

By far, her favorite places were Montezuma Castle and Montezuma Well. She especially loved the Well. Like the locals, Allie understood that shade and water were luxuries here and they drew her as other luxuries couldn't.

Almost home, she drove past the blackened frame of a house set in a plot of scorched weeds. She thought, *they need to tear that down and build again.* She was glad the Verde Valley had escaped the ravages of immense wild fires that had devastated the eastern portion of the Rim not long ago. She sighed and squinted against the last rays of the sun reflected off her untinted windshield.

A quote about Arizona that she had read during an especially cold and dreary Long Island winter came to her. 'Arizona is where summer spends the winter and Hell spends the summer'.

Even unscarred by fire, the natural beauty of this area was sometimes hard to appreciate. In the searing days of summer the unrelenting sun in a vast expanse of blue overhead redefined for her the word *sky.*

A person could feel smaller, lonelier and more vulnerable out here under its immensity. At times she felt she had been opened up by the openness of the land and sky, and didn't quite know how to behave or what to do with herself. It was an environment and a way of life foreign to her, a native of Long Island, the area sometimes called 'New York City's parking lot'.

She wondered what had possessed her to come here. She certainly couldn't remember the labyrinth of thoughts, conversations, electronic paths and actions that had led her to this particular place rather than one of a dozen other places. *Maybe it was fated,* she thought. *Maybe I'm an instrument of karma and just don't know yet how it will play out.*

Chapter 2

She had the day off from her job at the hardware store but it would be a mistake to try to kill him now. It was too soon. The plans weren't finalized. She needed to focus on the details, the process, and not on *him*. When she thought about *him*, an image of a different horror from her childhood emerged, a neighbor boy hunkered in the dirt, his back an avid arch as he struck matches and with them burned insects alive. The look of savage glee on his face when he glanced up at her, trying to draw her in, was burned in her memory. "See," he said, "see how fun it is?"

Sickened, she had turned and walked away. Now she willed herself to mentally walk away from the man she planned to kill, instead, to consider every eventuality, reduce every risk. She pulled a bag down from the top shelf in her hallway closet and began to gather her supplies.

The rope and new roll of duct tape came from her utility drawer. She would dispose of the packaging and any unused remains in a construction site dumpster instead of bringing them home. That way they could never be matched as hers. She would take the little 32-caliber pistol, just in case. It couldn't be traced to her either, because the serial number had already been filed off when it was bought on the street in Phoenix. Now it lay sandwiched in a padded sleeve, tucked at the bottom of a spacious black gun bag, a Wal-Mart find from several years ago.

She loved Wally-World but Wally-World had security cameras. Smaller stores or even the local Wal-Mart were too risky, too close to home. In spite of security cameras, she decided the one in Flagstaff would be the best place to get the black clothing and other things she might need.

When she disguised herself it suddenly felt like fun, in the spirit of Halloween. She tucked her hair into a black baseball cap, pulled on jeans and a plaid cotton shirt, then tried darkening her chin and upper lip with black chalk to mimic a five-o-clock shadow. Her reflection in the mirror made her laugh. It might fool the camera but a too-close appraisal by the cashier or another shopper would give her away. That would attract attention she wanted to avoid.

She flattened her breasts with a tight sports bra and donned a pair of work boots, beat up and too large. She had scavenged them from a thrift shop and at first try on she thought they were a mistake but she practiced walking in them until she did it without tripping. Thus disguised, and unusually tall for a woman, she made a passable man.

Well after dark she left, grateful Wal-Mart provided a twenty-four hour venue. The stretch of highway between here and Flagstaff was a well paved, well lit, two lanes in each direction with some downslopes but overall an inexorable uphill climb of four thousand feet.

On the road, the usual phalanx of semis resolutely labored upward, outnumbered by cute little cars piloted by college students, probably on their way back to Northern Arizona University in Flagstaff. Their cars and small pickups darted in and out between the trucks and her vehicle at reckless, speeds. The young drivers obviously believed they were immortal.

Darkness and solitude invited her to feel a sense of companionship with them, the anonymous camaraderie of travelers on any road anywhere. She wondered if the truckers were tired, if they had far to go. She wondered if the college students were hung over on their way back from a weekend of diversion or dissipation in Phoenix or Tucson.

She knew it was only idle speculation that lacked emotional connection. Because she had enveloped herself in a cloak of secrecy she wasn't able to see them any more than they could see her; she couldn't get inside them. She felt her difference from them as total alienation, as if she and they were different species who shared nothing but miles of road unravelling into emptiness.

So deep was her sense of detachment that she didn't notice when she entered the ponderosa pine forest with its energizing scent borne on crisp, cold air. Usually she breathed it deeply, with zest.

Fifteen minutes later the terrain leveled out. When she neared Flagstaff the highway crossed a main artery of East/West travel, I-40. The darkness of conifer forests abruptly gave way to bright lights and traffic. Alert and wary again, she threaded the congested streets, entered the parking lot of the Wal-Mart store and looked for a spot that was dark but not isolated.

The parking lot and the store were never empty but tonight was a slow shopping night, sans crowds. She felt unnoticed and safe when she got out and walked toward the store but when the automatic doors anticipated her approach and opened, her imagination provided a security camera picture of herself. A moment of panic threatened to overwhelm. She shook off the feeling that knowing eyes watched and instead concentrated on the pretense that she was just like anyone else out for an evening of low end shopping.

The cart she selected wobbled a bit. Not wanting to draw attention by replacing it, she headed for the department at the back of the store. She had to remind herself to slow down, look casual by stopping to examine some clothing, a few house wares, and islands along the aisles heaped with Halloween candy.

Her circuitous route finally ended in the right department. It took just a few minutes to find what she needed without the interference of a single clerk. The checkout went quickly, this time of evening.

Back in her car and on the road, she coasted most of the way down the mountains, relief and anticipation raising her spirits. Dawn had not yet brightened the eastern horizon when she arrived home, a deliberate timeline calculated to avoid the curious eyes of neighbors. Mission accomplished, no speed bumps.

Finding and buying the stun gun proved more of a problem. It would be too risky to buy it in person. These days you could buy anything on the computer but she knew that meant you also left a cyber trail.

She drove the short distance to Prescott, to the beautiful new library on the side of a hill. She found a spot at the end of the row of computers reserved for patrons, strategically located at the back of the room.

The web site she found was impressive. The 'self-defense' company had a Better Business Bureau rating of A+. They were listed with Dun & Bradstreet. They accepted all major credit cards and Pay Pal. They had just what she wanted.

Now, how to pay for it, provide the e-mail address they required and get it shipped to her but not to her own address? In other words, how to keep her anonymity? She created a new e-mail address on the library computer, then rented a mail box at the friendly Mail Boxes Special just down the highway.

She knew those steps would be a waste of time and money if she couldn't solve the payment and shipping issues, but somehow she knew it would work out. Work out it did, a week later with the help of an elderly aunt, for whom she often did errands and shopping.

Auntie was afflicted with both diabetes and arthritis. She seldom left her house except for infrequent visits to the doctor, with a friend or relative driving.

Aunt Iva's house was as old as Auntie, but she managed to keep the interior, with its 1950's furniture and hardwood floors, clean and neat. A few male relatives helped tend the small front yard. When Auntie telephoned for shopping help this time, she wanted some moderate ticket items from the Target store in Cottonwood.

She must have been watching from the window as her young helper mounted the wooden steps. Not waiting for a knock, she made her way to the door with wide placed steps and a rolling gait, as if she walked on the deck of a wave-tossed ship, her painful progress the result of degenerated hip joints. She carried her purse in her arms. It was a once colorful but now ancient bag reminiscent of home made pot holders, woven from thin ropes of stretchable yarn.

In the open doorway, the old woman accepted a kiss on the cheek then withdrew a list and credit card from her purse with fingers shaken by a fine tremor. She handed over the card and list with a smile that said, "I trust you completely; I have confidence in you."

At Target the would-be murderer shopped for items Auntie wanted, with special attention to a toaster oven that approximated the cost of the stun gun she had selected from the web site. She mentally calculated the price of the stun gun plus shipping. Not exact. She added the price of one of the gun's optional accessories. Better. The cost of the toaster oven matched the price of her items within pennies. At the checkout counter, she kept the toaster oven in her cart while she paid for the other items with Auntie's credit card. Then she paid for it in a separate transaction, with her own cash.

A hurried trip back to Prescott to place the order on line with Auntie's credit card completed this part of the plan. She doubted the old woman would notice the discrepancy on the receipt or the credit card statement but if she did, she would reassure her that she hadn't lost any money from the silly computer error, it was just a comical glitch in inventory data that listed a toaster oven as a stun gun.

It had been a challenge. Now all the supplies were in the gun bag, safely stowed in her car. They included a long handled pitch fork with three curved prongs and a rubberized handle grip. It wasn't made for what she had in mind, but it would do. Now she had to wait for the right time. Soon. She hoped it would be soon. She could picture it clearly.

With a start she recognized her eagerness and sternly told herself that it was not something she wanted to do; it was a thing that she *needed* to do. Then why did a thrill of anticipation course through her to ride up her spine in slivers of ice? And why did it subside into a warm tingle between her legs?

***

Allie arrived at the apartment complex but before she drove into her covered parking space she stopped at the bank of metal letter boxes near the office. She slid out of the car seat, found the small key on her key ring and inserted it in the little mail box door with her apartment number. She reached inside, thinking, *Surprise me, will you?*

No surprise. She let out an exasperated groan at the envelope from The Department of Education, her nemesis. She had told friends that her chief goal in life now was to pay off her college loans before she retired or died of old age. *Oh, well, the price of a good education and the price of being my own person again.*

The other envelope bore the familiar handwriting of her ex-husband. After almost twenty years she had escaped the marriage with the last of her dwindling self confidence and the only material possessions she valued, a few sticks of antique furniture for the sentiments they embodied and an aging, deteriorating but valiant Subaru for freedom of mobility.

She had left the marriage and the last of a succession of office jobs to return to college for the education needed to do what she somehow knew she was meant to do, counseling. This was the career she was destined for since the age of sixteen, although she hadn't known it at the time.

That summer she had gone to the library as usual, but not as usual, had lugged home just one book. It was a heavy tome with tissue thin pages filled with tiny print. *The Complete Works of Sigmund Freud.* She had waded through it with frequent helps from the dictionary.

All around her, other teens were working on their tans, getting a job or getting pregnant. She began to wonder if perhaps she wasn't normal. When her interests came to include astrology and mythology her self doubt increased. It didn't help that her best friend confused her yoga practice with that new milk product, yogurt. When Allie wondered out loud if there was anything to numerology, her friend accused her of flirting with witchcraft. Allie decided she certainly wasn't a witch and probably wasn't normal but she was okay with that.

The radically changed life style she was now living wasn't typical or perhaps even normal, and it hadn't come easily. Her first steps, fraught with economic, mental and emotional danger, were as tentative as those of a tightrope walker on a wire above the Grand Canyon. It took all the courage and persistence she could muster to sit in classrooms with students young enough to be her children.

She remembered one classmate not long out of her teens who told her, "When I'm your age, I hope I'm just like you. You don't say much but when you do it's important and it's smart."

Allie wasn't sure whether to consider this a 'when I grow up' or a 'when I get old' comparison but she felt touched and took it as a compliment. Since then she had come to realize that her quiet nature was a personal asset and silence could be a valuable tool for a therapist, who couldn't listen and understand while talking.

Looking at the mail in her hands she hesitated over the note from Paul. She knew from his text message yesterday that the super storm ravaging the East coast had left his house–what had been their house– untouched. He was safe. Her intuition said this note would be another plea for her to come back, to come 'home'.

She didn't open it. Slowly, without emotion, she tore it in half and dropped it in the nearby trash can. It slipped down and out of sight, settling amid empty Coke cans and heaps of junk mail. Paul and the marriage were years ago and thousands of miles behind her.

When she entered the apartment she reminded herself to be happy it was new and fresh, although very small, less than four hundred square feet.
Management had decorated it in neutral colors. 'Earth tones' they called it. *Ha,* she thought. *I see plenty of earth tones every time I step out my door.* On Long Island most of the ground had long ago been paved

over, built on, carpeted by grass, or was covered with planted or native shrubs. The common view in most neighborhoods was limited to the neighbor's house or a highway.

In the Verde Valley, Nature's palette consisted of shades of grey and brown splashed across vast expanses of bare dirt and rock, relieved only here and there by patches or threads of dusty green. The blotchy pattern on the hillsides reminded her of camouflage fabric.

She had whimsically wondered what these mountains and valleys hid from. Perhaps the sky itself. The vast landscape of nearby hills, distant mountains and towering rock formations was encompassed by a vault of blue sky where sometimes clouds lowered enough to dampen her outstretched fingertips.

Allie had enlivened her apartment when she hung colorful prints on the beige walls and inserted touches of blue, yellow and green with sofa cushions and plants. That helped but there was nothing she could do about the brown carpet except keep it clean. The tiny bedroom appeared a little brighter with a spread in vivid pinks, purples and blues that matched a valance over the single window.

Closing the door behind her, she hung her car keys on a hook, dropped her purse on a side table and went into the bedroom to take off her shoes. She planned to change into lightweight exercise clothes and go for her usual power walk. Instead she plopped down on the bed, realizing she felt drained.

It was the usual routine, the usual places, the different clients with the same problems, the iron bond of debt, the enervating pull of a love she no longer shared and the barrenness of a life alone. The thoughts invaded her mind leaving her overwhelmed, empty.

She began to take stock of her life, something she hadn't done often in the past years because they were years dominated by the exigency to survive and achieve.

Long ago, within a year of marriage, she and Paul had produced Brian, the beautiful, perfect baby who had blessed her life. Grown now, he lived in Boston, working on a degree in electrical engineering. She loved him dearly but this distance, this physical and emotional separation from him gave her no distress. It was healthy.

She picked up the stuffed rabbit that he had cherished as a toddler. When she had packed to move out of their house she discovered it in the attic and brought it with her to this new place, a talisman of love and family happiness. Now it again held the place of honor on a bed. Without conscious intent, she had begun a morning ritual. On days when she had time, she amused herself by posing it on the pillows with its floppy ears and limbs in an expressive arrangement to match her mood.

Still seated with her feet on the floor, she let her upper body fall back on the bed. She thought of Paul and as the memories returned she stretched her arms above her head then allowed her relaxing muscles to recall another body next to her in bed, the warmth of touching, cuddling, and the deliciousness of sweaty, energetic coupling.

Hum, she thought, *if that's my problem, I can always have sex with Bob.* Their friendship of almost a year hadn't progressed to the 'benefits' stage yet and she felt comfortable with the status quo. Bob had let her know that he wanted more but so far he hadn't pressured her. Bob was handsome, very handsome, with tanned skin, dark hair, golden brown eyes, a dazzling smile and a nicely muscled body kept in shape by his construction job. He was smart and sweet and there was no reason she shouldn't want him fiercely, but she just didn't. She wondered what subtle biological or psychological force was missing. Hormone deficiency? Was she getting that old?

What is it that I want? I have what I thought I wanted. I'm free and independent. My life is a great adventure out here in the West. I love my work, even though I sometimes wish I could live up on Second Mesa and counsel the Hopi.

But that really was a fantasy. She knew this empty yearning couldn't be filled by work featuring a different set of clients. The one-way intimacy that any good therapist rigidly structured in counseling would apply to any and all clients, even the Hopi.

Now her life was dominated by those relationships of one-way intimacy. That explained it. Those professional relationships lacked a free, mutual exchange of thoughts and feelings; they lacked the zest of unlimited possibilities, they lacked a multitude of intriguing unknowns but most of all they lacked warmth and passion.

The image of Paul's letter slipping down into oblivion came to her with a twinge of doubt. *What did I throw away? Is the counseling really satisfying enough to replace that?*

Then, *Second guessing myself again. I thought this was over, resolved, done!* This was just like her. In college, when she took tests she often went back over an exam and changed right answers into wrong ones.

She brought her feet up onto the bed and rolled over on her side, idly examining the small array of books atop her dresser. They were sandwiched between two rabbit-shaped book ends. *If I were a Hopi, I would be in the Rabbit Clan, or maybe the Star Clan.* The thought brought an immediate inward rebuttal. *Not that I could choose, of course. It's not like pledging a sorority. You're born into a clan. I would have to take what I got.*

Then the *I Ching* caught and held her attention. She considered it, hesitated, then surrendered to the impulse. She gathered a pen, three coins, a notebook and her worn copy of the book. She sat on the floor with her back against the bed and began to mentally formulate her question. It couldn't be "Will I ever get married again?" or even "Will I ever get laid again?" Years ago, a friend had introduced her to this book as a way to gain insight into personal issues. She quickly learned that it was pronounced 'E-Ching' rather than 'I-Ching'.

While others might consider it a system of divination or fortune telling, over the years she had learned that to use it with such 'yes-or-no' or 'will-I-ever' questions yielded confusion and frustration instead of answers. Asking for elucidation, counsel or insight proved more in keeping with the esoteric, philosophical nature of the ancient work.

She had read that Confucius, the very personification of ancient Eastern wisdom, had consulted the *I Ching* when in crisis. She was even more impressed by a forward to the book by a famed psychiatrist. He advised Western minds to overcome their science-blinded world view to accept the validity of the *I Ching*. Somehow that reassured her and endorsed her interest in the time honored guide for wise and correct behavior.

At last she wrote down, *"How should I conduct myself and what should I expect regarding a love life?"* As she wrote she recalled she had asked this question before, perhaps more than once, but she couldn't remember the answer. Or maybe she just hadn't been satisfied with the answer.

She would throw the coins six times to create a diagram of six lines, beginning at the bottom and working toward the top. Her first throw showed two tails and a head. The next throws gave a mixture of solid lines and changing lines. The changing lines would reveal specific details about the question.

The name of this hexagram, number two out of the sixty-four that comprised the book, was 'The Passive Principle'. She began to read and skimmed some parts that were very abstract or didn't seem to apply. Phrases about relationships between men and women were more understandable.

In part, the text read, 'The superior man...' (she had penciled in 'wo' to make it 'woman' and long ago ceased to notice the sexist bias of the text) '...If the superior man wants to lead, he fails; but if he follows, he finds help'.

Next, she read the additional messages given by the two changing lines, which referred to a mare, and being passive. She smiled. *How strange, being compared to a female horse.* Parts of this ancient tome could only be described as inscrutable but it seemed to say that she, the receptive and superior woman should do nothing, and let her prince come to her. She was too old for fairy tales, she thought, but her mood brightened.

She drew the second hexagram. This was hexagram number four. She turned to the page and saw, 'Youthful Folly. The young fool seeks answers. Only once will I inform him. If he asks two or three times, he is revealing his importunity.' Further down the page an explanation of the text clarified, in no uncertain terms, '...the text gives one answer only and refuses to be challenged by questions suggesting doubt'.

The testy accusation made her laugh out loud. Yes, she had asked this question before. The oracle was scolding her for asking it again. Still smiling, she put the book away and went for her walk.

***

Halloween brought just a few children to her door, decked out in the same kind of super hero, pumpkin, and princess costumes the smaller children everywhere wore, along with older kids sporting bloody masks and other gruesome details.

Their numbers were far less than the hordes she had enjoyed back East. She was left with bags of candy that she knew she would consume, followed by massive guilt, unless she took them to work to share with her coworkers and clients.

The staff's gathering place at the office served many purposes. It was kitchen/break room/mail room/copy room in one. Located directly behind the reception area, it was accessible to both the east and west wings through two doors at right and left, with glass double doors at the rear that led to a small, walled patio. Since the building lacked a conference room or group therapy room, the therapists came here to discuss cases.

Ralph VanDeusen's wife, Sherry, was a counselor who had an office in the building. He would on occasion present a case in the conference room for her and the other counselors. He was here in the break room today, sitting at the big kitchen table of pine wood, his legs crossed, sipping coffee from a huge mug that bore a crest and the name VanDeusen in gold script.

The psychiatrist was a tall, lanky man whose clothes looked too big for him, although they were in good taste and of good quality. Today he wore dress slacks, a long-sleeved, blue shirt and a tweed sports jacket. Bony wrists poked from his sleeves and the hands attached had long, thin fingers.

Doctor VanDeusen wore his salt and pepper hair short. His face was partly hidden by a beard and moustache, also greying. One of the therapists had joked it must be his Freud disguise.

Allie thought his face lacked the refinement obvious in photos of Doctor Sigmund Freud. Some quality about Ralph's sharp and uneven features prevented a description of attractive. He might claim distinguished except for a slight inward cast of his left eye. At times it was barely noticeable. He had a way of minimizing the defect by turning his head so he never seemed to look at a person straight-on.

Allie greeted him, collected her mail, made a copy of some handouts she wanted to give Crystal, then poured her own cup of coffee and sat down at the table.

"How are you, Doctor V? Your wife tells me you're flying back to Ohio for Thanksgiving."

"Yes, Sherry's family is there. It will be nice for her but I'm not looking forward to the nasty weather. How about you?"

"Probably stay here, do some sightseeing." She briefly pondered Ralph VanDeusen. His practice of psychiatry was limited to prescribing and managing his patients' regimen of psychoactive medications. Like most other psychiatrists, he had priced himself out of competition for counseling. That left psychotherapy to professional counselors and psychiatric social workers like Allie. For a fee, Doctor V had begun to provide licensing supervision for several therapists who worked in the building.

Among her peers, Allie had gained quite a reputation for her insights and ability to diagnose and problem solve difficult cases. She believed it was her intuition which enabled her to identify many core issues that bedeviled her clients, rather than expertise in psychology.

Dr. V intruded on her thoughts. "So how are you doing with our little borderline, Crystal?"

"Oh, she's a little slow to open up, but I think we're going to be able to work together."

Doctor V shook his head. "Better you than me."

It made Allie wonder again whether, in spite of all his psychiatric training, Doctor V understood women at all. He was especially judgmental of those with borderline personality disorder. It was a malady that rendered clients incapable of regulating their intense and sometimes extreme emotions. As a result, they struggled with relationships. Every aspect of their lives was disrupted.

The term 'borderline' signified that clients with the diagnosis were so compromised by emotional extremes they were at times on the edge of actual psychosis. The latest research indicated this particular mental illness might be a kind of posttraumatic stress disorder caused by severe physical or sexual abuse in early childhood. Doctor V didn't know or didn't care.

Allie remembered his comment about his experiences as a staff psychiatrist in a private psychiatric hospital. "I could always tell the borderlines. When they walked down the unit in their jammies and came into my office clutching their teddy bears, I knew I had another borderline on my hands."

Allie thought about it now and mentally corrected him. *Not a borderline, Doctor V, a person who suffers, with the emphasis on suffers, from borderline personality disorder.*

Wanda, the receptionist, came in for her morning break and joined them at the table. She didn't speak and Allie was glad. The woman had a way of saying or doing precisely the wrong thing at the wrong time. She turned when the door popped open as if from a sudden gust of wind.

"Oh my God I had a night!" Heidi Alarcon talked to no one or anyone within listening distance as she entered. Heidi was a young intern working toward her license in counseling. Sherry VanDeusen was her supervisor for licensure.

Heidi had a few individual therapy clients and also worked for the agency that provided mental health services to people in crisis. For the agency, she put in five nights and two weekends per month and was on call during the week. She had to sandwich her appointments here at the office between her other duties.

Heidi pressed a few keys on her android phone before she sat down at the table. Allie looked at the younger woman's face, marveling at her firm, smooth complexion. It fairly glowed, her cheeks lit by the vivid pink flush characteristic of plump, energetic, fair-skinned. She looked like an excited child to Allie, who found her youth and enthusiasm endearing. Allie lifted her coffee cup at Heidi with a question on her face.

"No, I can't drink coffee any more," Heidi said. "Not since I started crisis work at the agency. I'm now addicted to kava-kava, l-tryptophan and anything else that's legal and helps calm my nerves. Last night I had to do a Title Thirty-Six *and* a *Tarasoff!*"

Doctor V smiled. "Proud of yourself?"

"Not really," Heidi shot back. "It was not fun and it kicked my butt. I'm exhausted!" She pushed her blond hair back from her face with both hands and smiled, as if to indicate she was stressed but certainly not defeated by the challenges of crisis work.

Title Thirty-Six refers to the Arizona law that permits involuntary evaluation and commitment of anyone deemed to be a danger to self or others. Additional provisions in the law allow the same seventy-two hour commitment of someone who is 'gravely disabled' or 'persistently and acutely disabled' by a treatable mental illness.

The latter criteria are narrower and less obvious, therefore less frequently used by mental health professionals, than the 'danger' definitions. These assessments are often done in a medical hospital, where the patient is first tested for drug use or other signs of medically induced mental deterioration.

Doctor V asked, "How did the hospital staff treat you?"

"Not bad."

"You're lucky," he said, and leaned back in his chair to stretch his long arms toward the ceiling. "They don't always welcome the attempted suicides or other 'crazies'. Look at it from their perspective. They spend all their time and energy trying to preserve and prolong life. Why would they want to waste that effort on someone who doesn't want to live?"

"I guess I can understand that, but I also go there sometimes to evaluate clients for *Tarasoff*. You'd think they'd be happy to cooperate in preventing violence. Less trauma for them to treat later. So many of the mass shootings, even the shooting of President Reagan, were done by deranged souls."

'Tarasoff' refers to *Tarasoff v. Regents of the University of California*, a precedent-setting legal case from the 1990's, still upheld nationwide. It mandates professionals to warn an intended victim of violence by a client of theirs if they believed the threat is immediate and real.

That caveat, 'imminent and real,' creates an ethical and practical dilemma that demands a judgment call. A wrong decision might cost a crisis worker her license, her career and all the worldly possessions a lawsuit could wring from her.

Doctor V lowered his chin and looked up sideways at Heidi, "Let me guess. The Title Thirty-Six was for a borderline."

"She does have that diagnosis. She took a bunch of pills in a suicide attempt then changed her mind and called nine-one-one. She couldn't convince me that she wouldn't do it again tomorrow, and she was very depressed because she broke up with her boyfriend. She needed to get back on her antidepressants, the sooner the better. The psych hospital was the best option, the safest option."

"I'm not questioning your clinical judgment," Doctor V told her. "The final decision isn't yours anyway. The crisis agency psychiatrist has the final say, and the final liability, I might add. What was the *Tarasoff* about?"

"Some people reported their neighbor was ranting and raving and acting strange. They were afraid of him. They did a petition for involuntary evaluation. He seemed pretty squirrelly, all right. When I went to talk to him he said he was inspired by mass shootings. He wanted to make it clear he was not a terrorist, but he said so many people who didn't deserve to be alive were ruining things for him. Then he went on to describe how he would like to kill them."

"Well, I guess that was a slam-dunk," said Allie. The need to hospitalize the man was clear and unmistakable. By this time, Heidi had her full attention as well as that of Wanda.

"I'm not sure he could do it, as disorganized and psychotic as he was, but 'c-y-a' is my motto."

"It's a pity that has to be a factor, but you're right," said Allie.

"Sometimes it's damned if you do and damned if you don't," added Doctor V "They can hail you as a hero one day and sue the pants off you the next for the same decision."

Allie nodded and sipped her coffee. "The client who loves you today may hate you tomorrow, and in both cases, for actions that are clinically necessary."

Heidi said, "Yeah. But I've been in trouble more than once in situations that *look* like a slam-dunk but aren't. Have I told you about my beach client?" She hesitated a second before she continued.

"The client was from San Diego and she was really, really homesick. She cried every time I saw her. She told me she loved the beach. It was the only place that made her feel calm and relaxed. So I suggested she would feel less anxious if she made her apartment more like the beach. She loved the suggestion, and she just loved me. It was going so well. Then she came in one day mad as hell at me. Her landlord threatened to evict her. She said it was all my fault. Turns out, he came into her apartment to do some routine maintenance and found she had dumped two inches of sand all over the living room floor."

Heidi jumped when a buzzing sound interrupted their laughter. She reached for her phone, which had been on vibrate.

"Great startle response," Doctor V said. "A clear case of what we used to call pager anxiety."

Heidi looked at her message. "For sure," she agreed, without looking up. Then, her mind still on clients, "You're right, Allie, they either love you or hate you and it has absolutely nothing to do with how good you are at your job." Her voice had risen in volume and her face looked tense. Allie recognized the signs of an anxious attempt to gear herself up for another crisis call. The text message had been a summons from the crisis agency.

Heidi stood up and hooked the phone on her belt. "Oh, before I go," she said, "I have to tell you about one of my first crisis evals last spring." She drew a deep breath. "She was just sixteen years old, and her mother called the crisis line because the girl wouldn't eat or drink; she was distraught for some reason.

"When I went out to see her, I got that she wasn't suicidal, she was just very upset because she wanted to go to the prom and they had no money for a dress.

"You know how these kids go ape-shit about the prom. She didn't want to tell her mother what had her so upset for fear she'd make her mom feel bad. I talked to the girl for a long time about self esteem, valuing herself for what she is instead of what she wears. I told her in the long run, clothes don't make the man--the woman--she knew what I meant. I thought everything was fine. A few weeks later her mom called to tell me the girl showed up at the prom stark naked and got arrested."

Allie and Doctor V laughed. Even Wanda looked amused.

Doctor V said, "They're supposed to warn you in school to beware of unintended consequences."

"Evidently I'm the queen of unintended consequences," Heidi said.

"I might contest you for that title," Allie told her.

Heidi exited the room as abruptly as she had arrived, smiling at Allie over her shoulder.

Doctor V drained the last of his coffee and looked at the clock. "I thought Sherry would have an hour free to talk about our vacation plans, but I guess she got stuck with a client. What's on your agenda for the day, Allie?"

"I'm seeing both Crystal and my anger management client later today. But not back to back. They live in the same general area and I think they might know each other, so I don't want them to run into each other at the office."

"Ah, our little borderline, Crystal," said Doctor V, with a tilt of his head and a snide smile.

Wanda turned to Allie, "Have you noticed that whenever Doctor V talks about a borderline he goes cross eyed?"

Stunned by the woman's rudeness, Allie blurted, "Wanda, he always looks like that."

In the same instant she silently screamed at herself, *That did not come out right!*

She turned to him. "Doctor V, I didn't mean...". He stopped her with that tell-it-to-the-hand gesture. She searched his face, expecting to read hurt or anger. Instead, the psychiatrist met Allie's eyes with a look of appraisal, an intense expression that culminated in an almost imperceptible nod of self assurance. Without a word he got up and left the table.

Wanda also went back to work, leaving Allie alone in the room, trying to regain her composure. *What just happened here?* She hadn't meant to insult him but her gut told her he had felt disrespected. Now she wasn't sure where she stood with him. She had to respect the man, but sometimes he was such a jerk. If he was angry there might be no more referrals. She could accept that, no problem. It was being at odds with people that disturbed her.

***

Crystal appeared to shrink into herself when she rounded her shoulders and squeezed her knees together. "I think it happened. I mean, I know it did, but I don't remember it actually happening."

"How is that?" Allie asked.

"I remember playing with one of my friends, a little girl named Mary-Kay. We were on the sidewalk in front of her house. We wrote on it with chalk. We drew hop-scotch squares. We drew in some numbers. I don't think we wrote 'home'. We didn't know how, so. I think we were probably four or maybe five years old." She stopped and took a deep breath, avoiding Allie's eyes. She reached for her hair, twirled a lock round and round between thumb and forefinger, again and again. Her head drooped and her eyes fixed on the blue skirt draped over her knees. Her gaze relaxed, softened, lost focus.

Allie knew she had momentarily lost Crystal, who was experiencing a drifting sensation that would take her into a misty state of no thought, no feeling, no memory, into what Crystal felt was safety. Allie kept her voice neutral in tone as she inserted it into the forming void, "You remember that very well."

Crystal's head jerked erect and she stared at the wall in back of Allie's face. "We were just playing like kids do. It was in the spring time. It was warm and cool at the same time. We were sitting on the sidewalk in the sunshine. Then I remember I said to her, 'I was in bed with my uncle, and he was doing nice things to me and I was doing nice things to him'."

She stopped, motionless, lifeless but for the almost imperceptible rise and fall of her chest. Silence hung in the stale office air for long seconds before she continued. "Then, maybe the next day or a few days later, I went over to play with Mary-Kay again.

"Her mother came to the door and asked me to come in the house. She had never done that before. I don't remember what it looked like inside. I don't remember how her mother looked. I felt like I was in trouble with her, like something was wrong, but I didn't know what. When I was inside she sat down and started to brush Mary-Kay's hair. Mary-Kay had beautiful blond hair. Then her mother said, 'Mary-Kay told me what you said about being in bed with your uncle. Is that true?'."

"What did you say?"

"Nothing."

"You didn't answer?"

"I couldn't answer, like I was paralyzed. Then she said, 'Nice little girls don't say things like that about their uncles. I don't want you playing with Mary-Kay any more'."

The outraged comment Allie wanted to make went unsaid. She was incensed at the woman's lack of empathy and understanding but it was the client's feelings that mattered, not her own. She asked, "What did you do then?"

"I guess I just stood there like a statue. Then she said, 'Don't come over here any more, understand? You can't play with Mary-Kay any more'. Then she just got up and went over and opened the front door for me."

Allie wanted to curse but instead she said, "That really hurt you, didn't it?"

"Mostly I felt scared, because I told. I told after he warned me not to tell!" Her voice rose to half a decibel below a scream. "He told me not to. He told me about the bad things he'd do if I told."

"What bad things?"

Crystal's face drooped, emptied of emotion. She whispered, "I don't remember." She slumped back in her chair.

"It's all right that you don't remember," Allie said. "If you need to remember, and when you're ready to remember, you will. Until then, just do all the things we've talked about to take care of yourself, okay?"

"Yeah."

"Crystal, this uncle--is that the man you saw a few weeks ago? Before you came to see Doctor VanDeusen and me?"

Crystal nodded.

"Have you seen him since then?"

"No."

"Can you stay away from him? You don't have to see him, do you?"

"No."

"Good. If he did molest you, we'll have a lot to talk about."

Crystal's head jerked up. "Like what?"

"Whether to report him or not; whether to press charges or not. The statute of limitations against sexual abusers in this state is two years from the time a person first learns about or remembers the abuse, so we'll have time." Crystal's eyes widened but she didn't speak.

Allie sensed her mistake. *Damn, why did I bring this up now? It just spook her more.* Anyway, don't worry about that. Don't think about it, just do what you've been doing, and I'll see you next week. If you need me before then, you have my number here at the office and my message number, right?"

"Right."

"Are you all right, Crystal?"

"Yes."

When she had gone, Allie went back to the office but rather than sit to complete paperwork, she began to pace the small open area of her office, thinking about the uncle who had betrayed her client. With sexual abuse, she knew it wasn't always the act itself that did so much damage, unless it involved a brutal, physical attack.

The damage often went straight to the survivor's sense of safety. It cast doubt on her trust in herself , trust in others, in the world in general. It could impact her ability to know and speak the truth. The demand for agreement to a blatantly untrue statement was confusing at best and crazy making at worst, statements like, "That doesn't hurt, that feels good. That's what all kids do with their uncles, ...fathers, ...brothers, ...neighbors...".

Allie felt the blood rise to her face in a rush of anger fueled adrenalin. The lies, the secrecy, the shame! Early on during her internship and therapy practice she had refused to work with offenders. She wanted nothing to do with them because her ability to feel empathy or compassion had its limits. Pedophiles were far outside the boundary of her compassion. If the truth were known, she wanted them all dead.

***

The client slept and dreamt. In her dream, she trudged a wind-swept desert. Thirsty, exhausted, she lay down on her back, spread-eagle in the sand to rest. She gazed up to see the sky lowering. pressing her down.

She floated above herself and saw her own body rise up and walk away. It left a perfect imprint of head, arms, buttocks and legs in the sand, a sand angel.

Wind came up, carrying streams of sand that flowed like water over the surface of the dunes, drifted over the impression of her body, blurred it, filled it, leaving no evidence that she had been there.

Then she was on her feet again. The landscape had changed to farm land in heartland America. She saw a house in the distance, pastures, and in front of her, an old fashioned well. The circular housing of mortared stones rose as high as her waist. Wooden four by four beams on either side supported a low peaked roof and a shaft to crank by hand, around which coiled a rope with a bucket attached.

She began to turn the handle to lower the bucket. When she looked down she saw a face in the water, a man's face. His mouth opened to shout for help. She saw the red mouth and white teeth but she couldn't hear him. Suddenly she herself was in the well. She tried to shout, cry for help, but no sound emerged from her throat. Again and again her mouth strained to emit the shriek echoing in her brain, but she was mute. She couldn't make a sound. She woke in anguish.

Chapter 3

The shadows in the hollows were charcoal dark while the shoulders of the frosted earth were ghostly pale. The new moon, low on the dark horizon, was a silver blade poised to cut its way upward through the blue-black fabric of the sky.

His house sat on a ridge in the sterile landscape of rocky, hard-pan earth dotted with low creosote bushes, desert broom and prickly pear cactus. Its roof was a dark smudge against the sky, its frame all but invisible. She knew the garage squatted beside and slightly below the house, backed into the hill. Distant lights from the highway to the north were the lone signs of life.

She had chosen this day for a dark phase of the moon. She arrived unseen in the early evening and found a place to crouch in a shallow declivity between the trunk of a scraggly mesquite tree and a large boulder, where she could watch his comings and goings. She needed to make sure there was no one else in the house to witness what she would do, no victim of his that she might unintentionally victimize even more.

When he left an hour later, she guessed he was headed to town to get his mail from the packaging store or maybe buy take out food from one of the dozens of fast food restaurants that littered the exit from the highway.

As soon as his car was out of sight she unfolded her body from the hiding place and hurried to the front door. She knocked. No answer. The handle didn't turn. He had locked the door. She went around to her right where on this side of the house the un-curtained window gave her a view of a kitchen table, chairs and a refrigerator. No sign of movement. Continuing around to the rear of the house she saw a small window that had been left open a few inches. It was set too high to look into.

One by one, she tore three large, flat rocks from the dry earth. By stacking them she built a wobbly platform under the window. She balanced precariously, pried out the screen with her pocket knife and let the screen fall to the ground. She pocketed the knife then lifted the window with both hands.

She stood on her tiptoes, managed to part the curtains and saw a bedroom that contained little else but a bed covered by limp and dingy sheets. Grasping the sill with her gloved hands she heaved herself up, levering first with her knees and then her feet against the siding. She pivoted her body and tried to straddle the window in order to lower herself down but lost her balance and crashed to the floor.

She lay on her bruised shoulder and hip holding her breath to listen. No sound in response to the racket she had made.

When the pain subsided she scrambled to her feet and looked around the dimly lit bedroom. The furniture had the raw, unfinished look that decorators of cheap motels described as rustic. The walls were bare except for one framed print that featured a pair of hand tooled, yellow leather cowboy boots. She edged a little closer to the bed to search the print for some detail that might reveal a meaning, but discerned none.

She turned back to look at the other piece of furniture, a dresser that held an old television set, the screen grey with dust. She opened the top drawer beneath it to see three rows of old boxed cassette videos. 'The Magnificent Seven, True Grit, High Noon,

The Good the Bad and the Ugly'. They were all there, every Western genre film she had ever heard of and others with unfamiliar titles. Where were the horror films, the slashers?

She went to the closet door and feeling both frightened and foolish, held her breath as she opened it. No one tied up in there, nothing but clothes hanging from the wooden rod, a shelf that held several cowboy hats and on the floor, shoes and boots. A glance into the bathroom revealed the toilet seat upright, marked by yellow stains. That was enough.

She turned and walked through the other door into the hallway. The house had been cheaply constructed with a shotgun floor plan, named for the narrow hallway that bisected the house from front door to back wall.

From the front entrance, the kitchen and dining areas were to the right, the living room to the left and the two bedrooms at the rear, with the bathroom between them. Like most houses in this rocky, upper desert area, it had no attic or basement. She reminded herself she had to finish and get out of here before he came back.

The living room held a few more pieces of roughhewn furniture, the sofa upholstered in a cheap Southwest fabric picturing horses. Above the sofa, the head of a dead deer gazed into eternity with glass eyes. The television here was a newer flat screen. The row of DVDs beneath it held what she expected. horror and slasher films in every category and sub-category from vampire to zombie flicks.

She turned, went to open the end table and there she saw it, the gun she remembered so vividly, the cold blue Ruger. She stared at it, fighting the memories. Then it occurred to her that it might be a problem later. Should she take it? No, she couldn't bring herself to touch it. His essence was here in the house. It infected every object down to the molecules of the air, but this gun embodied him.

When she had checked every room, rifled through drawers and closets, peered under the bed and the sofa, she went back to the hallway, assaulted by new questions. This house wasn't the show place a typical real estate agent would want to own. It was rumored he had made a lot of money from his early days in real estate sales, but this house flatly denied affluence. She thought that its sole asset must be that it sat on several acres of land, isolated from its neighbors.

So, where did his money go? Did he spend it on his perversion? Trips to the Middle- and Far-East, where she had heard that child victimization was a despicable shadow industry?

There were no actual victims here, but what about virtual victims? She hadn't seen a computer or any scrap of hard copy child porn. Then she spotted his smart phone hiding in plain sight on the seat of the sofa. She picked it up, then put it down again to pull off her thin, transparent gloves. With bare hands she pressed the icon to see his pictures.

Oh, God! There they were, childhood degradation in livid color. Some included his own image engaged in horrifying acts. She focused on the small faces. Most of them looked Asian, but no, maybe they were actually Native American.

She couldn't be sure. Resisting the urge to throw the phone down and crush it with her heel, she stilled herself, told herself to think. *He's smart not to own a computer for this dirt. The phone is small and he almost always has it with him but he can plug the charger into a USB port on any computer to sync it for sharing with other perverts. So what of it? It's proof, but it doesn't matter. I'm going to kill the worthless piece of trash.*

Yet, for some reason, she looked again at the smooth black oblong, turned it over, pried off the back, then with her fingernail lifted out the tiny micro SD memory card that she knew contained the photos as well as saved text messages and other data. It looked virtually paper-thin, no bigger than a button. She held her breath as she scraped it off her finger into the breast pocked of her shirt. Then she put the back on the phone, returned it to where she had found it and pulled on her gloves. He wouldn't know the memory card was missing until he tried to access the pictures. She had been in the house less than ten minutes but she sensed she didn't have much time left.

Back in the bedroom, she rubbed out the scuff marks her sneakers had left on the vinyl floor then lowered the window to its previous position. She returned to the front of the house, where the door had been locked by a simple turn of a lever on the door knob. She opened the door a crack to peek out. When she saw no one, she turned the lever to lock herself. She shut the door, ran around to the back of the house, kicked down the platform of rocks and erased the few other faint signs of her break in.

Five minutes later she watched from her hiding place as he returned and parked his car. It had been too close. He emerged from the garage carrying a small grocery bag and a hand full of mail.

**

On Thanksgiving Day Allie gathered four other orphans, those who had no family in town, to her apartment for a traditional dinner. Her oven provided a tight fit for the twelve pound turkey. On the plus side, its heat warmed the tiny apartment to midsummer temperature. She opened the door and all the windows to let in the cool outside air.

It was a challenge to hold a dinner party in this limited space. She added a folding table and chairs to the small table in the dining area. Covered by blue table cloths, set with Blue Willow dinnerware, she thought it would do.

Up since seven o'clock to get the turkey and dressing into the oven, she barely had time to shower and dress before Sue, the woman who lived alone in the apartment next door, knocked. They hadn't socialized much but they were cordial neighbors. Sue held a covered casserole dish that exuded the oniony aroma of green bean casserole.

Betty, a colleague from the office, arrived next carrying a huge bowl of mashed potatoes. "Betty, you look wonderful," Allie said, as she put the bowl in a shallow pan of hot water to keep it warm.

Betty was a tall, slender older woman who wore her long white hair swept back from her face. The way she carried herself suggested no apologies for her low-slung breasts and bloodless uterus. It was obvious she had sailed through menopause undaunted. Now she encouraged other women who were at that certain age to say they had 'power surges' rather than hot flashes. "It's just vascular instability," she told them. "We're stronger than that."

Betty licked a dab of mashed potato from her finger before holding her hand under the faucet. "Maybe I look wonderful *for my age*," she said to Allie. "But I know where I stand since a friend told me I'm at that awkward stage for a woman."

At Allie's puzzled look she smiled. "The awkward stage, the years between when men open doors for us because we're hot, and when they open doors because we're old."

Allie laughed. "Was she implying that men have a gap in their motivations between the ages of lust and respect?"

"Let's hope not." Betty gave Allie a quick hug that produced a flutter of her clothing with a hint of fragrance.

Allie loved that Betty always smelled of sandalwood incense and wore loose, flowing clothes in natural fabrics. Today she could have been a run-way model displaying a long dress made of raw silk in shades of purple and blue with an uneven hem line. The sweeping, abstract pattern of the cloth and ripple effect of the hemline reminded Allie of ocean waves.

Heidi and her new boyfriend, a local sheriff's deputy, were the last to arrive, bringing salad and rolls. Allie kissed Heidi on the cheek and shook Mike's hand. "Don't let me forget to serve the rolls," she said to Heidi. "I don't know why, but I always put them in the oven to warm, then forget them."

Later, when she looked around at her guests, she missed the sound of children gathered around a smaller table and the aura of closeness that only family could create. She reassured herself that this dinner was traditional in at least one sense, obligatory overeating and mutual compliments about the food.

When second helpings had been consumed and everyone complained they were stuffed, Allie herded them to the living room for conversation, dessert and coffee.

Mike and Heidi sat on the sofa with Sue. Allie and Betty took the easy chairs. Allie offered a choice of pumpkin pies. The one with pecans or the one with whipped cream. After she served them, for several minutes there were no sounds but the clink of silverware against china and a few murmurs of appreciation.

Allie again noticed Mike's huge frame. She wondered if he might want a second piece of pie. He wore blue jeans, scuffed cowboy boots, and a blue shirt whose color paled in comparison to the electric blue of his eyes. Set in his warmly tanned face, those eyes were arresting, she thought, then inwardly smiled at her unintentional pun. He did make a virile contrast to his fair-skinned, soft-figured girl friend.

"Would you like another piece of pie, Mike?" He nodded.

"Were you born in the Verde Valley, or did you come from back East, like most of us?" she asked, as she handed him the plate.

"Thank you ma'am. It's good pie. My momma used to serve it with pecans, too. And no ma'am," he added, "I'm not from around here. I'm from Texas."

She smiled. "Whenever someone calls me 'ma'am', I know they're either ex-military or from the South."

"Yes ma'am. Ah...no ma'am. I mean, I was in the Air Force but I don't really think of Texas as part of the South." To her questioning look he said, "We're just-- Texas."

The others laughed at his implication that Texas deserved a locational category of its own. To ease any embarrassment he might feel, Allie said, "I'm from New York State, Long Island."

"Delaware," said Heidi.

"Colorado," Sue said.

"Well, I'm from here," Betty finally told them. "Near here, anyway. I was born in Prescott, believe it or not. Most of us born here have the good sense not to leave the Rim."

"Some of us don't want to leave even to go home for a visit," said Heidi.

"How about you Allie?"

"My son is with his father for Thanksgiving. My only other family is two sets of elderly aunts and uncles and several cousins that I hardly know. We're not a big enough incentive to each other for a long flight for a short visit. What I do miss is the fall color this time of year."

"Gone by now, probably," Heidi said. "It's cold and dreary back there."

"It's late in the season, but remember the leaves? The red, gold and scarlet, the smell of them, the crunch under your feet, and the big piles kids jump in?"

Betty said, "If you want fall color, take a drive up Eighty-Nine A, along Oak Creek to Flagstaff. The oaks and maples are gorgeous this time of year. Fall comes a little later here than back East."

Mike turned to Allie. "That drive up Oak Creek Canyon is pretty, but be careful on the way down, especially on the switchbacks near the top. One in particular is a killer. Literally. Not all the cars landed there by accident, either. So many wrecks down in that ravine it looks like a junk yard."

"I wonder what the locals here do on Thanksgiving," mused Sue, "besides drive up Oak Creek for the foliage or watch football on TV, of course."

"They drink beer, smoke dope and beat their wives and kids," said Mike. "Just like everywhere else."

Heidi tilted her chin at him. "I thought you weren't into that cynical cop stuff," she said.

Mike nodded at Allie's offer of more coffee. After a thoughtful sip he turned to Heidi. "It's because people do such danged, stupid ass things. Uh, excuse me ma'am. But yesterday we had a guy sittin' on his front porch, threatening to kill himself.

"He had a rifle to his forehead for God's sake, a nice little Remington Varmint twenty-two made for hunting, not blowing your brains out. For more than an hour we tried to get him to put the thing down. When he finally lowered the gun he covered the end of the barrel with his hand and shot himself right through the palm. Made a hole as big as a golf ball. Why would someone do that?"

"Therapists never ask why," said Betty. She smiled when she saw a question form in his mind. She explained, "When we ask why, clients see it as a challenge. We get excuses, rationalizations, justifications, instead of honest answers."

"Or outright lies," said Heidi. "I've learned that when you ask someone if they've thought of suicide and they say no, it's a lie. Everyone has *thought* about it."

Betty said, "It works to ask the reporter questions, 'what, where, when, who' and maybe 'how'. The most important question is, 'what comes next?'"

Allie had great respect for the older woman's clinical judgment, yet she felt as if someone had just told her the sky was green. She said, "Isn't 'why' the most important thing of all? If we help people understand what motivates their behavior, they gain control, they make better choices. 'Why' is the heart of it."

Betty pursed her lips. "If you have the luxury of working with people who are not seriously mentally ill, people who just have existential issues, I guess that's true."

The others appeared thoughtful but no one commented until Heidi spread her arms wide in an emphatic gesture. "The holidays! They drive people nuts, even the opposing team." She glanced at everyone in turn except the neighbor Sue, a bookkeeper who she obviously did not consider a member of the opposing team.

Allie cocked her head at Heidi. "Wait a second, let me get this straight. The opposing team is us, mental health professionals, law enforcement, and the other team is...?"

"The rest of us, I guess," said Sue.

Heidi shook her head. "I'm sorry. I didn't mean to insult anyone, but sometimes it does feel like a game, people trying to hurt themselves or someone else and us trying to prevent it."

"No offense taken," Sue said. "But if you're the 'opposing team', then who are we? What's our team name?"

Heidi said, "Depends. Clients used to be called 'patients' but that represents the medical model for mental health treatment, driven by psychiatrists. That's old fashioned. These days some agencies call them 'customers'. In some places they're 'consumers' or 'members'."

Sue smiled. "Nothing new about being a 'customer' I can identify. But if you call me a 'consumer' it sounds like I could gobble up mental health services like someone wolfing down a burger. And who in heaven's name would want to be called a 'member'? A member of what, the local 'crazies' club?"

Heidi said, "Good point. I still like 'client' although the guy who shot himself in the hand could start a fine 'crazies' club."

"Wait a second," Allie interjected. "I'm a little confused about which team I'm on. The reason I'm a pretty good therapist is because I've either suffered from or have friends or neighbors or family members who've suffered from just about every issue or diagnosis in the book. I refer to the DSM, of course."

She started to explain to Sue and Mike that DSM stood for *Diagnostic and Statistical Manual of Mental Disorders*, the reference book for psychiatrists and other mental health professionals. Before she could speak, Betty said, "You're not alone, Allie. A lot of us got into the field that way. It can be compelling to find a perfect description of Uncle What's-His-Name or even of yourself on page something-or-other in the DSM.

"What most of us don't realize is that even though we have certain features of a diagnosis, like being obsessive about certain things, that doesn't mean we have the diagnosis. There are lots of criteria for any diagnosis. Together they have to interfere with daily life in order to reach the level of a mental disorder." She smiled at Heidi, her eyes soft with compassion. "And it really isn't an 'us against them' game, even though it does seem that way at times."

Sue pursed her lips, gave a little 'humph', then said, "Maybe the guy who shot himself went to Sedona and some guru told him that all the spiritually advanced people have holes in their hands."

Heidi said, "Or maybe he tried for a stigmata look without realizing he wouldn't be able to shoot the other hand."

Mike grinned. "We joked about it, too. I told the guys, 'That hand sure would be a loss in a game of peek-a-boo'."

"Or a '*hand*icap' in a game of catch?" said Allie. Her pun was followed by a few amused groans from the others.

Betty smiled. "I like the Sedona explanation. I had a client who went there to see a psychic. She told the psychic, among other revelations I'm sure, that her sister had recently died. And then, that she had a lot of pain in her feet. The psychic said her sister's ghost was attached to her feet. That was causing the pain."

Allie managed to say, "For heaven's sake." She noticed the expression on Sue's face and wondered if

Sue regretted that her comment had headed the conversation in this direction. "Black humor," she said to Sue, shrugging her shoulders in apology.

"Darn right," said Heidi. She leaned forward to put her glass of water on the coffee table but almost lost her balance, several inches short of the target.

"Sorry," said Mike.

Heidi realized they had pushed the table further away from the sofa to accommodate Mike's long legs and feet with size thirteen boots.

She smiled at him and turned to Sue. "You know, tasteless jokes are an occupational hazard or maybe a defense mechanism. I guess we all get a little calloused. We see such horrible things and hear such horrible stories. Sometimes we have to laugh because it helps us cope, helps us forget. Otherwise, some of those images would haunt us."

Her face softened. She looked away, then down at her feet clad in Teva sandals and green socks.

Sue put a hand on Heidi's shoulder. "You're too young to be cynical, Heidi. I wouldn't do your job for all the money in the world. It gives you such a limited perspective on life."

"Ah, ha," said Mike, looking at Heidi, "Someone else noticed you being cynical. I reckon that means the pot called the kettle black."

"Yeah, maybe I am cynical or maybe I'm just worn out. Here's one on me. I got a call from the hospital at about three in the morning last week, to come and evaluate an attempted suicide. I was sound asleep because I was *really* tired, but I had no choice. I dragged myself out of bed and drove down there. I went in and started to do my job but when I saw the look on the nurse's face I realized I was still in my pajamas."

Within an hour the conversation lost its momentum. When the guests began to leave the coffee pot was empty and only crumbs remained in the pie plates.

Allie saw Mike and Heidi out the door, then Sue, making sure they had the dishes they had brought. The containers were now washed and refilled with leftovers covered in foil.

Only Betty lingered to help with the clean-up. Allie insisted Betty wear one of her own seldom-used aprons to protect her beautiful dress while she scraped plates and helped load the dishwasher. They chatted about past Thanksgiving holidays and about the weather.

"Hey," Betty said, "did you notice how Heidi and Mike looked on the sofa together?"

The question took Allie by surprise. She shook her head.

"Six feet four inches of brown skin over bulging muscles next to peaches and cream. Beefcake and cream puff. Can you imagine what their children would look like?"

Allie laughed. "I'm picturing some little dude in diapers with size thirteen feet and a ten gallon hat. But we may be jumping the gun. So far, I think they're just friends."

"Friends or more than friends, I hope he's able to give her some TLC, some support. I worry about her. She works too many hours at a tough job. She seems just too stressed out."

"I know. She should cut down on the crisis work and increase her individual therapy sessions. I think I'll have a talk with her."

Betty nodded her approval.

Allie put the table cloth and napkins in the washing machine then turned to Betty. "Done. Thanks for your help."

"You're always welcome, Allie. And now I have a favor to ask of you. Can you cover for me with a fragile client while I'm out of town next week? He may not be able to make it by himself for ten days. "

"Of course. Tell me about him."

Chapter 4

Night fell early this time of year. The gathering hush of twilight yielded to the distant hum of a few cars on the road, and the first tentative *yip-yip* of a coyote.

When darkness completely curtained the land its lone voice was joined by another, then another, until the wild celebration of night climaxed in an ululating chorus from the whole pack.

Strangely, it comforted her. She remembered an old film in which cowboys around their lonely campfire called coyotes song dogs. The Navajo, who knew them more intimately, called them tricksters. *A creature of many guises*, she thought, *like me*.

The luminous hands of her watch said eight-fifteen. No one had entered or left the house. She was reasonably sure he would spend the rest of the evening alone.

She gathered herself upright on legs and feet stiff with cold and inaction then took off her gloves. She warmed her hands with her breath then worked her feet and legs until the muscles were warm and flexible again. Tenderness in her shoulder and hip reminded her of her clumsy fall just an hour or so ago. There would be black and blue marks tomorrow. She wondered how she would explain them as well as the newer scratches and bruises inflicted by thorny mesquite branches and sharp rocks that lined her hiding place.

Ignoring the discomfort, she patted her jacket to feel the hardness of the little thirty-two weapon in the inner pocket. *For backup.* She felt good. She felt ready.

She made her way on silent feet toward her car, which she had parked a hundred yards away, downhill and behind a crumbling adobe shack, where it couldn't be seen from the road. The interior of the car was pitch black. She fumbled with her key to find the ignition switch but resisted the automatic reflex to switch on the dome light. She took what appeared to be a cell phone from her jacket pocket. She engaged its tiny flashlight to see how to insert the key to start the engine.

When she pulled up close to the house she was careful to allow enough room for his car to exit the garage, then turned off her headlights. Beside the front door a small light fixture cast an anemic glow on something she hadn't noticed earlier. The skeleton of a cactus, that virtually indestructible native of the desert, stood in its coffin of concrete and dry soil. It was long dead.

The slab of concrete that served as a porch stood beneath a flat roof. It sloped downward from the house, supported on either side by battered four-by-four timbers.

Stepping onto the porch, she put what looked like a cell phone to her ear while she pressed the door bell with her left hand. She began talking into the phone as if to a friend, aware that he might peek out the front window to see her. After a few seconds she heard his footsteps. As soon as he opened the door and she was sure he heard and saw her, she finished the charade by pressing the gadget with her thumb as if to end a call.

"Uncle!" she said. "They told me you were in town again."

Nothing. Then he started in recognition. His eyes darted around then behind her into the darkness. He saw her empty car. His brows drew together in a question.

"Just me," she said. "I was thinking about old times, you know, the things we used to do together?" She shrugged and raised an eyebrow. He read the expression as an invitation. Without speaking he backed away and opened the door wider.

She stepped over the threshold into the narrow hallway. He closed the door. She noticed something else she hadn't earlier. This wasn't the house she remembered from childhood but it smelled the same, a stink of sweat, dust and sex.

The dark and quiet in the hallway was relieved only by the blue flickering light of the TV set in the living room with its background noise of screeching car tires and gunshots.

She felt him behind her. She turned to press her back against the wall of the hallway, as if to let him lead the way. Instead of passing he turned to face her. A sudden chill pricked her scalp, threatened to rise into panic. She hadn't expected fear.

She pressed the safety switch on the gadget in her hand. A tiny red light indicated it was enabled. Without a word she jammed the two metal prongs of the stun gun against the side of his neck, sending four and a half million volts of electricity into his body.

He jerked backward, slammed against the wall. Expecting it, she went with him, keeping the stun gun against his neck. His leg muscles were useless against the surging current. He slid down the wall, his arms and hands jerking. His mouth opened, dripping spittle.

She straddled his right leg to bend down over him, keeping her fist and the stun gun still hard against his neck. She felt his muscle spasms travel up her arm but no chargeback entered her body.

Adrenalin-infused, panting, she stood upright and backed against the wall. He remained slumped in a half-sitting position against the opposite wall, feet and legs twitching, eyes unfocused, moaning.

According to the product information he would be helpless for at least the next two or three minutes. She put the stun gun in her pocket and ran outside to grab her other supplies. In the open air, the soft sounds of the night were like a ripple of far away applause. The surge of clean, cold air against her face felt like a blessing.

When she raced inside again wearing her latex gloves she saw his head rolling from side to side against the wall. He tried to get up. *No problem.* Another three second jolt animated his limbs that jerked like those of a crazed marionette. He was helpless again.

Stepping over his legs she grabbed him by the back of his shirt collar and dragged him a few feet into the living room. She released the shirt as if it was poison. She heard the back of his head smack the floor.

The next two minutes were a flurry of swift, purposeful action. She pushed, pulled and ripped while avoiding his weakly protesting arms. Twice he almost succeeded in getting up but she subdued him again with quick jabs in the face with her fist. When the wrestling match was over he lay flat on his back, stark naked.

She tied his hands together, savagely yanking the rope into one knot then two. Not satisfied, she wound duct tape over the rope for good measure. When she bent toward his feet the sight of his naked genitals revolted her. She resisted the urge to spit on them. Instead she put her shoe against his hip and rolled him onto his stomach. She tied a knot around one ankle, left a few inches of slack, then tied the other foot, hobbling him loosely enough that he would be able to walk.

Panting with exertion, she smelled the stench of his sweat then a more disgusting odor. When she rolled him onto his back again she saw a puddle spreading on the dark wooden floor. Urine.

He tried to speak, "What are you...?"

"Shut up, Blood sucker! You and I are about to take a little trip." She reached for something to stuff in his mouth and retched when she accidentally touched his white jockey shorts. Incensed, she grabbed a sock and jammed it into his mouth. A glob of saliva smeared her wrist above the glove's protective barrier. She wiped it on the seat of her jeans with a violent swipe, then tore off another long strip of tape. The brisk ripping noise sounded vicious, a satisfying sound to match her mood.

She pressed the end of a strip of duct tape over the sock in his mouth, grabbed a fist full of hair to lift his head and wrapped the tape around over his mouth again. She thought, *If someone tries to rip it off, it will yank out his hair.*

On her feet, she considered him while she caught her breath. He was out cold but from the rise and fall of his chest she knew he was alive. The tape stood out in grey bands against the whiteness of his fleshy body. *He looks like a maggot*, she thought, *but trussed at both ends, more like a fat, pale sausage waiting for the frying pan.* Of its own accord, her right foot crept forward and poked a slow motion dent into his belly. The toe of her sneaker left a dusty print in his flesh. She looked at it for a long time, as if it might be the sole clue to some ancient mystery she must solve.

***

The morning after Thanksgiving, Allie was making her bed when she remembered she had three more days off counting today. She propped pillows against the bedstead, satisfied with her choice of pattern and hue in the lovely shams. Then she arranged her son's ancient stuffed bunny against them in a pose of abandon, with its limbs spread, head back, long ears akimbo.

When she was finished with her morning exercise routine of *qi gong* and yoga she set out for another visit to Montezuma Well National Monument.

She loved the pleasant drive, a breezy cruise down Highway 260, a brief race north at seventy-five miles an hour on I-Seventeen, then an exit at Maguireville onto Beaver Creek Road for the last leg, completing a thirty minute drive to a destination in the middle of nowhere. She turned off the access road and jerked to a stop when she saw the driveway to the Well's parking lot still blocked by the entry gate, a rather flimsy structure composed of two metal pipes chained and padlocked together.

With a look at the dashboard clock she realized she was early. The ranger wouldn't arrive until nine a.m. to open the Park. Since it was less than a fifteen minute wait she backed the car up and pulled over. The sun shining through the half open window gave just enough heat for comfort. The air was cool with the scents of sage and creosote. She leaned back, stretched long and hard. With a contented sigh she ceded all track of time to memories.

On her first visit she had found an informative brochure at the trail head. The first thing she learned about the Well was that Montezuma had nothing to do with it. It had been discovered by Native Americans thousands of years ago and rediscovered more than a hundred years ago by soldiers at war with Native Indians. The Well is still sacred to local tribes, who use the water in religious ceremonies. Montezuma Castle and Montezuma Well both are destinations for tourists from all over the world.

They would be well-advised to visit in Spring or Fall, she thought. On her first visit in July the temperature was a sweltering ninety-five degrees by noon. On that day, the half mile long access road gave her time to wonder if this sight seeing jaunt was going to be worth it. The road ended in a one-way circular drive that gave onto a dozen or more parking spaces and continued past a tiny frame building, the visitors' information booth. It also served as the ranger's air-conditioned refuge.

That day she had approached the concrete walkway and ascended a series of stone steps with no expectations. She reached a concrete landing which led to another set of steps with a handrail made from a length of metal pipe. Under the blazing sun at mid-day the rusty pipe felt hot to the touch.

More steps and more landings, this time with signs that told her the Well is a funnel shaped, limestone sink, three hundred and eighty-six feet across, a hundred and fifty feet deep in the fissures at bottom, where springs that feed the Well bubble up at the rate of one and a half million gallons of water every day.

At the summit she gazed down hundreds of feet into the Well, thinking that it was much more than a well. In this parched land, it was a miracle. Vegetation outlined its steep banks with beautiful shades of green. Islands of algae and pond weed floated on its surface. The greenery gave cover to ducks and other aquatic life in a testament to the miracle.

Her eyes were drawn to the walls of the Well where cliff dwellings a thousand years old were visible four stories above the water. Grey limestone overhangs served as the roofs. The walls had been constructed of adobe brick and stone, built by the *Sinagua* Indians whose name means 'without water.'

She looked at the stone facades for a long time but they told her nothing. The openings for doors and windows were dark, mysterious oblongs unpenetrated by the strong rays of the sun. With a heavy, uneasy feeling, she took a last look then continued on the concrete pathway that led down into the Well.

After several steps, she saw wild grape vines growing by the path, mallow weed with orange flowers, and tall spiky shrubs called Mormon tea. To the right, the wall of the Well had collapsed some millennia ago, leaving huge boulders and slabs of rock a foot from the pathway. One slab the size and shape of a large speed boat balanced on an even bigger boulder. On top of the 'speed boat,' in what must have been an inch or two of rocky soil, a prickly pear cactus grew.

Allie wiped the sweat from her forehead with a tissue. She noticed that the further down the steep path she walked, the cooler it grew. Then the shrubs formed an archway, casting dense shade over the path. Down a little nearer the water, willow trees with silvery green leaves appeared, along with water loving Arizona walnut and hackberry trees.

Where the path leveled out she saw a Datura plant, a poisonous flowering weed whose white blossoms open at night, then in the shallows at the edge of the Well, large patches of reeds and cattail. She wiped the last beads of sweat from her forehead and breathed in the cool, damp air.

Abruptly, here on the floor of the Well, more ancient native dwellings appeared along the right side of the path. They were roped off now but some of the smoke stained walls were marred by graffiti, dates and names of miners, soldiers, and pioneers who lived more than a century ago. Passing the dwellings, she came to the end of the path where she found found a rock to sit on.

From above, the surface of the Well had appeared as a tranquil mirror reflecting a sterile landscape of sky and rock, but from here she spotted turtles churning across the surface or sunning on rocks, ducks paddling their way among water plants, clouds of dragon flies, like scraps of iridescent orange and blue gauze, skimming and soaring a few feet above the water.

Suddenly she felt a chill that came, not from an errant breeze, but from deep inside her. Time stopped while an image, a memory, or perhaps a warning struggled to reach her awareness. It was akin to a déjà vu experience, but then, not quite. She shrugged and rolled her shoulders, trying to dispel the ominous sensation, trying to return to the present.

Gradually, she became aware of a hollow, gurgling sound that suggested water running through a narrow opening. The outlet! She had read that the outlet for the one and a half million gallons of water the well produced daily is called a 'swallet', an underground tunnel a hundred and fifty feet long The water rushes through the swallet to empty into its natural outlet, Beaver Creek, as well as into a channel dug by the Hohokam natives hundreds of years ago to irrigate their crops.

When Allie found the outlet she saw the roof of the tunnel was set low, almost flush with the surface of the Well. Determined to see where the water emerged, she retraced her steps back up the trail into the blinding light of the sun, then around to her left and down again until she saw the creek on her right. To the left, the irrigation channel flowed with water.

The concrete path wound its way close to the irrigation canal, which in turn hugged the cliff, the outer wall of the Well. Entranced, she followed the path to its end, where an enormous sycamore tree bent toward the creek. The smooth, pale trunk had extended horizontally for five feet before it turned to grow upward. Its wide, spreading leaves were like open palms warming in the sun. It would take three people with outstretched arms to encircle the massive tree trunk. Allie had never considered herself a tree hugger, but this magnificent, living being made her want to run her hands over it, recline against it, embrace it.

This place, unlike the Well itself, was not haunted by the departed souls of countless natives. This place lived and breathed, a lush, soothing ambiance that emanated from flowing water, vegetation and soft, dark earth. The shade felt like a cool cloth on a fevered forehead. It was given as a gift, cast by sycamores, ash trees fifty feet tall and willows in abundance draping over the path and the creek.

From the overhanging bank, where lambs quarters, salt bush, and Spanish dagger grew, drops of water fell from their leaves onto the path.

Below a small embankment, the creek, wide and shallow, burbled happily in the sun. The irrigation channel on her left appeared just two or three feet deep, its banks lined with water cress, maidenhair fern, penstemon and golden columbine. She bent down and trailed her fingers in the clear water, almost touching long, white filaments that flowed like mermaids' hair in the current. She sat down on a large rock. For a long time she remained there, soaking up the life giving peace of the place.

**

That memory had almost soothed her to sleep when the sound of tires on gravel interrupted her reverie. She saw the Park ranger had arrived to release the chained-up gate. They waved at each other then he followed his white pickup truck into the parking area.

"I've seen you here before, haven't I?" he asked, as they exited their vehicles.

She nodded. "I come here as often as I can."

"Welcome back. Nice to see local people who appreciate the place. Mostly we get tourists and some of them think it's just a big hole in the ground."

"In all the times I've been here, I've never been in your little visitor's center. What have you got in there?"

"Come on in. I'll show you."

They walked to the building, where he unlocked the door and stepped aside for her to enter. The structure consisted of one small room with a window that enabled the ranger to greet and converse with park visitors from inside his shelter. It provided space for two desks, a waste basket and a small bookcase. The walls were lined with shelves filled with an assortment of objects--part of a plant called a devil's claw, animal skulls and what she could only identify as dead things floating in jars of liquid.

The ranger was a man in his forties who looked to Allie as if he worked behind a desk in an office, rather than in the sunny outdoors. He bent to switch on a small space heater. When he looked up Allie was peering with a puzzled face at the glass jars.

He picked up one. Nodding at its contents he said, "That right there, you're lookin' at somethin' you won't see anywhere else in the world. That's Motobdella montezuma."

Allie peered at several pale, wormlike creatures about three inches long floating in the jar. "What are they?"

"They're leeches."

"They don't look like leeches."

"The actual color is black. The formaldehyde bleaches out the color, and they're not fat and snail shaped like most leeches. See, the water in the Well is filled with carbon dioxide. It's very alkaline because of the dissolved limestone. Fish can't live in it but the amphipods can. That's what the leeches feed on.

"Amphipods are tiny little crustaceans, like miniature shrimp. I don't have any in here to show you, but they're in the Well, all right. The leeches are at the top of the food chain here, and there are millions of 'em. They're blind but they come up at night, big, dark clouds of 'em, up from the bottom of the Well to feed."

"I thought all leeches feed on blood."

"We have a few blood sucker kind that live in the shallows around the edges of the Well. But these don't suck blood. They just swallow the amphipods whole. Most people, even locals, don't know that. Maybe we don't mind if they're ignorant of it Maybe the thought of millions of leeches in the water keeps the skinny-dippers and partiers from sneakin' in here, nights. And this here," he continued, picking up another jar, "is a water scorpion."

Allie accepted the jar from him. She inspected the insect floating in it. "It doesn't look like a scorpion, either," she said. "Those two little hair-like things at its end aren't stingers, are they?"

"Nope. Just feelers. These eat the amphipods, too. They spear those amphipods, just suck 'em dry, more like a spider than a scorpion. Like I said, these species, you can't find anywhere else in the world. 'Course we have the usual animals, too." He picked up a tiny skull to show her. "Rabbits, squirrels, foxes, raccoons, coyotes, all the ones you'd expect to see hereabouts."

***

Allie's session with Kim had just begun when Kim said, "I saw you at the Well last Friday."

"Oh! You were there too? Do you go there often?"

"The Well is sacred to my people. Also to the Navajo and the Hopi. We get the water to use in ceremonies."

"I've heard that. It's a place that feels sacred to me, too."

"Do you know our legend about it?"

"No, tell me."

Kim relaxed against the sofa and looked straight ahead. Her eyelids drooped a little, perhaps a sign she was focusing inward or backward in time. She hesitated. When she spoke, her voice sounded as soft as a child's.

"They said the lake had no bottom. The people lived around there and they were happy for many years, but there came a bad drought. The chief was an evil man and it was an evil time. He touched his daughter while she slept, in a bad way. She grew very angry. She cast a spell on him that made him sick, sick enough to die.

"When he was dead, she called a flood down on all the people. Then a corn stalk sprouted from the heart of her father's dead body. The people climbed on it, out of the water. For a long time they lived. Then she called another flood and one woman alone lived through it. The people all came from her, First Woman, and from Father Sky."

Allie said, "Sort of a creation story. And a story about abuse and anger. When you said 'he touched her...in a bad way' you were talking about sexual abuse, weren't you?"

"Yes. Our people didn't know exactly what words to call it, but it happened anyway, even back then."

Kim did not look or sound childlike now. Her fists clenched at her sides, her jaw line set in a rigid square.

Allie said, "Thinking about it makes you angry."

"Doesn't it make you angry too?"

"Yes it does. Maybe it's no comfort to you, but sexual abuse is probably as old as the human race. Stories of women trying to protect themselves from it or seeking revenge on people who've victimized them go back to the beginning of recorded history."

"I know." A flush rose to Kim's high cheekbones and her eyes narrowed as she rushed to articulate her feelings. "I've read about chastity belts in medieval times. Even today, in some places, they sew the young girls' vaginas shut. Disgusting!"

"Yes, it is," Allie said, her voice calm.

"You know, there's a legend about a woman from our tribe being chased through the desert by a *cowboy*." She spat the word like an expletive.

"She knew he was going to catch up with her and she knew what he wanted. He was bigger, stronger than she was. She couldn't win a fight with him. So she stopped and she packed sand into...into it."

Allie refused to release the gasp in her throat. She said, "That must have been...horrible," while her imagination struggled with the images that implied an unyielding determination in the face of violence and evil.

Kim's face settled into a grim expression, as if she were thinking the same things.

Into the silence, Allie said, "Life is strange. Sometimes even tragic."

"Life is brutal," Kim said. "I lean toward just killing them all."

Allie shifted in the easy chair she had taken instead of her task chair, in order to equalize her relationship with her client. She felt both disappointed and fearful the session might drift out of control.

"Careful, Kim," she said. "Anger can be your best friend or your worst enemy. The way you lean is the way you go and if you lean far enough it's the way you fall."

"Haven't we talked enough about things that make me angry? And what my anger thoughts are, and what my anger signals are, and how I can calm myself down, and what I can say to myself to make the anger go away?"

"According to your court order, one more group and two more therapy sessions will be enough."

Kim didn't speak for half a minute, then drew a deep breath, as if surrendering to the inevitable.

"Kim, haven't you learned anything in the group or in here that's helped you?"

"I learned that if you focus anger into a plan, then you don't get in trouble, then you're free to be guided, an instrument of karma, like we talked about."

Allie said, "I've been thinking about that, about being an instrument. Being an instrument sounds like you have no choice, that you're being used, maybe without even knowing it. Wouldn't you rather be an 'agent' of karma? An agent is someone who takes responsibility for his or her actions."

Kim took a peppermint candy from the dish on the table and turned it in her fingers, crackling the cellophane. "I think an agent of karma would act like a judge, jury and executioner, instead of someone who's guided by a higher power. Weren't you the one who told me that when you know something, when you're sure of it without knowing why, you don't question it?" She put the candy in her mouth.

"I guess I did."

79

Kim said, "You were an instrument of karma when you came to Cottonwood, not an agent of karma." Her eyes locked on Allie's. "You didn't even know where the Mogollon Rim was. You came without meaning to come, guided here."

Allie's elbow was propped on the arm of her chair with her chin in her hand. This woman had been a pleasure to work with and something of an amazement to her.

She straightened. "I'm not sure karma brought me here at all. But this is about you, Kim. The point is that whichever it is, agent or instrument, I hope you don't break the law again and get in trouble. That's what brought you here, and that's what I'm supposed to be helping you with."

***

When Allie returned from lunch both Doctor V and Sherry were in the break room. Sherry stood at the copier, making handouts for clients from a workbook on anxiety. Allie murmured a preoccupied greeting then went to the refrigerator to stash the remains of her lunch. As she turned to leave, Doctor V crossed to where his wife stood and pressed his body against her back. She leaned into him, turning her head to smile up at him. He gave her a quick slap on the bottom before moving away.

Allie glanced away in embarrassment but when she headed for the door she heard Sherry say, "You really perk up with just a little vacation time, don't you, Ralph?"

"After last night I'm the perking up champ," Doctor V laughed, his meaningful gaze not on his wife, but on Allie.

Sherry also looked at Allie. "Ralph is really very manly," she said, "and he understands what women like."

Allie was at a loss for words. She smiled at them politely then retreated to her office. She had just been given an unexpected glimpse of the couple's personal life that she hadn't asked for and she knew it was distinctly unprofessional behavior for a workplace.

She had never thought of tall, gangly, intellectual Doctor V as a sexual person. This new perspective brought no pleasant images but for some reason her mind drifted to the early days of her marriage to Paul.

Often her first chore in the morning was to change the tangled and stained sheets. Over the intervening years, lusty excitement had faded to healthy passion, then to routine release. During the last year or so before the divorce, the marriage bed became tangled only by Paul's restless tossing and turning and stained only by the sweat of her frustrated insomnia.

This morning she had slipped out of a bed virginal in its freshness, putting it in order with wistful hands making a few tucks, tugs and smoothing motions.

Abruptly, her reverie ended. The pen she twisted in her hands hit the desk with a small 'thunk'. Memories of her intimate life with her ex-husband had always been pleasantly erotic but now, she realized, they were by some strange psychological osmosis, connected to that image of Doctor V and Sherry. *How gross is that?* she wondered. *It's ridiculous. I'm not even attracted to him.*

The phone rang. The voice of Wanda at the reception desk refocused her thoughts. "It's that client of Betty's on the phone, the one you agreed to fill in with while she's away."

A start of alarm went through Allie. "Oh, yes, Tim Smith. Put him through."

"Wait. That client of yours, that tall Indian girl? The last time she was here, she called me 'Auntie'. I'm not her Aunt. You should tell her not to call me that."

Allie shook her head in silent exasperation. "Wanda, Native Americans often call older people Aunt or Uncle as a sign of respect. It's a compliment."

"Not to me, it's not."

"Just put him through, Wanda."

The voice sounded soft, timid. "Hello? Mrs. Davis?"

"Yes, Tim. But call me Allie. Betty told me you might call while she's away. What can I do for you?"

"I had a fight with my mother. Then they left. They're on vacation and won't be back for two weeks days."

"You sound upset."

"She said I don't deserve to live, that it's my fault, after...after what I did."

"Your mother said that? What, what's your own fault?"

"The pain. She told me not to complain, that I deserve it."

Allie needed time to think, time to overcome stunned disbelief. Why did his mother think he deserved pain? Or had she really said those things to him? Betty had told her about this young man and his uncaring, narcissistic parents, but she was having a hard time grasping the reality of it.

"Is someone helping you with the pain, Tim? Do you have a doctor? Are you on medication?"

"Yes."

"Would it help you to come in and talk about it some more?"

"Yes, please."

"Then let's make it today, at say, five-fifteen?" She heard a relieved sigh, and a soft, "Okay."

***

82

Crystal sat on the edge of the chair, clutching her small purse with both trembling hands. Allie knew at first glance that this client was not doing well, either.

"How are you today, Crystal?"

The question was just an invitation for her client to begin. She was not prepared for the disturbing report that followed or for the flood of emotion.

"I saw him again! I took the kids to Dairy Queen on Sunday for a treat and he was there!"

"Your uncle?"

A nod. Crystal placed trembling fingers over her flushed cheeks. Tears began to flow.

"Did something else happen, Crystal?"

"He came over and tried to hug me. I wouldn't let him. I wanted to hit him. I wanted to run but I couldn't leave because the kids were about to get their ice cream. He looked at them and said how cute they were."

Violent trembling in her hands rose up her arms and body then erupted in loud, wet sobbing. Crystal's face reddened, twisted in rage. She grasped her purse until her knuckles turned white. Suddenly she threw it across the room. Allie jumped. The purse smacked the wall and fell to the floor.

"I'll kill him!" Crystal screamed. "He's dead. He's as good as dead." Her face streamed tears and mucous.

"Crystal! I get it. I hear you. You're angry, but you need to calm down. We need to talk about it."

Allie leaned forward, trying to penetrate the storm of anguish. "Take some deep breaths for me. Here, use the tissues. Take a deep breath. Here's the wastebasket. Another deep breath. Try again."

Obedient, Crystal wiped her nose, mopped her face then discarded wads of tissues. Her heaving chest subsided. Gradually her eyes refocused on her therapist.

"Okay, now that's better," said Allie, with what she hoped was an encouraging tone.

Crystal dropped another wad of sodden tissues in the wastebasket then closed her eyes. For a moment, a peaceful silence prevailed.

Allie said, "What else happened, Crystal?"

"I remembered. When I got home, I remembered what he did. What he made me do."

"What? What was that?"

"You know what it was! He molested me. He raped me! Don't expect me to tell you any more, because I won't. And I swear he won't come near my children. I'll kill him first." She started to cry again, her face twisted with emotion.

Allie clenched her teeth. *That threat! I can't believe she's telling me she's about to kill him.* She said, "I can understand your fury, Crystal. Lots of people talk about killing when they don't really intend to do it."

"Oh, no, I mean it." Crystal's voice was now a whisper. Her face serene, she rose and walked across the room to retrieve her purse.

Allie shook her head in disbelief. *This can't be happening. She's not capable of it.* "You're telling me you actually plan to kill him? How?" She didn't wait for an answer. "Remember what we talked about? The limits of confidentiality?"

"I have a gun. It will be easy."

"Crystal, we have to stop right now. We've talked about the fact that I can keep almost anything you tell me in complete confidence except a plan to hurt yourself or someone else. I have no choice now."

"What do you mean, no choice?"

"The law requires me to warn him. It also requires me to arrange an evaluation to see if you need to be hospitalized to keep you from hurting him. What's his name?"

"Hospitalized? You mean the psych hospital? The looney bin? I can't go there. Who would take care of my kids? There's no one but my husband and he can't take time off from work." Her voice rose in volume again. "You're supposed to be helping me. I thought you were on my side!"

"I am on your side Crystal, believe me, but I also have to do what the law requires me to do. It's the best thing for everyone."

"Everyone? You want to do what's best for that blood sucking monster? Do you actually think he deserves to live?"

"It's not my place to judge...".

Before she could finish, Crystal leapt out of her chair, jerked the door open and darted down the hall. The office door slammed against the door-stop then swung half closed again, punctuating the end of the session with an exclamation mark.

Allie felt exasperation and disappointment rise in her chest. She followed her own advice and took a deep breath. She got up to close the door. Wanda was striding down the hall toward her.

"What was that all about? She...".

"Never mind, Wanda. I'm taking care of it."

Wanda's usual scowl turned into a grimace but she retreated to the waiting room.

Allie sat at her desk. *Tarasoff.* She reached for the telephone before she realized she couldn't warn the uncle because Crystal hadn't revealed his name. Her alternative was to call law enforcement. The Sheriff's Department had jurisdiction where Crystal lived. *Damn it to hell, I don't want to do this, but I've got no choice. She might actually try to shoot him.*

The dispatcher put her on hold once and transferred her twice while the receiver grew slick in her sweaty hand. When she finally heard a deputy's voice, it was Mike's voice with its soft Texas twang.

She explained the situation as quickly and concisely as she could.

She knew that both the Cottonwood Police Department and the Sheriff's Department had received training on how to handle mental health emergencies but Mike was even more knowledgeable about those situations because of his relationship with Heidi.

He reassured her that he would do whatever needed to be done, both to warn the man and get Crystal evaluated by the crisis counselor on duty. Allie hung up the phone and sank back in her chair. *So this is what it feels like to be on the 'opposing team'. It sucks, big time.* She looked at the clock. She had four scant minutes to compose herself before the appointment with Tim.

***

In his early twenties, Tim appeared average in height and weight, but pale and puffy looking. His eyes appeared colorless until she saw they were grey. The outer side of his lids drooped toward his cheeks, giving him a sad clown appearance.

He wore beige slacks with a black t-shirt printed with the words, 'No boundaries'. The hand she shook felt thick. She saw ropes of scarring on the palms. The tips of his index and middle fingers were missing. The remaining skin had the slick, tight texture of burn scars. It fit with what Betty had told her.

Tim was familiar with the counseling routine. There were few preliminaries. He said, "I'm having surgery again in a few weeks." He held out his hand for her closer inspection. "They say they can restore some range of motion by operating on the tendons. I might be able to use it again."

"I hope that works out for you. Are you having any thoughts of wanting to hurt yourself again?"

He leaned back against the chair cushion and stared at his hands, palm up in his lap.

"No," he breathed, as if talking to himself alone. "I won't set myself on fire again. It was too painful and it didn't do the job." He looked up at Allie with a wan attempt at defiance. "I hated the hospital. They kept me for six weeks. I had pneumonia from the smoke getting into my lungs. The worst part was the skin graft, a split thickness graft, they called it. From my back, to cover the burns on my chest. My tattoo got ruined. I'll show you."

"No!"

Unheeding, he stood and yanked up the tee shirt to show his chest, where a patch of healthy looking skin about eight inches square was surrounded by puckered scarring. On the smooth skin she saw the head and torso of a figure clothed in green. Before she could make it out, he turned to display smooth, pink skin on his upper back. Beneath it was the image of a pair of legs and feet, also clad in green.

Allie was puzzled. What was she was seeing?

He put his shirt down. "It's Peter Pan, my favorite Disney character. I got it as soon as I turned eighteen. It used to be on my back. They called my back the donor site. When they grafted the skin, the top half of the tattoo came with it, right onto my chest. I thought about asking them to get the bottom half too, but I knew they wouldn't."

Allie's mind raced to understand. A grafted tattoo. Peter Pan, the eternal boy, a joyful free spirit without a mother or knowledge of what mothers do. What could she say? Finally she managed, "You must like that character a lot."

"He doesn't have parents and he can fly. What's not to like about that? We all wish we could fly. So, when is Betty coming back?"

"Next week, didn't she tell you?"

"I guess she did. I miss her."

"You've been seeing her for two or three years now, haven't you?"

"Four years, since the first time I tried to commit suicide. I love her."

Allie's discomfort must have shown, because he blurted out, "No, not like that. Not sexual or anything. She's wonderful. She's really special."

"Yes she is. But aren't there other people in your life who care about you, Tim? And don't *you* care about you?"

"That's a funny question." He fell silent, thoughtful for a long moment then said, "A couple of years ago, when she moved into her place here, she sold some of her old office furniture. I bought her chair. Sometimes when I'm really depressed I sit in it. It makes me feel better."

Allie pictured him in Betty's chair, trying to soak up the concern and caring of his therapist, as if through some magic he could experience the balm of love. She gulped, fighting back tears. She told herself, *Cut the water-works. Be a professional here, for heaven's sake!* She needed to refocus the session on the problem Tim had presented when he called, a fight with his mother. Maybe she could help him with that.

Soon she found her attempts to engage him in problem solving went nowhere. He told her that neither his mother nor his father had ever in his memory hugged him or told him that they loved him. He probably expected her to conclude, as he had, that it was hopeless.

He said, "So, she'll be back five days from now?"

Allie nodded. With that they both realized it was almost time to stop.

He said, "She told me she was going to San Diego, to the beach." He obviously didn't expect a reply.

Allie felt drained, empty and inadequate. She reached for her bowl of transitional objects, rocks and shells. She showed it to him. "Why don't you take one of these? Every time you look at it, you can think of her having a good time on the beach, and know she'll be back soon."

His good hand hovered over the container until at last he selected a small, pink shell.

"Thank you." He gave her a weak smile. That facsimile of a smile still on his face, tears slipped from under his lids and began to roll down his cheeks. He closed his eyes, silent. Allie waited. Tears streamed down his face now, unchecked. Still he remained silent.

Allie asked softly, "Tim, what are these tears for?"

He reached for a tissue, although his face, neck and the front of his shirt were already wet. "She hugged me. At the end of our last session when she said goodbye, she hugged me."

Alone again in her office, Allie put her elbows on the desk and her head in her hands, willing to have no thoughts, no feelings. *That song said it best, 'just breathe'.* It didn't work.

She could feel Tim's anguish for a denied birthright, love he had never known and never would know. The hug had given him a taste of what he lacked from the two people who had given him life, the love needed to keep any human being alive.

She wondered why some parents, like Crystal, were willing to kill to protect their children, while others weren't willing to just love theirs.

With a weary effort she raised her head to look at the framed drawing of the Navajo girl. *So pure, so simple. Before the turmoil of puberty, embraced by tradition and tribe, in a landscape of sere beauty, at ease in her cotton and buckskin, holding a food that sustains life.*

She rose from the chair, went to the sofa, lay down on her side with her forehead against the back cushion and her back toward the office. *I'm good at projection, too.*

***

The session was going well.
"I had that dream again last night," the client said.
"Which one is that?"
"The ones I have all the time. The details are a little different, but it's always me being chased or beat up or killed. Someone trying to hurt me. I'm afraid and trying to get away. I try to scream but I open my mouth and nothing comes out. I try and try to scream but nothing comes out."
"What do you think it means?"
"I don't know what it means! That's why I'm telling you."
The therapist was silent. Then, "I'll tell you what. Let's try a little lucid dreaming. You understand about lucid dreaming? It's a way to bring consciousness into your dreams, to interact with them in a meaningful way. It can be difficult, but with a little practice most people can do it. It will help you understand what your dreams are trying to tell you. And they're always telling you something, something you need to know about yourself. So tonight when you go to bed, ask yourself

that question: 'why can't I scream in my dreams?' Then, if you have the dream again, bring that question into it. Ask yourself that question while you're still dreaming."

"That sounds weird. Can a person actually do that?"

"It works for lots of people. If you do it you'll feel sure of the answer you get."

"Putting it back on me, huh? Making me answer my own questions."

The therapist just smiled.

Chapter 5

He came around with a shudder that started in his chest, roiled like a snake under his blanched skin and ended with a jerk of his foot. His eyes opened. Unfocused, they were nothing but empty reflectors of the flickering glow from the TV. He blinked, turned his head from side to side, trying to see, trying to orient himself. Even when his vision returned, he couldn't see her because she had opened the door against the stench of him and moved behind him, out of his line of sight.

He must have sensed the thin, cold caress of the night's breath on his torso and genitals because he raised his head, looked down the length of his naked body at his bound hands, then the doughy mound surrounded by its dark thatch, to the rope around his ankles. He gasped. His dazed brain had finally registered his condition. She heard the sharp intake of breath and laughed. Like a shadow materializing from the wall she walked around to stand between him and the TV.

Even in silhouette, her image penetrated his fog. Now he knew the danger. With a muffled shout he tried to stand. He struggled against the rope that hobbled his feet, then torqued his body to the right and pushed himself up with his bound hands. He wobbled but remained on his feet, then turned toward the end table and took a shuffling step.

"Too late," she said, bringing up the Ruger in her left hand, pointing it at his head. He stopped, turned back toward her. "It's uglier than mine," she said, pulling her own gun from her pocket with her right hand, "but mine can blow your brains out too." She pointed both guns at him, arms straight, hands steady. "Now you're going to do everything I tell you to do because if you don't, one of these guns will be the last thing you see. Do you have a preference?"

Abruptly her voice changed. She no longer mocked him, she demanded. "Get going. We're taking a ride in your precious Z." She put his gun in a pocket, grabbed his keys from the coffee table, motioned toward the door with her right hand.

He remained frozen in fear but responded with a few whining sounds, which might or might not have been attempts to speak through the gag. As if instinctively, he raised his bound hands to his mouth, trying to tear away the tape.

"If you pull it off you won't live to regret it," she said. "One word out of your foul mouth will be your last! Do you understand?"

He searched her shadowed face with desperate eyes, then apparently sensing not an iota of compromise or compassion, he began to shuffle toward the open door, every movement an agony of reluctance.

***

Allie waited until the next morning to call the Sheriff's office to ask about Crystal, grateful that Mike was working the day shift.

He said, "Good news and bad news, Ma'am. She was mighty near as closed mouthed as a preacher on Saturday. She wouldn't tell us her uncle's name either, but her husband was more obliging. Uncle by marriage is Frank Upshall. The aunt, her mother's sister, has been dead twenty years. After his wife died, Frank stayed here in the Valley. He's a real estate agent, sold a lot of properties around Camp Verde. Moved away about eight years back, returned this October."

"Did you talk to him? Did you tell him?"

"Yes, Ma'am. We paid him a visit. He didn't seem surprised when we told him about the threat. He appeared very nice, very polite. Too polite, too nice. He's hiding something."

He paused. When Allie didn't respond, he said, "Uh, Ma'am--Miss Allie--why was she threatening to kill him?"

"She didn't tell you?"

"No, she just kept saying he's a vampire and he deserved it."

"I don't know what to tell you, Mike. It's a private thing, is the only thing I *can* tell you."

"I get it. Need to know, confidentiality. I guess I can do without knowing as things stand now."

"What happened with Crystal? Did you have to Title Thirty-Six her?"

"You can't Title someone who's going in of their own free will."

"Yes. I'm glad you didn't have to force her into it."

"And she doesn't have a gun. Not that we could find, anyway. Her husband said he never saw one or heard of her buying one. Like I said, husband's a good old boy. He let us look around for an imaginary gun. All the time, she's following us around, apologizing, crying a river. The two little kids are following her around, crying."

Allie managed a muttered "Damn!"

"Yeah, reminds me why I don't cotton to the idea of getting married. Uh, sorry, Ma'am. Not your problem. Anyway, after we had a nice sit-down with both of them, she agreed to go into a psych hospital in the Phoenix area."

"I thought maybe that's why you didn't call me. Thanks for doing all that, Mike. Now she's safe, everyone's safe. She's going to feel a lot better after she gets on some meds. Maybe I'll go visit her tomorrow."

"Uh, I don't know about that."

"What do you mean?"

"She's right pissed, uh, angry at you, Ma'am, says she'll never speak to you again."

"I guess I can't blame her. She feels like I betrayed her."

"Affirmative. She feels like might-near everyone betrayed her."

***

At noon, Allie went to get her lunch from the refrigerator in the break room, planning to eat it out on the patio. The temperature hovered near freezing today but whenever she was outdoors, no matter how cold the air, the blazing sun warmed her enough for comfort. When she opened the door to the break room, Ralph VanDeusen and Sherry were at the table talking, their faces solemn.

Doctor V turned to her. "Allie, you've heard?"

She opened the refrigerator door. "Heard what?"

"About the Smith boy, Betty's client?"

"No. What?"

"He killed himself last night. Hanged himself. They called me to come ID the body."

Allie closed the refrigerator door and clutched her lunch bag to her stomach, feeling as if she had been punched.

"Why did they call you?"

"They found my card on his desk, near the body. Anyway, it's common knowledge that I was treating him. His parents are out of town for a week, second honeymoon or something." He paused, then shrugged and said, "I thought his prognosis had improved considerably after we changed his meds the last time. The conzalidraline seemed to be working. Who would have thought he'd decomp?" He raised one eyebrow at her. "You saw him yesterday? It must have been quite a session."

Allie couldn't speak. Doctor V continued. "The police notified the parents of course. I called Betty." He interrupted his monologue when he sensed the level of Allie's distress.

He unfolded his long frame from the chair, and went to her. Without a word, he took the lunch bag out of her hands. He put it on the counter then pulled her into his arms, his beard against her forehead. Now she felt shock for a different reason. She pushed away from him.

Sherry had been watching every move. "Come and sit down," she said, moving a chair away from the table for Allie. "You look pale."

"I'm fine. I just need to process this. This is a shock."

When she turned to leave, Doctor V pulled a business card from his pocket. "Allie, I know you're alone here in the Valley, single, no one close to talk to. I'm giving you my cell phone number. If you need me, call me." He scrawled a number on the back of the card and handed it to her.

Allie took it without a word and left the room to return to her office. After a few seconds she realized Wanda was following her down the hall, approaching at a fast walk that exaggerated the swing of her wide hips. Allie stopped at her office door to let Wanda catch up with her.

"Here," Wanda said, thrusting something into Allie's hand. "Yesterday on his way out, Tim Smith asked me for an envelope. Then he put something in it and asked me to give it to you. I just heard about him. I figured it might be important."

She followed Allie into the office, her eyes glued to the envelope. Allie put the business card and the envelope on her desk. She turned to glare at Wanda, who got the hint and flounced back to her desk, curiosity unassuaged.

Allie tore open the envelope. Nothing. Then she saw the little pink shell he had taken from her collection. *What...why?* She couldn't begin to think this through. She felt as if her brain had frozen. When the phone rang she jumped and looked at it as if she had never seen such a device. Then a San Diego area code appeared on the caller ID. When it registered she picked up the receiver.

"Betty...Betty I'm so sorry. I saw him yesterday. He was depressed, but he told me he wouldn't hurt himself again. I believed him. I had no idea. I'm so sorry."

"I know you are sweetie. I am too. What a thing to hear on your first vacation in five years!"

Neither spoke for a moment, then Allie murmured "I'm sorry," again.

Betty respond immediately. "Allie, don't you for a minute blame yourself. I don't want to hear any of that nonsense. You know that if they honest to God want to do it, there's nothing we can do to stop them. I spent four years trying to help Tim find the will to live. No one would expect you to do it in one session."

"I know, but...".

"No buts. All we can do is try to help them discover their own courage and their own wisdom. It's not our job to fix them, remember?"

"I know the buzz words," said Allie. "We're supposed to 'empower' them instead, because fixing them implies there's something inherently wrong with them. I'm sorry! If anyone ever needed to be fixed, he did."

"He was broken, alright, but remember, we weren't the ones who tore him up. As much as we might like to fix a person we are not that all-powerful."

Allie sighed and looked up at the diplomas on her wall. "Yeah, I know You're absolutely right."

"I just called to let you know that I'm cutting my trip short by one day to get back in time for his funeral. Not that his parents will give a damn I'm there. I'll be lucky if they don't blame me and try to sue me. But I want to do it for him."

She paused. In a softer, more thoughtful voice she said, "One thing I'm glad of. Before I left for my vacation, during our last session, I hugged him. I had never done that before."

Allie hung up the phone, realizing she felt chilled. She crossed her arms across her breasts to rub her upper arms, but the goose bumps wouldn't subside. When the thought hit her another chill raced up her spine. *My God, he didn't tell me he wasn't going to hurt himself. He said he wouldn't set himself on fire again!*

Regret and guilt rose again in a mind-numbing miasma. She struggled with the implications of what she had just realized. *Was he planning it, even while he sat in my office?*

Betty's voice came back to echo, "We can't stop them if they really want to do it." It rang true, making her wonder if her feelings were self indulgent or even self important. Betty was right. Allie had spent less than one hour with the poor man. How much influence could she have had?

Still, she couldn't stop mentally reviewing and processing the session. A vivid picture arose. Tim's face in despair, tears streaming down his cheeks, his voice filled with a deep yearning. "She hugged me."

The picture persisted while her mind swirled, until a thought pierced her. *He did it because she hugged him*! Betty had become his surrogate mother, perhaps the only woman in his life who had displayed affection and good will toward him. When she hugged him, that bit of affection was like the taste of honey on the tongue of a starving man. It overwhelmed him with the awareness of his deprivation, causing him more pain than he could bear. Dying was the one way he knew to escape.

She waited for another explanation, an argument of fact, a rebuttal, but none came. Then it occurred to her that this idea might be an unconscious attempt to absolve herself of blame by projecting it onto Betty. Unaware that she did it, she shook her head. That was not the case.

My God, the suicide was an unintended consequence of something she did with the purest of intentions. But she doesn't know it. I'm glad she doesn't know. I certainly won't tell her. I can't ever tell anyone.

She called Wanda, asked to have her remaining appointments for the day cancelled. Then she went home.

***

Back at the office the following morning, Allie looked up the contact information for the psychiatric hospital whose name Mike had given her. When she called and asked to speak with Crystal Naven, a woman's brisk voice said, "I can neither confirm nor deny that such a person is here at this time. However, our general policy in cases like this is to take a message, and if that person is here and if that person wants to speak with you, they have the right to call you."

"I know that," said Allie, with an edge to her voice.

"I think she has my number but here it is again." She gave the number. "Please ask her to call."

By the end of that day, Wednesday, still no response. On Thursday she made the call again but Crystal didn't return it. At the tail end of a busy week, on Friday close to five p.m. when she had completed the day's counseling notes, the now familiar number appeared on the display as the telephone rang. She knew there was relief in her voice when she answered.

Crystal spoke softly and sounded very calm when she said "Hello."

"How are you, Crystal?" In the silence that followed, Allie heard other voices and activity in the background. Crystal didn't respond. "I'm glad you decided to call."

"They told me I can't leave until I have a discharge plan, an after-care plan. I guess you're it."

"You mean for out-patient counseling. Sure. We'll just continue where we left off." Allie knew Crystal's explanation for making contact was an excuse. Since her hospitalization was voluntary, an after-care plan would be recommended but the hospital couldn't refuse to release her if she refused to complete one. Besides, Crystal could choose to see another therapist for outpatient counseling.

Allie decided not to make an issue of it. Crystal needed to save face after her angry outbursts. Instead, she said, "I was planning to come see you there, but if you're about to be released...".

"I'm leaving Sunday around six o'clock, but you could come earlier that day. The nurse said she wants your signature on the discharge plan."

Allie hesitated, thinking of her hiking club, the all day outing scheduled for that Sunday. "Sunday," she said. "Well, okay. I'll see you then."

When she left the office half an hour later, she met Sherry in the hallway. "Did Ralph call you last night?" she asked Allie.

"Uh, no. Why?"

"He said he wondered how you were doing after that client committed suicide. He wanted to call you. He mentioned it at dinner, and again while we were getting ready for bed."

"I'm fine," Allie said. "Betty is the one who could be devastated but she said she's determined not to take it personally. I'm just following her good example."

***

The inpatient unit was a sixteen bed, free-standing facility, not affiliated with a medical hospital. It was known to mental health professionals as 'The Puff', an acronym for Psychiatric Health Facility. Its official designation was Level One Facility, indicating it housed patients with a high level of psychiatric acuity and was licensed as such Allie had never been to this particular facility to visit a client.

There were a dozen cars in the parking lot as she drove in, but she saw no one else as she approached the building, an unadorned grey concrete structure with no windows in front. The open porch displayed the same grey concrete. Its sole concession to comfort or décor was a concrete bench beside the doorway.

Allie pulled the handle on one of the two large steel doors but it didn't budge. She tried the other; both were locked. She looked around. Only then she recognized a camera and speaker security system on the otherwise unadorned concrete wall. She pushed the buzzer by the door.

After a few seconds a voice answered with a questioning "Yes?"

"Hi. I'm Allie Davis. I'm here to see Crystal. Crystal Naven." She felt the unseen eyes inspecting her through the camera.

"Just a minute please."

A loud buzz in the lock signaled she had been approved for admission. The door was heavy; it opened with effort and swung closed behind her with an emphatic slam.

She found herself in what appeared to be a deserted building, staring down a long, dark, empty hallway. Her few steps down the hall revealed two much shorter hallways branching to the right and left with what she guessed were three offices opening onto each.

Several yards ahead, a windowed reception booth was dark and unmanned. Trying to decide whether to knock on a door at random or explore further down the hall, Allie saw someone emerge from a door about fifteen yards away.

The woman came close enough for Allie to identify her as a nurse, a blond haired woman wearing medical scrubs printed in bright yellow and orange.

"You've never been here before have, you?" the woman asked briskly. She didn't wait for an answer but continued in a honeyed, southern accent that contrasted oddly with her businesslike manner. "I'm the charge nurse, Linda. Crystal and the other patients are in the cafeteria finishing lunch. I'll show you around until they're ready to visit." Allie followed, grateful for a guide.

"This is the twenty-three hour unit," the nurse said, indicating an open door on the right. "It's for patients in crisis who don't need to be admitted; they just need a time out."

Allie glimpsed a well lit day room with sofas, chairs and the ubiquitous TV set but no patients.

"We're pretty empty right now, but it will sure pick up around Christmas and New Years," Linda said. Further down the hallway on the right, she indicated the closed cafeteria door then the open door to a very large room at the end of the hallway. "This is the conference room where we do staffings and where the Title Thirty-Six hearings are held," she said. "Room enough for the judge, the lawyer, and our staff."

A long oval table lined with chairs filled the room. On a large table against the wall, a very large, flat screen TV claimed most of the surface except for an electronic device about the size of a loaf of bread.

"For tele-med," Linda said, leaving Allie to think about the value of high tech applications for mental health work.

The nurse stopped in front of another door. From her pocket she hefted a large key ring that contained seven or eight heavy metal keys. Allie had vague intimations of medieval jails and their keepers until she noticed the keys had colored plastic borders around square heads.

The nurse selected the key marked with red. It opened the door to a tiny room that contained nothing but a copy machine, a bulletin board and a door opposite the one they had just entered. She chose a blue key to open the facing door then turned to smile at Allie.

"It's like an air lock, isn't it? To slow down the runners. Some can dash through the first door when we open it, but the second is apt to stop them." They entered the unit.

The nurse's station with its locked, swinging half door was on the right. As they walked past it, Allie noticed another nurse and several staff members there. "The techs," Linda said, not bothering to introduce them. Allie knew their full title: behavioral health technician.

Looking around, she noticed the concrete floor had been treated with a mustard-yellow epoxy paint. The walls were white plaster rather than dry-wall. A few feet beyond the nurse's station, Linda indicated an open room empty of patients. It was barren to the four walls except for a stretcher-like table bolted to the floor in the center of the room with wide leather straps hanging down both sides.

"Seclusion and restraint," she said. "We don't have to use it often." She flashed a now familiar grin at Allie, who was impressed by the woman's charming drawl and chipper personality. She wondered if the woman was genuinely good humored or was she practicing a defense against the drab, prison-like environment?

"There's a row of offices for the psychiatrist and the social worker through there," Linda said, motioning to a door with a small, steel mesh reinforced window. Through it Allie saw another long corridor with office doors along one side. They approached the end of the building, where wide doors with reinforced windows gave a glimpse of a small lawn outside.

"The patio and yard are through there," Linda said. "The patients used to smoke out there, but now we have them on nicotine patches. They hate not being able to smoke, but they still like to go out for fresh air."

They turned back to the large central common area which was lined by the open doors of patient's rooms. Each room was only eight by ten feet, holding nothing but a narrow bed and a single dresser. Most of the beds were neatly made but a few personal belongings scattered here and there added a human touch that contrasted with the otherwise military barracks atmosphere.

Allie suddenly felt like an intruder. People were living their lives in here, if only for a short time. A squeamishness overtook her, reminding her of how she felt visiting the zoo, a mixture of fascination and pity, and these were people, not animals. She was relieved they had come to the end of the tour.

Set across the far end of the unit, opposite the patio doors, were the closed doors of a craft room, two bathrooms and a shower room.

"There you have it," Linda said. "You can wait anywhere." She waved her arm at a group of several small tables with chairs around them, then at the sofas and easy chairs in the common area. With a last smile, she went back to the nurses' station.

Allie seated herself at one of the small tables. Soon a patient at another table caught her attention. The woman was a picture of industry, busily tearing paper. The small stack of intact paper to her left was dwarfed by piles of shredded paper in front of her. When the woman tore off a tissue-thin piece, leaving one like it in her hand, Allie realized she was not just shredding paper, she was separating the several layers that comprised each sheet. Allie watched her, aware the patient's face was serene. She appeared happily engrossed in the meticulous work.

When the unit door and the outer hallway door opened at the same time, she saw the patients, escorted by two male techs, ambling from the cafeteria as if in no hurry to return to the unit. All fourteen patients, male and female, wore identical blue cotton scrubs. Crystal entered last.

"Hello, Mrs. Davis," she said cheerfully. She sat down at the table with Allie, who thought Crystal looked wonderful. Relief flooded her.

"Hello Crystal. How are you? Your hair is so cute."

Crystal reached up and touched her hair with both hands, as if she had forgotten it was pulled back off her face, arranged in an intricate French braid. "One of the nurses did it," she said.

"So, they're treating you well in here?"

"Yeah, it's not bad. Except for these pajamas they make us wear." She tweaked her baggy shirt. "It's not as bad as I thought it would be. They put me on Prozac, said it was 'tried and true'. I've been on it just four days but I do feel a little better."

"Who's taking care of your children?"

"My husband. He must have thought I was turning into a real whack job, because he said he could use some time off, and he took vacation days."

"Have you told him everything? About your uncle?"

"Some of it. I think he understands. I made him promise me he wouldn't let the creep anywhere near our kids." The smile left her face and her hand went to the nape of her neck in a familiar gesture, but found no hanging strand of wispy hair to twist. Allie thought the gesture might indicate doubt or anxiety, but before she could question it Crystal stood quickly, her chair screeching against the concrete floor. She called out, "Kim!"

Allie looked up. She saw Kim Altaha enter the unit with another visitor, escorted by a nurse. Allie wondered if Kim was as surprised to see her as she was to see Kim.

"Hi, Allie!" Kim said, then took Crystal in her arms for a long hug.

"So you two do know each other. I thought you might."

"For years," said Kim.

"BFFs" added Crystal, laughing.

Kim said, "Before I forget, Crystal, your husband asked me to say he's not bringing the kids to visit today since they'll be here later to take you home."

"Thanks. He already told me." She motioned to a chair. Kim sat down with them.

Activity swirled in the common area now, the noise of the TV mixed with the voices of patients and visitors socializing.

Sound echoed off the bare floors and walls, amplifying what could have been a pleasant murmur into a strident, institutional clamor. Allie knew the walls and floors were uncovered, unadorned to prevent patients from using the most harmless seeming objects to harm themselves or others, but she thought the noise and stark surfaces must stress the patients and the staff. It felt stressful to her.

She noticed several patients, even one of the techs, staring at Kim. It it occurred to her that Kim's striking appearance was even more noticeable here, like a bright splash of color swept across a muddy canvas. One of the young men sat down at a table near them, staring at Kim, listening to their conversation without guile. Kim ignored him.

"Time for service, time for service," announced a deep male voice. A tall, heavily muscled male tech escorted two other men toward the craft room. The tech's face was pock-marked by acne scars. His features were rough, except for his eyes, which were large, brown and bracketed by smile lines.

He passed them, looking pointedly at Kim. He raised both eyebrows and pursed his lips in a silent whistle of appreciation, an unspoken 'Wow!'

Walking on the tech's right was a bearded man wearing wrinkled, stained scrubs, his shock of wildly tousled hair hanging in his eyes. On the tech's left was a medium sized man with blond hair and a ruddy face above a white clerical collar and a dark suit.

"I don't know who that guy is," whispered Crystal, indicating the cleric, "but the other one is Jacob. He's got schizophrenia. He's on twenty-four hour obs. The nurses told me I shouldn't be scared in here because the violent patients, the ones who committed crimes, are in the State Hospital in Phoenix. In the forensics unit, whatever that means. But Jacob punched one of the other patients and then spit in the nurse's face. That's why the techs are with him. Close obs means observation. They have to keep him within eyesight or arms length twenty-four/seven. He scares me. I wish he wasn't here."

"Tonight *you* won't be here," said Kim, "that's even better. Let's find out what the pastor has to say." She rose, nodding toward the craft room, which evidently doubled as a chapel.

Allie and Crystal looked at each other, then Crystal shrugged and followed her friend while Allie followed her, wondering at this very strange visit and this particular unexpected turn of events. They walked toward the craft room/ersatz chapel.

Kim said to Allie, "The nurse told me there's a law in Arizona that says people in psych hospitals are entitled to practice their spiritual beliefs, so the hospital has to provide that as well as food, clothing and shelter."

There were four rows of folding chairs across the width of the craft room facing a table which the pastor now prepared as his lectern. Allie sat in the middle of the second row, Kim and Crystal to her left, the tech to her right with his patient Jacob on his other side at the end of the row.

The tech turned toward Allie and leaned down to say, "All our Sunday speakers are volunteers, different ministers or priests or a rabbi from the community. We've had some good speakers. One woman, she's a Baha'i I think, brings her violin to play for us. Her name is Kate. She reads some nice prayers that sound like poetry. We sing a few songs and everyone feels better afterward."

"That's nice...".

The pastor's voice interrupted. "Welcome everyone. I'm Reverend Dean. I'm happy to be invited here to share this sacred day with you." He looked down to consult his notes one more time. His pale hair fell across his forehead. He put his fists on the table. Leaning forward on straightened arms, he began.

"Today I want to talk to you about attitude. Attitude, my friends, is everything. Attitude is the difference between a cup that is half full and one that is half empty. Attitude makes the difference between hope and despair. And attitude, for some of you here, can make the difference in having to be in here, or being free in the Lord."

He stood with his arms folded now, and Allie noticed his face had turned pink and mottled. "For some of us here today, as the Bible puts it in the Book of Wisdom, Chapter Five, Verse Six, 'We, then, have strayed from the way of truth, and the sun did not rise for us'. A sad condition indeed. For that sad condition, some of the patients here may blame their dysfunctional families, their selfish or abusive mothers or their alcoholic fathers. Or they may even blame God Himself! But these excuses from the past do not help any of us in the present."

While his voice escalated in volume Allie noticed beads of sweat on his forehead, although the room felt cool. Several of the patients stirred in their folding chairs, perhaps sensing the start of a real sermon. The close obs patient stared straight ahead. He began to rock back and forth.

The Pastor continued. "To make such excuses proclaims that we are helpless and powerless before God and our fellow man. Are we helpless? No. Because God has given us the power of free will, and the free will that changes our *attitude* is the *power* that changes our lives.

"An attitude adjustment. That's all we're talking about. So, what is the right attitude and how do we adjust ours to get it? Let me ask you this. Have you ever, any of you here, ever seen a newborn baby with a *bad attitude*?"

Allie smiled, but when she glanced around she didn't see another amused face. The pastor continued, either unmoved by, or unaware of his, audience's reaction.

"Second Timothy, Chapter One, Verse Seven reassures us that we have all been gifted from birth with the right attitude." His voice took on a different tone as he quoted, 'For God hath not given us the spirit of fear; but of power, and of love, and of a sound mind.' A sound mind! That is our birthright, friends!"

A rift of sharp screeches startled Allie, the sound of metal chair legs against the concrete floor. Jacob was rocking faster and harder.

The pastor continued. "The right attitude. Philippians, Chapter Four, Verse Eight tells us how to get it. 'Finally, brethren, whatever is true, whatever is lovely, whatever is of good repute, if there is any excellence and if anything is worthy of praise, let your mind dwell on these things'."

Jacob now rocked in his chair so violently he was in danger of pitching forward onto the floor. The tech stood and with a quiet, deep-voiced command and a firm grip on the patient's arms, got Jacob up and out of the room. In less than a minute the tech reappeared without the patient, and reclaimed his own empty seat.

The pastor appeared unaware of the disturbance. He fixed his eyes on the wall at the back of the room and swiped his hand across his face.

"Let's sum up, then.The right attitude is an attitude of love and of forgiveness. It is truth, honor, beauty and excellence in any form. Now, I know you're asking how we can rediscover this life-affirming attitude in ourselves. I can tell you, it's not by lying on a psychiatrist's couch or sitting in some therapist's office, although God can work through just about anyone. And not by reading self help books, unless it's the Good Book." He waved his Bible at them. "No, we can't find this perfect attitude in books or therapy sessions. We get it from letting our minds dwell on the right things.

"I know, my friends. I hear your thoughts. You're saying, 'Death, disease, falsehood and despair are everywhere. If life were different, I could have a better attitude' but I say to you, that's backward thinking.

"What I'm telling you is that what you *believe* about a matter is so much more important than the *facts* of the matter, and what you *believe* guides how you *feel*.

"What is fact, after all? Five hundred years ago it was 'fact' that the earth was flat. A hundred years ago it was 'fact' that humankind would never set foot on the moon. So you see, facts are mutable. Facts are relative, facts are irrelevant to the *right attitude*. So called facts and judgments about facts are inventions of mankind. But the, *right attitude* friends, is a true gift from God."

He closed his Bible and folded his hands. "Let us all pray that this gift we were invested with by Divinity at birth will be restored to us and to our loved ones, through the grace of God. Amen."

Silence. Then quiet sobs. Allie looked to her left, to see Crystal crying, face in her hands.

The pastor still appeared oblivious to the members of his tiny congregation. He concluded the sermon, "Go in peace, my friends." Then he grabbed his notes and his Bible and left the room before anyone could stir.

A pause. As if released from a spell, the patients and visitors began to rise and leave. The tech turned to Allie. "First time I ever felt like a hit and run victim of a man of the cloth."

"Yes, he certainly didn't want to linger afterward. It was a little strange. Maybe he felt uncomfortable here."

The tech smiled. "It can have that effect on people."

A patient near by inserted himself into the exchange. "I thought it was very powerful and the absolute truth."

The tech replied, "True, possibly. Powerful, yes. Maybe a little too powerful for people that are stressed or have a sensitive nervous system."

Allie said, "I guess he put us mental health professionals in our place. Or at least he tried to."

"He wouldn't be the first, would he?" the tech said.

Allie noticed Crystal was still crying. She vacillated between thinking about the provocative content of the sermon and wanting to attend to Crystal's distress. Crystal held a sodden tissue to her nose and mouth but couldn't stifle her heart breaking sobs.

Allie's indecision became resignation. She turned back to the tech, who was ushering out the last patient. "I think Crystal and I need to talk. Can we stay in here for some privacy?"

"Sure."

Kim said, "I'm staying too," and put her hand on Crystal's shoulder. She turned to Allie. "All the preacher did was confirm what Wilma Mankiller said."

"Who?" said Crystal, looking up with tears streaming down her face.

"Wilma Mankiller. I love what she said. She said, 'I believe in the old Cherokee injunction to be of a good mind. Today it's called positive thinking'."

"Who's Wilma Mankiller?"

"She was a Cherokee tribal leader. She wasn't a man killer. That was just her family name, like people named Smith and Baker aren't actually blacksmiths and bakers. White New Agers think they invented positive thinking, as if Natives have no intellect, no philosophy. Wilma Mankiller is one of my heroes. President Clinton gave her the Medal of Freedom."

"Did you understand what that was all about?" Crystal asked, referring to the pastor's sermon.

Kim replied, "Yes. I liked it. I believe so-called right and wrong and good and bad are no more than personal opinions. John Kennedy said kind of the same thing. Here's one of his quotes. He said, 'A man does what he must, in spite of personal consequences, in spite of obstacles and dangers and pressures. And this is the basis of all human morality'."

Allie felt she could be drawn into an interesting debate here, but chose not to comment. Instead, she turned to Crystal and asked, "What's going on with you right now? What did he say that made you cry?"

"I don't know, maybe just about kids and how innocent and sweet they are. It made me think of my kids, and then it made me think about my uncle. Kim and I call him the blood sucker."

"The blood sucker? Kim, you knew him too?"

"We lived on the same street, him and my family and Crystal's. It would have been hard to live in Camp Verde and not know him. He was one of the few real estate agents in town. He was in and out of his house all hours of the day and evening, every season of the year."

Allie said nothing but questioned with her eyes.

Crystal nodded. "We started going over to his house in the summer when he was home because he would give us ice pops and soda." She slumped further down in her metal chair, as if weighted by memories.

Kim said, "None of the parents minded because he was our neighbor and everybody knew him. Then one day he asked if we wanted to go for a ride with him to look at a new listing. I still remember how he talked about his car and how proud he looked when he told us he had a new 1978 Datsun 280-Z Two-plus-Two, as if we knew what that meant."

Crystal said, "I didn't understand, either. He said, 'Let's go look at my new house', and from then on I thought the empty houses were all his."

Kim continued, "He told us to go ask first, the ones who had parents at home to ask. Then he piled us in the car, two in the front with him and four kids in the back. I think Crystal was the youngest one there. He put the air conditioning on high. Our parents didn't have air conditioning in our cars. We loved it."

Allie knew, but asked anyway, "What happened?"

Kim chose not to answer.

Crystal had begun looking around the room with anxious eyes, inspecting its open cubby holes full of paper, glue, paints and fabric scraps. As if satisfied, she leaned back in her chair, her face calmer, and said, "It's quiet in here. It feels safe in here."

She stared at her hands in her lap without seeing. "Nothing," she said. "Nothing happened that day. It was fun to run around in the empty house and on the way back he bought us all a Dreampop, you know, those orange and vanilla ice creams on a stick."

Allie thought, *He had a new car and he let six little kids ride in it? Gave them ice cream? He was grooming them, picking his victims, planning it.*

Both her clients were silent. Allie waited.

Crystal continued with a wavering voice. "We trusted him. We thought he was our friend, that he just liked kids. After that first ride, I went with him a lot. Sometimes the houses were empty but sometimes they weren't. Those felt creepy and I didn't like it. I thought they must belong to someone else but he acted like they were his. He used the kitchens, the bathrooms and--and the bedrooms.

"I really don't remember much about how it started, and then only parts." She paused and drew a deep breath. "One thing he did--he used to make me take off all my clothes and lie in the bed on my stomach with my legs together. Then he put his--thing--in between my legs, near my butt, and push. One day when we were at his house...one day he pushed inside of me. It hurt, it hurt so bad." She began to sob. "My face was shoved against the bed and I could feel the pain of him doing something to me, I didn't know what, and I felt like I was going to die."

Kim reached for her friend. She held Crystal while the woman sobbed against her shoulder. At last Crystal stopped crying. She reached down to pull more tissues from her purse. Her face had become hard, set in anger. She wiped her eyes and continued, "When it was over and he got off me, I tried to run outside. I didn't care that I didn't have on any clothes. But he caught me. I screamed at him. I told him I was going to tell my parents. He didn't say anything, he just took me in the bathroom and cleaned me up, wiped away the blood and stuff. I guess he knew he couldn't let me go until the bleeding stopped.

"Then he took me into his living room and put a movie on. It was a vampire movie. He kept making it go fast with the remote control to get to the scary parts. When the vampire would come on he'd say, 'That's me. That's what I'll do to you and your parents if you tell anyone. I'll fly into your house at night, when you're asleep and kill you. Then you'll turn into a vampire too'. That scared me the most. I didn't want to be a vampire. I didn't want to be like him."

Kim broke her uneasy silence. "He did the same with me."

Allie looked up in shock. Kim had never told her about being sexually abused, but then the focus of her therapy had been managing anger, not exploring childhood traumas or seeking the etiology of her anger.

Kim said, "I believed his vampire stories too, until I turned eight years old. Then I told him it was just a movie and there weren't any vampires. He grabbed me by the arm and sliced it with his pocket knife. Then he licked off the blood. I still remember the look in his eyes and the smear of blood on his chin. I guess he wasn't sure he had me convinced, because then he showed me his gun. It was an evil looking thing, a shiny, dark blue color. I remember thinking I'd rather he shot me than drink my blood.

"I guess he decided he hadn't cowed me enough because he put me in his car and took me out to the desert. There were empty shell casings on the ground all around, so I think other people went there to shoot, too.

"He set up some full cans of Pepsi. He shot each one. When they exploded, he'd say, 'That's your mother', or 'that's your brother Wayne...', until he named every member of my family. After that I never questioned him any more. The f-ing pervert!"

Allie had never heard such horrific details of abuse. It both stunned and infuriated her. "You're right. He is a pervert, a pedophile, a sexual predator. I can't believe he's walking around free. Hasn't he ever been arrested?"

"I don't think so," said Kim.

"When did he stop? What made him stop it?"

Kim said, "I remember wanting to stop it but being so afraid for my family. Then, when I was about to turn ten years old, I remember the idea of having lived a decade impressed me. It made me feel like I was almost grown up. I told myself that when my birthday came at the end of January, it would be a new year and a new me, that I wouldn't have to let him touch me any more. And I didn't."

"How?"

"It was a dark night, the new moon. When he...I'm not going to say any more. He never tried it again after that, after what I did and what I told him. Every January on the new moon I think about it and celebrate." Kim's chin tilted upward in a small gesture of triumph.

Crystal took her friend's hand and squeezed it in a gesture of empathy. Then she turned to look at Allie. "He'll never touch my kids," she said, wiping her nose with the soggy tissue. "I'd rather die first. I'd rather they were dead!"

She glanced at Allie in alarm. "I didn't mean anything by that. I'm not going to do anything!"

Allie hesitated. "I'm glad you didn't mean it." She sensed that Crystal would say no more today because she felt she had already said too much. Her cathartic revelation was ended.

Allie said, "We can talk about this a little more next week when you come for your appointment, right?"

Crystal nodded. Allie fervently hoped Crystal's retraction of her new threat against Upshall was sincere. Even more horrible was the implied threat against her own children if Upshall ever tried to molest them. But she had to believe her instincts that Crystal's denial of future violence was genuine.

In any case, she suspected that Crystal had learned to play the mental health game. In the game, a denial that she presented a danger to anyone might or might not be sincere but in either case it relieved mental health professionals of 'the duty to report' or any *excuse* to report, for that matter. Allie had no mandate to inform law enforcement, warn the uncle, or try to force Crystal into further treatment.

***

The session was going well.

"Any more nightmares? That one about not being able to scream?"

"No. I haven't had a chance to use that lucid dreaming technique you talked about. I'm not dreaming much at all, or at least I'm not remembering them." She paused, thoughtful, then, "Did you ever just wake up and question everything you believe, everything you're doing?"

"I'm guessing you did. When did this happen?"

Allie appeared not to have heard. "I don't even know why. Maybe something someone said or something different in the way I feel...I can't explain it."

"A certain amount of introspection or self examination, if you want to call it that, is healthy. Is that what you're experiencing or is it something more?"

"I'm not sure. I'm second guessing some decisions I've made and starting to wonder if my life is headed in the right direction after all."

"Maybe I can help you get a different perspective on things. Let's talk about specifics. What decisions are you second guessing?"

A long silence. "I don't feel comfortable talking to you about them right now."

Chapter 6

His gun felt obscene in her hand. Kim threw it onto the sofa as she followed his shuffling steps out of the house. She closed the front door behind her but left it unlocked. When they moved out of the small pool of light on the concrete step she took out the stun gun and switched on its flashlight, the illumination little more than a pin point in the gloom of night.

They felt their way across the rocky earth toward the garage, he with bare feet that suffered every rock and cactus spine, judging by his muffled grunts and moans.

When they reached the garage she commanded, "On your knees!" He remained standing. She kicked the back of one knee, sending him sprawling. He remained face down in the dirt while she went into the garage to start the old two door Datsun. She had noticed earlier it gleamed with sparkling new metallic paint. Now she saw the interior appeared in mint condition, too. He had been restoring it.

She didn't need to move the seat forward; her legs were as long as his. When she inserted the key into the ignition the car's V6 engine roared into life on the first try. The manual transmission presented no problem.

She backed the Z out of the garage then replaced it with her own car after removing the last of her supplies, the long handled pitch fork. She checked, saw her prisoner sitting in the dirt picking thorns from his bare feet. She methodically closed the garage doors. Best to keep appearances normal in case of unlikely visitors.

The Datsun's white paint made it a little easier to see what she was doing next. She lifted the hatch back, which had been fitted with black louvers, then went around to tilt the back of the front seat forward so she could reach into the rear. She had to put the gun down on the floor in order to use both hands to pull the levers on the ends of the seat back at the same time, which lowered the seat back to form a cargo compartment.

She picked up the gun and turned back to him. He knew she intended to put him in the compartment. He shook his head. She wondered if he was remembering children he had confined there, what he had done to them there and elsewhere.

"Get up," she growled. Watching him, she felt a sick emptiness in her stomach. *I want this whole disgusting job to be over.*

Watching him struggle to his feet, then cover his genitals with his bound hands as he stood in front of her infuriated her more. Now he was modest? Now he was chaste?

Her anger flared. Then she remembered the sensual pleasure she had felt earlier in planning his humiliation and defeat. Earlier today the surveillance and break in had produced an adrenalin rush accompanied by just a tinge of sexual arousal. It had faded tonight the second she saw him standing in his doorway. Then she felt only rage and now, as well, a secret shame. *It's not normal to get excited by anger and fear and violence. It's sick! Oh, God, am I as sick as he is? Damn him to hell!*

She put the gun in her pocket and picked up the pitch fork, resisting an urge to bash him over the head with it. She didn't want to touch him. Instead she used the back side of the curved prongs to prod him toward the low slung sports car. He made his way to stand at the rear bumper. One good shove with the handle toppled his upper body into the compartment. She started to use the pitch fork again to lift his legs and feet but he saw her intent and quickly folded himself inside.

A phrase she had heard from a friend in the Air Force came to her, *self-loading cargo,* a description that dehumanized any unessential or unwanted passengers. *How appropriate.*

It wasn't until she closed the hatch and stood with her hand on it that she began to wonder what came next, what route to take to get to the Well. Strange, she thought. Her planning hadn't gotten that far and now she had a choice to make. Go the shorter, more direct route on I-Seventeen to the exit at Maguireville or head south on Highway 260 to the Forest Road?

The shorter way would get her there in less than twenty minutes. The back way was twice as long. She recalled seeing state troopers on the local stretch of Interstate 10. They patrolled it regularly, hoping to ambush drunk or disgruntled drivers leaving the casino in Camp Verde. The thought of being stopped by a trooper while carrying self-loading cargo, naked, bound, self-loading cargo, decided her.

She got in, headed in the opposite direction from the Interstate, careful to keep to the speed limit. She was relieved that she met not a single other car on the way to the turnoff onto Forest Road 618. As she bumped onto the dirt road, she heard a groan of discomfort from her prisoner.

The washboard-like road stretched dark and deserted, a thread strung across an inhospitable landscape. She accelerated until she felt the car's vibration chattering her teeth. She liked the way the car handled as the road dipped into a canyon, passed an abandoned salt mine, then rose onto a plateau.

The cliffs here were horizontal layers of rocky earth in shades of chalk white, tan, and tarnished-copper green, but tonight they were nothing but blanched shadows banking the road. When the banks gave way to flatter terrain, the vegetation, creosote bush, scrub mesquite, rattlesnake brush and yucca, appeared like small, malignant mounds against a stark horizon.

A machine gun-like clatter and hum startled her. Then she knew: the tires going over a cattle guard. More of the iron barred inserts in the road ahead failed to startle her.

She recognized the halfway point when she passed a side road marked by a typical ranch gateway, a twenty-foot tall, square structure with a wrought iron sign that said 'D-Diamond Ranch,' its cattle branded with the 'D' inside a diamond shape.

Impatient for the destination, she pressed harder on the accelerator. The car began to fishtail on the loose, graveled soil. She cursed under her breath but wary of losing control, slowed the car that was doing thirty-five miles an hour on a dirt road that was fit for maybe twenty-five.

As if in recognition of pushing the limits, she felt an impact on the undercarriage. The car's suspension failed the challenge of another rapid series of bumps. A muffled whine from her prisoner indicated his concern for the car as much as for himself, then another machine/human duet as she bottomed out again.

Reluctantly she slowed a little more, wary she might slide into a ditch or disable the car before she reached her destination. She glanced into the back to check her naked passenger, pleased that the beating the car was taking pained him and the jouncing would keep him off balance enough to prevent an escape attempt. The brief glimpse of his pale, curled form reminded her again of a maggot.

Thirty minutes later, by the time the car crossed the bridge over Walker Creek, she felt hypnotized by the headlong rush into darkness, the incessant road noise, the constant vibration. She could almost believe that time had stopped, that she would ride this road for eternity.

A small sign on the shoulder appeared. Trying to read it in the dark pulled her back but she already knew what it said: 'Dead Wood Draw.' She slowed a little, not wanting to attract attention from the roadside campground when the car crossed Wet Beaver Creek. The campground appeared silent, dark, still, then *gone* as they passed it in a split second.

The road was paved again here but soon became a roller coaster of steep hills and sudden turns that challenged her driving skill. At the metal 'no shooting' sign marked by dents and bullet holes she turned left, onto another dirt road. She hadn't seen another car or another person since they left Camp Verde.

Almost there. Her eyes searched into the distance. She made out a pale haze like the imminent break of dawn but the dawn was hours away. A mile later the haze revealed itself as a large cloud of mist writhing upward against the backdrop of the star studded night sky. It appeared like a living thing but she knew it was only vapor produced by the contrast between the lukewarm water of the Well and the freezing cold air.

The road was paved here, the ride smoother, but for some reason inexplicable to herself she slowed her approach toward the column of mist that marked her destination.

She thought of the countless people, both Native and non-Native, who had been killed or had died at the Well. Her imagination conjured ghosts from the ethereal mist. The smaller tendrils were the Native babies who had been buried in the floors of the cliff dwellings, literally beneath their grieving parents' feet.

Her eyes returned to the road. She caught a glimpse of something streaking in front of her. She heard the thump before she could tap the brakes. In the rear view mirror she glimpsed an indistinct form at the edge of the road. She braked, threw the car in reverse and backed onto the shoulder.

She left the engine running and got out. The tiny beam of her flashlight showed the dog-like animal with a reddish-tan coat, a magnificent, plumed tail and a twisted, bloody mid-section that leaked a glistening rope of intestine. The coyote's eyes turned toward her. It made a single yipping noise as she approached. Its legs twitched with the urgent need to run.

The nausea that had assailed her earlier returned. She felt this tragedy in her own gut while she sensed rather than saw the coyote's fear and suffering.

"I'm sorry, little brother," she said, pulling her gun. "I meant you no harm. I was in the wrong place at the wrong time."

The shot pierced the silence once then twice as it echoed off the nearby hills but the bullet did its job. She saw the coyote's limbs loosen and the light die from its eyes. She closed her own eyes for a second, the gun shot still echoing in her ears.

Her thought held the scolding tone of an angry mother. *So much for stealth. Curse this whole nasty business.* Then her mind evoked other words spoken by a president, *'A [wo]man does what [s]he must, in spite of personal consequences, in spite of obstacles and dangers and pressures.'* She took the coyote by its tail to drag it off the road. Even through her latex gloves the coarse fur was warm, alive. She felt a fleeting urge to stroke the coyote's head.

When she returned to the car Upshall was on his hands and knees trying to climb into the driver's seat. Without thinking she bashed his forehead with the hand that held the gun. Her wrist absorbed the impact of metal against skin and bone with a shock of pain. Upshall dropped back, blood trickling down his face. She attempted to cool her simmering rage by telling herself that at least he hadn't removed the gag and tried to speak to her.

She got in, put the car in gear and peeled out, leaving a spray of gravel in her wake. Her wrist hurt, contributing to a savage mood, her thoughts still dark and confused. *Stay here, stay with this,* she coached herself, *'in spite of obstacles and dangers'.*

A sudden scrape, a definitive clank from beneath the car followed by a loud, impressive rumble, the Z's newly un-muffled exhaust. *What? What next?*

She rounded the last turn and saw the access road to the parking lot head. An ominous 'flop-flop' noise from the road on the passenger's side squelched her relief. *No! Beyond belief!* But it was unmistakable. A flat tire.

No problem. I'll just get on my phone. Not the stun gun that looks like a phone, my real smart phone, and call Triple A! They'll be very happy to change the tire on a car with a naked man stuffed in the back. Instead of slowing, she gunned the car, determined to make it the last few hundred yards to the Well, even if it was on the rim of the wheel.

***

Wanda stood in the doorway of the break room, one hand on the door frame, the other on her hip. To Betty, she said, "Henrietta just called and said she's sick and can't keep her appointment this afternoon."

She turned and left without waiting for a response.

Betty and Allie were alone in the break room, where Allie had just poured herself a cup of coffee. "We both have a free hour then," Betty said. "How often does that happen?"

"Not often enough. It's nice to be able to relax at work for a change." She leaned back in her chair, relishing an unexpected break in the day. "I noticed Wanda didn't have to tell you Henrietta's last name. With a first name like that, you know who she's talking about. Not many Henriettas around."

"As scarce as Adele or Cher."

"But not the same at all, really. More like Jolene, Rayetta, or Jamie, all those men's names masquerading as women's names. But I'm one to talk. Allie is short for Alexandra, which is just a feminization of Alexander."

"Maybe parents should go ahead and name their baby girls Alexander or Harold or John. There was that movie star named Darryl...".

"Have you noticed there are no masculine endings on feminine names for boys?"

Betty smiled. "What, like a male Wanda named Wando? Or like Bettybo, or Ruthboy or maybe Jennifer-dude?"

Allie put her hand over her mouth to keep from spraying coffee on her friend. She grabbed a napkin and when she stopped choking said, "I love it when you're silly."

"Me too. Being serious is an occupational hazard for us, isn't it?"

"During my internship a few years ago, I did a therapy group for depressed clients and everyone had to tell a joke during check-in. I told them it was their price of admission."

"How did that go over?"

"Some of them liked it and actually told a joke. I had to remind some that we wanted *clean* jokes. Others were too--too depressed. Wow, it seems like that was eons ago."

"That's because you've turned into a very good therapist in the three years you've been doing this, Allie."

"My clients seem to like me but I know that doesn't mean much. So many of them just need an un-judgmental ear, honest feedback, and maybe now and then some common sense advice."

Betty nodded. "But for others, nothing you can say or do is good enough. So much depends on the client, not the therapist."

"Most therapists can get by if they don't insult or abuse clients or try to have sex with them. During sessions we have to be just polite enough not to fart and well groomed enough not to stink."

They both laughed. Allie said, "You know, sometimes I think if people could get just three statements, three rules to really live by, they wouldn't need us at all."

Betty raised her eyebrows until Allie continued. "First, *shit happens.* Second, *it is what it is. Accept it. That doesn't mean you like it, you just allow it.* And third, *God didn't make anyone perfect so don't expect anyone to be, including yourself.*"

Betty tilted her head. "You minimize what we do. What about the training we go through in order to do it? But I agree that there aren't many objective criteria for measuring a therapist's competency, much less her proficiency. It's not like other professions; the proof isn't always in the pudding."

"I know. Even the best therapists sometimes have clients who need to be hospitalized or attempt suicide. Even if we don't have those negative responses, how do we measure the positive ones? Occasionally I feel like I'm in limbo, waiting for a definitive sign of improvement in one of my clients. Like Crystal, for instance."

Betty pushed her glasses back up the bridge of her nose and smoothed her silver hair from her temples before she spoke. "The changes can be very subtle, but still profound. Sometimes the deepest changes don't manifest until the therapy is over or the improvements might continue long after the sessions end. The most important thing in helping clients is just what the research tells us. Be compassionate and empathetic."

Allie shook her head. "I don't seem to have a problem with that. Sometimes when my clients cry, I cry a little with them. But I read so much about 'compassion fatigue' and 'burn out' and 'secondary victimization' in the journal articles. It makes this profession sound downright hazardous. It makes me wonder if hearing so much horror and witnessing so much pain and suffering is going to make me jaded or even sick."

"Another occupational hazard. The best thing we can do for ourselves is follow the protocol we set for our clients. Laugh at every opportunity and talk it out."

When Allie got up to wash her cup at the sink and put it away in the cabinet, she turned back toward Betty. "Okay then. I've been worried about Crystal."

"We're not paid to worry about them, Allie."

At that, Allie tilted her head back and put both hands on her forehead. "I know."

Betty put her empty cup down and gave Allie a conciliatory smile. "What's going on with her that's got you so concerned?"

"Just the feeling lately that she's not telling me everything, that's she planning something or doing something that's dangerous. And my intuition's pretty good. To tell you the truth, I think the reason I'm as good a therapist as I am is not my training, it's my intuition."

"Then listen to it, Allie my friend."

"Of course. You're right." She smiled at Betty, considering whether to ask, then softly, "So how are you doing with thoughts of Tim?"

"I'm at peace with it. Not that he committed suicide, but that I did the best I could for him."

"Any repercussions from the parents? They playing the blame game?"

"No, not so much as an 'f- you.' I think they're just relieved to be rid of him, as horrible and sad as that sounds."

***

Back in her office, Allie checked her voice mail. To her surprise there was a message from Sherry. Didn't they see each other often enough to communicate in person?

Sherry's voice on the message said her husband felt concerned about Crystal and her medication regimen, and wanted Allie's impression of Crystal's mental status. He would be busy all day, and requested that Allie call him that evening, at home.

Allie's initial feeling of uneasiness faded when she told herself that someone else shared her concerns about Crystal and together she and Doctor V might be able to help her more. That evening she called him, as he had desired.

If that had been the end of it the call would have seemed helpful but unremarkable, a routine exchange of clinical information and diagnostic impressions between two professionals.

The next morning she was with Sherry and Doctor V in the break room when he said, "Last evening when you called I was about to get into the shower. All the time we were talking, I was standing there stark naked. Could you tell?"

"Tell? Uh, no, I had no idea…I…". She sputtered into silence while both Sherry and Doctor V laughed. "We'll have to do it again some time," Doctor V said, raising one eyebrow at Allie.

She retreated to her office once again feeling an odd mixture of embarrassment and anger. But the image had been implanted: Ralph VanDeusen stark naked.

It was not an image that stirred her libido but over the next weeks she found herself thinking of him at odd moments, in wistful daydreams of intimate conversations, quiet moments of togetherness, tender exchanges of affection. Previously, in any fleeting fantasies of that kind she might picture a film star, an old flame from high school or someone unknown glimpsed in a crowd. Now they featured Ralph VanDeusen, a man she could begin to dislike.

***

The weeks between Thanksgiving and Christmas seemed to speed by. Just past three p.m. on the Friday before Christmas, Allie realized how tired she was. It had been an exhausting week and the office Holiday party they were all expected to attend today would be nothing but an energy waster, a feeble attempt to conjure the elusive holiday spirit.

That morning, unwilling to reveal to the others her Grinch-like mood, she had prepared her best dish for the potluck, a Lasagna Florentine infused with flavors of butter, mushrooms and garlic.

The staff only gathering crammed the small break room with bodies clothed in holiday sweaters or cute ties that sported reindeer, wreaths or smiling Santas.

She wasn't enjoying the noise and commotion or the food and drink as she sat elbow to elbow at the table with Betty, Heidi, Doctor V and Sherry, while other staff members leaned against the walls, balancing their plates and glasses.

"I wish Mike could be here," Heidi said, taking a sip of hot cider. "He's working double shifts lately because they're short handed." She looked at her alcohol and caffeine free drink with distaste and said, "I would commit any number of misdemeanor crimes for a three-shot espresso, or a bold mocha, or a caramel macchiato--even a latte for Pete's sake."

"Still on your caffeine fast?" asked Allie. For some reason she recalled the sermon about positive thinking and added, "Maybe you should consider it a cup full of nutrition, rather than a cup empty of caffeine."

"Excellent advice," Heidi said, "but if I engaged in positive thinking, I wouldn't be able to complain so much."

Allie laughed. "You're right. Excuse the psycho-babble. I'd better go outside to cool off and come to my senses."

"I'll be out to join you when I finish," Heidi said, pointing with her fork to her full plate.

Doctor V and his wife followed Allie outside to the patio where they sat down on the curved concrete benches that surrounded a large round concrete table. Sherry looked nice, Allie thought, in the obligatory Christmas sweater depicting a traditional St. Nick, paired with a long green skirt and black boots. Doctor V wore a long sleeve shirt and a sweater vest in an argyle pattern that reminded Allie of a different decade, the 1950's.

He drained the last of his coffee and put the cup on the table with an emphatic clunk that could have broken it. His bony wrist emerged from his sleeve. His palm brushed his mouth then closed around his salt and pepper beard in a single stroke.

"I've been thinking about you," he said to Allie. He looked at her hand curled around a cup of cider. "Is that an opal?" He touched the ring then took her cup and put it down to uncurl her fingers and hold her hand in his own. It felt like skin and bone to Allie, devoid of reassuring human warmth.

"Yes, it's an opal."

"Nice. Has a lot of color." He continued to hold her hand, turning it to the sunlight this way and that as if to catch the opal's fire, then looked into her eyes. "You know, I had a dream about you last night."

A puzzling cloud of doubt, maybe even dread, descended and weakened her voice to a feeble, "Oh?"

"I'd tell you, but it was what you might call x-rated." His gaze sought out her own, but she turned her head then withdrew her hand from his with a conscious effort not to jerk it away.

"Dreams are fascinating, aren't they?" she blurted. "I love to work with them in therapy. I've read a couple of really interesting dream books."

Without waiting for a response she rose from the table and walked away. She knew it was rude but didn't care. She tried joining others but couldn't focus on conversation after what had just happened. At the first opportunity to retreat she left the break room, went to her office and then to her car. She knew she was running away but she didn't care.

She intended to go home but instead of turning left toward Main Street she turned the car right and drove toward the hills, her thoughts and emotions seething. She couldn't bring this home with her, but she also couldn't skirt the issue any longer. It was crystal clear that Doctor V had been coming on to her and if it was a deliberate seduction, he had just delivered the coup de grace. She felt too stunned and too confused to sort it out. *Just forget it for now,* she told herself. *Just be here now. Stay in the present.*

Ahead of her lay the hamlet of Clarkdale, its neat stores and old-fashioned white bungalows not visible, yet the town identified itself from this distance by a huge 'C' painted on the hillside.

To the northwest, the rooftops in the smaller town of Jerome appeared nestled into the sheer cliffs. In reality, the houses were precariously balanced on the edge of a maze of cliffs. The town, a newly resurrected artists' colony, also proclaimed its identity on a mountain-side with a painted 'J'. Between those proud markers the ugly, five story tower of a cement plant inserted itself, bringing a sight seer back to earth with a crash.

Allie slowed the car, taking the numerous roundabouts in the road with patience. They were better than stop lights and the snail-like pace allowed her to do a little sightseeing without fear of being rear-ended by some impatient local.

There were subtleties in the landscape here that she hadn't seen before. The bases of the distant hills were mauve, touched with amethyst shadows while the nearby cliff tops were ochre above a layer of terra cotta. There were soothing shades of color and pleasing silhouettes in the hills and hollows.

She had to admit the beauty of the Verde Valley was growing on her. She appreciated the free, open feel of the place. There was a cheerful and expansive quality to life here that seemed to be supported and protected by the surrounding hills. It occurred to her that she had begun to feel as opened up as the landscape. It was good but maybe frightening, too.

She drew comparisons of this upland valley to her former home. Back East by now the ground would be covered with snow, Christmas decorations everywhere, children sledding and building snow men, houses warmed by ovens filled with roasting meats or baking desserts. It was an idyllic mental picture.

Smiling to herself, she revised her memories to include shoveling her car out of the driveway every morning, fighting traffic on treacherous, icy roads, enduring power outages and 'snow days', navigating mounds of dirty slush on every other venture outside and feeling cold much of the time from November through March.

As much as it pulled at her thoughts, Long Island no longer felt like home. Neither did the Verde Valley, even though she realized with a start that she loved it here.

At a sign that said 'Old Jerome Highway,' she found herself turning the car, or the car turning as if by itself, as if on automatic pilot. The road wasn't much of a highway, just two lanes built decades ago, so worn and neglected it lacked a yellow line down the middle. *Good*, she thought. If it had been there the car would have been straddling it since the road was wide enough for just one vehicle.

She met no others on the road as it wound gently up, up and around, ascending further into the foothills. The real estate here would be described as high end, homes on two acre lots in natural terrain. Today the homes appeared deserted, neglected, not one home owner out trimming his shrubs or relaxing on a small patch of lawn, no other cars on the road. She was alone.

She stopped the car on the road and climbed out. Turning to her right, she noticed a few lowering clouds begin to cast dark shadows over the ridge. If they descended much further, they would engulf and obscure it. Turning to look back the way she had come, she took in a spectacular view. From up here it was a panorama. She could see as far north as the red rocks of Sedona, the Secret Mountain Wilderness to the northeast, Arizona's Black Hills to the southwest, and on and on into the west, where mesas, plateaus and mountains layered themselves into the sky to meet the clouds, softly billowing clouds in purest white to soft, dove gray. Like the view from an airplane or the middle of an ocean, it dwarfed human existence.

At last satiated with the numinous beauty of the landscape, she turned around. With a jolt she descended to the mortal and mundane. Atop a weathered wooden post, a small sign said 'Old Pioneer Cemetery'. Dozens of graves lay on the slope amid jumbled rock, scrub brush and cactus.

The cemetery was set back only a few feet from the road. One thick strand of wire served as a fence. Most of the graves were small plots outlined by native rock and instead of headstones they were topped with rudimentary crosses of wood or two inch metal pipe. Not a blade of grass or a single tree survived in this graveyard.

Walking along the road, she saw one grave that had collapsed and was now a three foot deep hole ending in what looked like a tunnel dug by some animal. Repelled, she averted her eyes and within a dozen more steps spotted a few engraved headstones and some less weather-beaten crosses that displayed Latino names and dates from the 1920's through 1944.

Had any of these people, before they were interred in this desolate plot, stood admiring the view below?

Now her mood matched the melancholy of the venue. Natives and Hispanics had a long history here. By rights they owned the future of the place. She and her kind were relative newcomers. Maybe they deserved no future here. Maybe she had no future here. What was she doing here, in this place and in this profession, trying to help people when she couldn't untangle her own problems?

Then the story came back to her. Of her own volition, she had taken the first steps on this career path, but the story had propelled her onward. This was it:

After a particularly violent storm at sea, a man walked along the beach in the morning to find hundreds of star fish that had been washed up by the tide. They lay dying in the sun. He began to pick them up, one by one, and throw them into the water.

Another man came along. Seeing what the first man was doing he said, "You're wasting your time. You can't save them all. What you're doing doesn't matter."

The first man silently picked up another starfish and tossed it to safety. "It matters to that one."

She loved that story, sometimes told it to clients. She continued walking.

The wind sprang up, raising goose bumps on her arms and down her spine. Chilled, the name Ralph VanDeusen came from no where, pierced her like an icicle in the brain. She stopped short, sending pebbles rolling under her shoes, then doubled back and returned to the car.

While she drove home the clouds thickened, obscuring the last light of the setting sun, sending a cold rain sputtering from the steel gray sky.

She pulled up at the mail boxes near her apartment, the windshield wipers on high. The pounding rain didn't deter her from getting the mail.

She thought, *Don't surprise me. I have enough on my mind already.*

There were two items in the box, a business size envelope from the National Health Service Corps and another letter from Paul. Through computer searches, she had discovered that the National Health Service Corps would wipe out her college debt in exchange for a two year commitment to work in an underserved community mental health center.

That would mean she must relocate to a different, less populated rural area, or to an inner city location where other professionals were loath to work. An old TV show had popularized the concept with a setting in Alaska but she had found there were many qualifying locations in almost every state and every large city.

Unable to wait until she got inside, she opened the business envelope with damp fingers while drops of water fell from her forehead onto the paper. The cover letter said her application had been accepted. Next spring, in four months, they wanted her to sign a two year contract and begin a new job in a new location. It was a two year commitment.

In her apartment she held the unopened letter from Paul, unsure why she hadn't discarded it. It felt different. She shed her jacket, sat down on the sofa, and opened it.

She read in disbelief that he had found someone new, a new love, and he would not be contacting her any more unless they needed to talk about their son. *At last!* The note remained between her fingers while she stared at nothing.

I should be happier. I should be happy for him and for me. Yet this strange feeling, wasn't this a feeling of rejection worming its way into her gut? *How juvenile, how pathetic! I'm damning the poor man if he does and if he doesn't.*

Impatient with herself, she discarded the letter and went to pull on fleece exercise clothes, a worn sweat suit and light jacket. Without care or thought, oblivious to the rain falling outside, she left for a walk. She often walked after dark, feeling perfectly safe in this little town trying to become a city.

Outside, she turned down Sixth Street toward First, where the road ran straight and long. Usually she chose a maze like but familiar path through a residential neighborhood but tonight she was in no mood to pass by a hundred cozy homes filled with happy people while she walked.

She quickened her pace from a brisk walk to a jog. It might help her stop trying to assimilate the latest news from both the Health Service Corps and her ex-husband. Instead, she mentally replayed the earlier encounter with Doctor V.

A relationship that had been cordial, comfortable and professional was now changed forever. When, how, and why? She had never felt the least bit attracted to Ralph VanDeusen until the past month or so.

Maybe it started when she came back from a therapists' training. She and some of the other therapists, along with Doctor V, chatted over coffee while she told them about the training. The presenter was from England and had one of the more educated and easy-to-understand British accents. At the end of the training session, he told his audience, "I have a plane to catch now, so it's goodbye, my dears." The 'my dears' sounded so ridiculously inappropriate, sweet and romantic, it melted her heart. The next day Doctor V started addressing her as 'my dear', without regard to who else might be present or listening, including his wife.

Allie stopped short in mid-step and almost stumbled, a mental connection sparking. Most of

Doctor V's seductive behaviors had happened in his wife's presence. Sherry had actually initiated some of the incidents. Sherry was fully complicit in this game of seduction.

The shock of realization brought with it the self-awareness of wet feet, wet shoulders, dripping hair and the stares of people passing by in their warm, dry cars. The feeling of revulsion in her gut competed with sensations of chill and physical discomfort.

She turned and slogged home, shivering, and went straight into the bathroom for a hot shower. By the time she toweled off she felt almost warm again. She put on a pair of worn flannel pajamas and lay down on the bed, idly playing with the oversized foot of her son's stuffed rabbit. For some reason, the issues of a possible commitment to a new job and a changed relationship with her ex-husband were overshadowed by questions about Doctor V.

As it frequently did when she struggled with a conundrum, the *I Ching* came to mind. It felt comforting to start the familiar ritual of gathering the materials. After much though, she formulated her question for the oracle, 'Help me understand what's happening with R.V.'.

The coin toss yielded six lines forming a single diagram, with no changing lines; thus it did not produce a second diagram. That signified a 'pat' answer about a static situation. The answer to this question was hexagram twenty-five, named 'Innocence'. The commentary and text were about innocence or lack of it, guile and ulterior motives. It ended with warnings about the unintentional or unexpected.

She read it over and over again. Could she be the innocent person? Or did this hexagram refer to Ralph V as innocent? No, she didn't believe that, not for a second. But what were the unintentional or unintended aspects of the situation? She couldn't fathom it. She was as mentally exhausted as she was physically bone tired.

Fatigue breached her defenses. Her emotions surfaced on a stream of tears. She scrubbed her hands across her face, as if to rub out her frustration. Damn! Her fantasies about Doctor V weren't even the product of genuine lust. If *she* had any ulterior design in this whole thing, as the *I Ching* might have suggested, it was to achieve intimacy with an intelligent, complex and even strange man, who just happened to be married. But that was hardly ulterior.

What if the ulterior design was his? If his motive wasn't the obvious, to initiate a sexual relationship with her, what was it?

She put the book away, feeling as frustrated as ever. At times she thought the oracle invited her to project her own solution to supersede whatever meaning the text might have, that its ambiguity invited her to read into it whatever she wanted the facts to be.

Then a conviction came with certainty. *I Ching* or no *I Ching*, the way to deal with this bizarre situation was simply not to indulge it. She had promised herself many times before and after the divorce that she would never have an affair with a married man. Nothing had changed. She told herself, *If I can't trust myself to keep my promises to myself, then who can trust me?*

***

The session was going well.

"I think I want to talk about men today."

"This is your hour. We'll talk about whatever you want to talk about. Is it one particular man or men in general?"

"Understand one, understand them all, don't you think?"

"Not at all. They're as individual as any human or any animal for that matter."

"I guess that's the problem. I'm trying to understand what makes one man so kind and supportive it takes you by surprise, while another is cold and uncaring"

"Can't you generalize to the human race, rather just the one gender? And I think you know the answer already."

"If you insist. It's in their inborn characteristics, plus the way they're raised, plus how they've interpreted their personal experiences. And I guess we shouldn't forget their intentions or purpose. You know, you're not helping much with this."

"Ask a general question and you get a generic answer. Let's talk about what's bothering you."

"What's bothering me is not understanding why we're attracted to some men who are creeps and not the least bit attracted to wonderful, sweet men, men who know how to nurture instead of dominate and control."

"Again I can only answer with abstractions but I do have a theory about that. Well, it's not my theory but something I've heard or read. It has to do with the roles we learn. Male and female children learn to receive nurturing, but when gender differences are stereotyped, little girls know it will be their adult job to provide nurturing. They've got all the dolls and all the cues from adults to help them learn how. They accept that role identity and if they also learn a little independence and competence, voila! A complete human being.

"On the other hand, some men who are socialized with those rigid gender differences never learn or at least never perfect the nurturing role. So many are jealous of their own children because they are, in essence themselves, needy children."

Allie said, "I know the kind. Older, unattached men like that aren't looking for a relationship between equals. They just want a nurse with a purse, as the saying goes."

The therapist laughed.

Allie continued. "So what about what men are attracted to? The type of guy you just described wants a mommy. And while we're at it, what type of creep wants a little kid for sex, and what type of man wants to seduce a woman just for the hell of it?"

"So many questions. I'll be happy to speculate, but first I want to remind you that I have a duty to report any actual or even suspected child sexual abuse if the victim or the perpetrator is known."

"Of course. I don't have names of any victims or perpetrators for you."

"Okay then. One question at a time. It happens I have a theory about the issue of pedophilia. Let me see how to explain it...". She paused. "You've heard about how newborn or newly hatched animals imprint on the first living creature they see? Well, maybe this isn't a good analogy, but suppose a person has his or her first sexual awakening prematurely, when he's a child himself, through sexual abuse or some other bizarre circumstance.

"From then on he could be fixated on children of the age and gender he was at that time. Some bizarre fetishes are conceived that way, pardon the expression. It's next to impossible to extinguish that kind of conditioning, even with intensive therapy. That's why there are so many repeat sex offenders."

"Makes perfect sense. But what about the guy who isn't fixated on, say, little blond girls between the ages of five and eight, but on any and all little kids?"

"I would guess he may not have a fixation at all. His primary interest is the process of seducing, controlling, corrupting the innocent and vulnerable as much as satisfying his sexual urges. For perpetrators who feel inferior or inadequate in some way, power over others can be a real goal. The need to be in control is a very common human drive, but when it's paired with lack of conscience and a hyperactive sex drive...".

She noticed Allie put her elbow on the chair and prop the side of her face on her hand. Allie finally said, "All that is very speculative. We could go on and on about the existence of evil, about sadism, about mental illness in general. Any or all of those things could play a part." She sighed, then straightened her head and shook it, as if in disgust. "Yeah, I think some men, some women even, are omni-sexual, poly-sexual, herbi-sexual for that matter. They'd screw anything from a pet poodle to a potted plant."

Chapter 7

Allie couldn't sleep. She got out of bed and opened the window half way, letting in a gush of cold air then got back in bed and pulled another blanket over her, expecting the warm cocoon of bed clothes in a cooler room to lull her into sleep. It didn't. Her mind swirled with thoughts of Paul, Doctor V, the Verde Valley, her clients, the National Health Service, memories of Long Island, and on and on. She got up and went to the kitchen to make a cup of chamomile tea.

She returned to drink it sitting up in bed. With her lower body under the covers, sipping her tea, suddenly she was six years old again, home from school with a cold, tucked into bed with a picture book and a cup of hot chocolate. She was tempted to succumb to that kind of elementary self soothing.

But no. She put her cup down on the night table, refusing to surrender to comfort. What was wrong tonight? She sometimes had trouble sleeping on nights with a full moon, but tonight the moon was a faded, translucent crescent in a black sky. Maybe it wasn't as much that she couldn't sleep, as that she felt she shouldn't sleep. Why?

Then the tornado of swirling thoughts touched down. *Kim and Crystal, Kim and Crystal. Why can't I leave them at work where they belong?*

Questioning herself didn't calm the turmoil. *Yes, Kim and Crystal.* This psychological storm had their names written on it. Something was up. Something was going on with them *right now,* something dangerous or harmful. She got out of bed and began to pace the floor. *What can I do? Call them in the middle of the night and ask what they're up to? Call the police and say I suspect some kind of foul play, some where, involving two people I can't name and can't even admit are my clients? Or I could wait until morning and consult with a priest, a minister, another therapist. Hell, maybe a psychic?*

She quit pacing and without conscious intent reached for the *I Ching*. She opened it at random, something she had never done before. Hexagram forty-eight, 'A Well'. She had received this hexagram many times and knew what it said. 'A city may be moved, but not a well...a positive misfortune'.

She threw the heavy book to the floor. It landed with a thud and a rustle of opened pages. A *'positive misfortune!' Crap! Another conundrum, an oxymoron, a dialectic, a bit of ancient oracle mumbo jumbo!*

When memories rose like lava, a volcano of thought, her pacing ceased. *It's January; there's a new moon in January, the anniversary Kim celebrates! The dream about a man in a well...'a city can be moved, but not a well.' It was a description of Montezuma Well! Kim and the Well!*

***

Kim clenched her jaw at the jolting ride on only three tires. She turned the car toward the access road and saw the gate barring it. She hesitated for a split second then accelerated into it. Two hinged metal pipes fastened with chain and padlock were no match for the Z. The gate swung open. The heavy chain lashed back, struck the top of the car's windshield, made a starburst crack the size of a baseball then slithered and clanked across the roof and down the rear bumper. They were in!

***

Allie didn't bother with underwear. She all but ripped off her pajamas, pulled on a sweat suit, jacket and short leather boots. Out of habit she grabbed her purse on the way out the door. The hard soles of her boots echoed in the silence of the parking lot as she made her way to her car.

Careful not to peel out, she backed out of the parking spot and drove with both urgency and skill, turning onto Highway 89A, then the long, straight shot down 260 to I-10, where she let her foot settle onto the accelerator with a delight in speed totally unlike her.

She took the exit at Maguireville a little too fast, the tires squealing in protest. Safely onto Beaver Creek Road she entered the sleeping town. She slowed to a crawl down the main street, its scruffy auto repair shops and fire station deserted but brightly lit.

Only then, making her way down the eerily silent street, did she have time to question herself. *It's one thirty a.m., for pity's sake. What am I doing in the middle of the night in the middle of nowhere?*

At the entry to the Well, the gate swinging ajar and the chain sprawled like a dead thing on the blacktop reassured Allie she hadn't been imagining things, wasn't having some kind of manic or psychotic episode after all.

Driving a few hundred yards further, *driving into trouble,* she told herself, she saw the car sitting at a random angle in the parking lot, but it sparked no recognition. She knew what Kim and Crystal drove, a late model SUV in candy-apple red and an older Chevy pickup, respectively. This thing looked beaten up, one tire a mere shred of rubber clinging to its rim and a thin stream of fluid, maybe oil, trickling from beneath the hood. *If fluid is still dripping it can't have been here long*, she thought. She wondered why someone had abandoned it, and again she questioned her reason for being here.

***

Minutes before, Kim had brought the Z to a lurching stop, turned off the engine and opened her door, but remained in the seat, unable to move.

After the rollercoaster-like ride, silence and stillness closed down around her. Her ears rang. She detected no sound or movement from her prisoner or from the darkness outside. The wedge of doubt that had penetrated her earlier inserted itself more insistently, split her wooden assurance, paralyzed her.

The dome light of the Z cast more shadows than illumination. She could feel the darkness outside the car trying to enfold her, suck her in. It felt like a black hole in space that could swallow her.

She shook her head as if to clear the image. *What, am I losing my nerve now, afraid of the dark like a little kid?* Then she noticed that the glove compartment had popped open at some point during the chaotic ride. In it she saw a large flashlight. She grabbed it and stuffed it inside her jacket, telling herself that finding it was a small stroke of luck but getting here at all was fate's endorsement of the plan, urging her to continue.

She got out and shut the door, went and opened the hatchback. He lay on his side in a fetal position with his eyes closed, pretending to be unconscious. "Get out!" she commanded.

When he didn't respond she prodded him with the pole end of the pitch fork. Fast as a snake, he grabbed at it with his bound hands but she had the advantage of leverage. She jerked it out of his hands, and turned it to use the business end. With metal prongs pulling and biting into his side, he stopped resisting, unfolded his body and climbed out.

Although Kim had never been here after dark, she knew this place, both the trodden and untrodden pathways. Rather than follow the concrete steps upward to the overlook and then down again to the Well, she prodded him toward the left, where she found her shortcut through the brush.

The dirt path had grown uneven and narrow, every inch begrudged by the chaotic growth around it. Branches, shrubs and weeds pulled and scratched at their legs as they passed. Above and ahead of them, the mist was a column of white that supported nothing. It was also a curtain they must penetrate.

When he realized where they were going the sounds from beneath the duct tape on his mouth grew loud and high pitched. He stumbled, caught himself by grabbing a branch with his bound hands then turned toward her as if to plead for mercy.

On the defensive, she aimed the flashlight into his face and recoiled in shock and disgust. His hair lay like a damp mat over his skull. His eyes were bloodshot, his face wet with tears. Snot ran in a steady stream over his duct taped mouth, dripping off his chin. Silently, she pulled the gun from her pocket and with the other hand brandished the pitch fork at him. He turned and shuffled onward.

Soon they reached the rim of the hill, and began to descend. Near the water she saw two small orbs of red looking up at them from the ground. She steadied her flashlight on the spot. The raccoon retreated with a rustling sound.

The path descended to within a few feet of the water. *As good a place as any,* she thought. She pocketed the gun, aware that she had the advantage of surprise. He knew his fate but not when she would send him plunging into it. One hard push against his back with the pitch fork sent him into the shallows.

He made a muted splashing sound while mud, algae and water plants swirled around and above him like ingredients in a blender. He thrashed and floundered, but his panic succeeded only in moving him toward the middle of the Well. Then he began to tread water, attempting with a clumsy dog paddle to return to the bank.

She extended the pitch fork and with the back of the prongs against his neck and head, sent him turning, spinning slowly away, until the mist wrapped around and engulfed him.

Looking at the place he disappeared, she envisioned dark clouds of leeches, leeches by the millions, rising from the bottom to worm their way into every tender, blood-engorged part of his body, attaching their hungry mouths to his feet and legs, his genitals, his stomach and back.

Silence. She could almost believe he was already dead, that he had descended into the depths as dirt and slime to be transformed into a wraith and was, this minute, rising with the mist into oblivion.

Now she heard him again. The splashing and inhuman grunting sounds grew louder. The mist parted, driven away by his frantic thrashing, revealing a white face infested with just a few dark blobs. *It won't be long,* she told herself. *He's getting what he deserves.*

A dizzy, rising sensation filled her head, then she was no longer present in her body. Her mind retreated to another desolate, dangerous place, the past. In a daze, she remembered the sick things he had taught her as a child.

He taught her to shoot his gun, aiming at cans of soda that had the names of her family members scrawled on them. He taught her that she did not belong to herself, that she and her body were at the mercy of anyone ruthless enough to claim it.

He taught her that sweet seduction could become savagery in an instant. He taught her that a scrawny seven year old's body could experience simultaneous pleasure and pain. He taught her many things she had been trying to unlearn ever since, but the worst thing he taught her was that any benefit, any favor, any scrap of good bestowed on another person was an unintended consequence of one's own intent or desire, an unintended consequence of one's own pleasure.

From deep inside her emerged a lullaby that her mother had sung to her long ago, and now she hummed it to herself.

When she felt cold air follow the trail of tears down her cheeks, she realized with a start that she was crying. Furious, she dropped the pitch fork and pulled the pistol from the inside pocket of her jacket. *This will end now. The leeches feasted on his blood. Now they can swim in it.*

The mist, her tears, and his wild but gradually weakening thrashing made it difficult to take aim. She struggled to find what couldn't be seen. A faint sound intruded. A car motor, the slam of a car door. For a moment she could not separate the sounds from the memories that had overtaken her. Then she heard footsteps on concrete, and knew it was happening now! She stuffed the gun back in her pocket, threw the flashlight, and ran.

Kim's panicked flight brought her a quarter of the way around the circle of the Well. She began to climb up the bank at a place she thought would lead to the junction of the Well's access road with Beaver Creek Road. The footing grew more treacherous, with loose rocks, cactus and dead branches creating an invisible obstacle course. In daylight it would have been challenging. In the dark it was bush-whacking at its worst.

Just over the crest of the bank, her heels slid out from under her on the unstable scree and she sat down hard. Deflated and confused, she remained sitting while she caught her breath and wondered what had just happened and what she should do now.

The only coherent answer was that she needed to put as much distance as she could between herself and the Well. She rose and continued to climb down the bank, placing her feet and legs at an angle to the incline to prevent another slide. She moved more deliberately now, focused on the next step and then the next.

When she reached the main road she wanted to whoop in triumph but the silence of the night prevailed against any fleeting expression of joy. She turned right, back the way she had come driving the Z.

***

Only momentum and stubbornness kept Allie at the Well in the middle of the night. She climbed the concrete steps to the top, looked down into the mist, sighed with relief when she saw nothing and turned around to leave then turned back again. A small shaft of yellow light had drawn her attention. What was that? And what was that in the water? The roiling haze parted enough for a glimpse of a moving object. *Something dark and round. An animal? A head...a human head?*

Lighting her footsteps with the flashlight, she descended the precipitous, twisting steps as quickly as she could, then stepped off the path to work her way left, around the lip of the Well. A dozen steps brought her to the small beam of yellow light: a flashlight upended in the middle of an agave plant. Careful of the needle like tips of the blade shaped agave, she retrieved the flashlight and pointed it, along with her own light, into the Well.

Stunned, she made out the head and face of a person. It really was a person, someone floundering in the water. For one timeless second she lived and breathed in the dream that haunted her months ago, a dark sky and darker water swallowing a man who shrieked soundlessly for help.

"Hey!" she yelled, and was startled by the sound of her own voice.

The figure in the Well turned toward her and began moving in her direction. As he approached she realized she needed to find something to fish him out with. She focused her flashlight on the ground, looking for a long, sturdy stick, but found instead a long handled pitch fork. Dropping one of the flashlights and stuffing the other into her jacket, she grabbed the gardening tool and extended it as far as possible over the water, yelling, "Here, over here, keep coming."

She held out the pole. All she could see through the mist was a pale half-circle that looked like half a face. As it came closer she saw something like a loose scarf sagging around his mouth and chin. He grabbed at the pole with both hands. Why were both hands together?

His sudden pull almost caught her off balance, tumbling into the water. Instead, she dug in her feet and pulled back, glad of the hard heels of her boots that sank into the earth to give her leverage.

The man, she could see by now that it was a man, kicked weakly then allowed her to drag him the last few feet out of the water and onto the muddy bank. He lay there on his stomach in the weeds, while she stared in disbelief at a naked man who had been hobbled, bound and duct taped.

She tossed the pitch fork aside, bent to grab his arm and help him to his feet. He wavered, struggled for balance then reached up and yanked the duct tape down from his mouth. It settled like a ragged necklace around his collar bones.

He brushed away several dark, quarter-sized blobs clinging to his face and neck and gasped, "Who are you?"

"I...my name is Allie. Who are you?"

"Never mind. Just help me to my car."

"Your car? That white thing up there? I hate to tell you but I don't think it's going anywhere. I'll take you to the hospital."

"Help me, get this crap off me," he demanded, indicating the rope and duct tape around his hands and ankles.

"I can't...I don't have a knife. Let me see...". Her mind racing, she realized he had to walk out of here, she certainly couldn't carry him. She had to get the rope and tape off.

She bent, acutely again aware of his nakedness, and began to untie his hobbled feet. The wet rope around his raw, bleeding ankles yielded its knots without too much effort. By the time she had it off, he had wrapped his hands around his upper arms to stem his violent shivering.

"Here," she said, stripping off her jacket and handing it to him. He stood holding it with both hands, until she realized he couldn't put it on with his hands bound. She draped it around his shoulders. "Stay here. I'll go get my phone and call the police and an ambulance."

"No! Just untie me!"

Pushing away the rise of resentment at his demand, she started to work on the duct tape and rope around his wrists. Her weak fingernails bent back, causing her pain without results. "It will have to wait until I get back from the car. I have a knife in an emergency kit." She turned back toward the concrete path, ready to run up the steps.

"No!" he growled, "I'm coming with you."

"All right then, go in front." She aimed the flashlight just ahead of his feet and followed him.

They went a few stumbling yards until he began to retch into the bushes. She waited until the gagging and dry heaves subsided. This was too much. She felt more puzzled and wary every second. "Can you make it the rest of the way? Maybe I should just go."

"No! I'm fine. I can make it."

They climbed the steep bank, then over and down the steps in silence. When they reached the parking lot, he stumbled to the white car and stuck his head through the open driver's side, then put his bound hands on the roof and hung his head. "Shit! No keys."

"Wait a minute. You can't be thinking of driving that thing. You need to go to the hospital."

His silent stare raised a clearer sense of alarm. "Who are you? Who did that to you?"

Without speaking he turned and took a few steps toward her. Something in his face and body language made her step back. *Wait a second! I am not afraid of this half-drowned man who has no weapon and is letting it all hang out.*

Yet without another word, she strode to her car, retrieved her phone from her purse, and while keeping her eyes on him, pressed nine-one-one.

The next few hours were a blur of vehicles arriving and uniformed strangers converging on her to ask questions she couldn't answer.

First the fire truck from Maguireville brought two volunteer fire fighters and an EMS tech. He wrapped the naked man in a wafer-thin, silver thermal blanket and returned Allie's jacket to her.

Relieved, she took it and went back to her car to turn on the heater and soak up its relative warmth. The jacket felt damp. Some intangible trace of him lingered there. Her better judgment told her to put it on. She couldn't bring herself to do it.

The EMS techs were about to load him for the trip to the hospital when the brown-uniformed sheriff's deputy arrived. Allie hoped she would see Mike's pleasant face but the deputy was not Mike. The Not Mike swaggered to the fire truck and began to talk with the other first responders. The victim sat on the bumper of the fire truck, clutching his warming blanket. She couldn't hear their exchange but she guessed the deputy finally determined the victim was in no imminent medical danger because he began to question the man.

The Arizona State Highway Patrolman arrived, climbing out of his cruiser with a posture of authority. He strutted over to the others, hand resting on his pistol.

Soon she heard their voices rise in disagreement. She rolled down her window and caught snatches of the argument about who should transport the near-drowning victim.

The trooper either won or lost the argument, she couldn't tell which. In any case, he returned to his car and drove off. He was followed by the fire truck with the patient inside, its siren bleating for attention as commandingly as if it entered a city street full of traffic to warn away. Vivid red and blue strobe lights accompanied the sound, illuminating the previously deserted parking lot before fading away.

***

After Kim's struggle through the brush, walking felt effortless on the level blacktop but after a few yards she paused to pick twigs and cactus spines from her jeans and took off one of her boots to shake out the pebbles she had just begun to feel although they had bruised the sole of her foot during her descent down the bank. As she made a final swipe to brush dirt and twigs from her jeans, she felt the keys to the Z in her pocket.

Without hesitation she pulled them out and threw them as hard as she could into the densest part of the underbrush, where they vanished without a sound.

Just then she heard another sound, the wail of a siren. That and the glow of distant headlights sent her scrambling back into the brush.

She crouched, her heart thumping in her chest, pulsing in her throat with the visceral fear of a hunted animal. Her chin bent to her chest, she didn't dare to look up. She held her breath.

The vehicle headed away from the Well, back toward Maguireville. She waited. Silence and quiet. She returned to the pavement. Feeling safe now, she was grateful for protective darkness and the complete absence of traffic on the road. Inexplicably, she was suddenly calm and confident. She took out her phone and pressed the number to speed dial Crystal.

***

Allie began to feel this experience was as unreal as a dream or a theatrical farce. *It might make a wonderful limerick. 'There was a naked man from Maguireville...'. Or maybe a joke. 'Five uniforms, a naked man and a therapist meet in a bar...'.*

Smiling to herself, she wondered if this was the black humor she had talked about with her friends, then decided she was too tired to question anything. She was sleepy, exhausted and just wanted to go home. She reached for the key in the ignition, then realized the deputy hadn't left with the others and was now walking toward her. Abruptly, he ordered her out of the car and began to question her. Soon she could tell he was as irritated as she.

"I can't tell you anything else," she said. She leaned back against her car and folded her arms. "I know it sounds strange, but I just had a feeling I should come here. I don't know the guy, and I certainly don't know who did that to him."

The deputy put a hand on his gun belt and looked at her with an expression of disbelief. He managed to curb it just before it became a blatant insult. Then he demanded to see her driver's license. He took it to his brown patrol car where he talked on the radio for several minutes.

When he returned he said, "Okay, Miss Davis. Everything checks out. Mr. Upshall said you didn't do it, he said you helped him. You don't have any warrants. I took your statement, so you can go home now, but we'll call you tomorrow to come in and clear up some things."

Allie registered the threat of more interrogation, then the name Upshall. She was wide awake again.

Crystal's abusive uncle was named Upshall. An echo of the denial she had just voiced, "I don't know who did that," came to her. Maybe she did know. At least she suspected this somehow involved Crystal or Kim. They were what lured her here in the first place. And who would have done that to Upshall except Crystal's husband or Kim's boyfriend? (Did she even have a boyfriend?) Or maybe even Crystal or Kim?

She tried to shake off the thought that one or both of her clients might have participated in a murder plot.

The anxiety-producing possibility rode with her all the way home.

The drive felt interminable. At last she parked the car and got out, careful not to slam the door. She reached her apartment before she realized she had snuck into her own home like an after curfew teenager. Why was she unwilling to be seen coming home in the early morning hours? Nothing a nosy, gossiping neighbor might imagine could match the bizarre scenario in which she had just played a part.

She stood under the hot water in her shower until she felt herself drifting off to sleep standing. She brought a dry towel to the bed and laid it across her pillow for her wet hair.

In bed, the questions in her mind were so many and so insoluble they at last ceased to demand answers and so she surrendered to fatigue. Sleep brought a soothing amnesia.

Her alarm buzzed three hours later. The troubling thoughts were back again, persistent as ever. Two of her clients could be killers.

Still in pajamas, while her coffee brewed she called Heidi. After the briefest, most edited version of the story she could manage to explain why she needed it, she got Mike's home phone number. She thought he sounded surprised. It was before eight a.m. on a weekday, but evidently he was too polite to ask. He waited to hear her explanation and request.

"Yes, Ma'am, I'll do what I can."

His response was so much like him, *the gentlemanly deputy*, she thought with relief.

"Getting information about a job like that, a kidnapped man tossed in a well. That should be easy. Law enforcement folks like to talk as much as anyone else."

Little more than an hour later he called her at the office. "I talked to the other deputy. They say Upshall's a little beat up, but nothin' a band aid and a sip of something strong won't cure. Hypothermia hadn't set in real bad, thanks to you. He's already fussin' to go home from the hospital."

"So he's not at death's door, like I thought he might be. That's a relief. Do they know who did that to him?"

"Two men. Other than that, the good old boy is refusing to say who hogtied him and threw him in the pond. Claims they wore masks and he didn't recognize their voices. He was more put out by what they did to his car than anything. I heard he moaned and caterwauled about that, no end."

"What's going to happen now?"

"Ma'am, if we arrest someone, like Crystal Naven's husband, for instance, it will be all over the local paper and you won't need me to give you more information."

"What? Why would you arrest Crystal's husband? Crystal threatened to shoot Upshall, but her husband didn't. And Upshall wasn't even shot."

"Sure enough. Their names came up right quick already in the investigation. But a little thing like her couldn't have won a wrestling match with Upshall, so who's involved who could have? Her husband."

"Maybe they don't have anything to do with it. If so, they got nothing to worry about." Silence. It felt like a question to Allie.

Then, "Is there something you need to tell me, Allie?"

"No. I mean, right, I understand. So, Mike, do you think this will get a lot of publicity? What about keeping my name out of the paper?"

"Not something I can control, Ma'am. The deputy's report has your name in it. Let's just hope the reporters don't get to diggin' around. If anyone like that does contact you, you don't have to talk to them."

"Right, that's right."

"But if you'll excuse me saying this, darned if I can figure out what you were doing out there at the Well in the middle of the night, unless it had something to do with one of your clients."

Allie didn't know what to say.

His voice a little wary, Mike said, "I'll do what I can, as long as it doesn't go over the line."

That cleared Allie's head, which swam with new alarm. "I do appreciate this Mike. I want to help Crystal as much as I can, but I'd never ask you to do anything unethical or illegal."

"Yes Ma'am, that's what I reckoned."

Next, Allie called Crystal, saying she had a scheduling problem and needed Crystal to come for her appointment that morning at eleven a.m., instead of the next day. Crystal said she would like to help Allie with her schedule but she didn't know if she could find a baby-sitter on such short notice. She would try.

When Crystal arrived at eleven she carried a little boy in her arms. He wore a red jacket, matching knit hat and mittens. His chubby cheeks and a little pot belly were those of a toddler, but he was almost half as long as Crystal was tall. Her face flushed red from the effort of carrying him.

"This is Toby," she said to Allie when she put her son down. "He just turned two a few months back. Kaylee is in pre-school, but I couldn't find a sitter for Toby. I hope you don't mind."

She didn't look up for an answer as she tugged off Toby's jacket. As soon as she pulled off his mittens, Toby reached up, snatched off his hat and threw it on the floor.

"Hi, Toby," Allie said, smiling at him. In spite of her misgivings she took in the sturdy little form with admiration, noticing his dark, baby-fine hair and enormous brown eyes fringed with thick lashes. He looked into Allie's face without a responding expression.

Crystal produced a handful of toy cars and trucks from a tote bag. "Here, Toby, play with these."

"Tonka trucks," said Allie. "I'm surprised they still make those. My son used to play with them." With an effort, she pulled her attention from Toby and turned to her client. She noticed dark circles under Crystal's eyes and her hair appeared loose and unkempt. Crystal looked tired and maybe even...depressed? Her client looked a little too much like she had when she first came in, less than three months before.

"How have you been Crystal?"

"Fine. Nothing new."

"Have there been any urges to cut or harm yourself lately?"

"No."

"Any thoughts of suicide bothering you?"

"No."

"I'm glad. Crystal, we've talked about your relationship with your husband and the hopes and dreams you have for your children. But we haven't talked much about your uncle yet, the one who molested you."

"We talked enough. More is too much. He's not worth it!"

"But you're worth it, Crystal. You shared some things with me that day in the hospital but other than that you've refused to talk about it and it's an issue I think you need to work on. I think you need to consider reporting it and having him arrested."

"Why should I drag up all that stuff from the past? What would that be like for me and my family? Why should I worry about it now? Everything's going fine. Its going so well I've been thinking maybe I don't need to come and see you any more."

Toby had abandoned his toy cars and now toddled over to Allie's desk, reaching for her computer keyboard with tiny, purposeful fingers.

Crystal rose from the sofa. "No, Toby, that's not a toy." She took her son's shoulders to guide him away. "Here, here's a coloring book, see, and crayons? Play with these."

As soon as Allie had her client's attention again, she said, "When you talk about the things that happened, that's healthy, that's what we call catharsis. It helps to get those memories out of you. I know that reporting him would take a lot of courage. I can't claim it would be easy. It's a decision should at least consider.

"And I think it would be a mistake to stop counseling. I'm glad you seem to be doing better, but I want you to know that these issues with being molested don't go away on their own. We've talked about what they can do to your self esteem and what a negative impact they can have on your relationships."

Toby stopped scribbling across the pages of his coloring book. Not bothering to stand up, he crawled purposefully toward Allie's bookcase. Crystal retrieved her son, and sat him on her knee, hugging him and kissing him on the cheek. "I told you I don't have any thoughts of harming him or myself or anyone, anymore. Isn't that what's important?"

Toby wriggled out of his mother's arms, slid down off her lap and walked back to the book case, where he began to pull Allie's books out, one by one. When Crystal started to rise to get him, Allie held up her hand.

"Let him," she said. She studied Crystal's face. "You haven't had any thoughts of harming your uncle, for instance, in the last few days?"

Crystal met her gaze with obvious discomfort. "No."

Silence. After a ten second pause, Allie said, "You're lying to me, aren't you?"

Long pause with downcast eyes. Then, "Yes."

"Tell me about it." Allie kept her eyes on Crystal, although she could see in her peripheral vision that Toby had pulled most of her books from the book case. He sat amid a great pile, leafing through one with a clumsy sweep of his chubby hand.

Crystal glanced over at her son, perhaps wanting a diversion, but Allie said again, "Let him."

"Well, then, I'll tell you. I did want to kill the SOB. When I saw that psychiatrist, that Doctor V-something, he said 'You're thinking of killing the wrong person,' and I knew he was right. I didn't deserve to die, my creep of an uncle deserved to die."

"What did you do?"

"I borrowed a gun from a friend. Don't ask me who, I won't tell you. And I sat in his garage one night, planning to kill him when he came in. But then...".

"Then what?"

Toby had tired of his bookish ways. He diaper waddled back over to his mother, legs of his corduroy pants swishing together, and climbed up into her lap. She embraced him, kissed him on the cheek again, then began a silent game of patty-cake while she looked up at Allie. "Then I gave the gun back to my friend, that's what."

"What about the Well?"

"What? What well?"

"Last night?"

"I don't know what you're talking about. You're not going to tell the police again, are you? That I was going to kill him? Because I'm not any more."

"I don't have a duty to report something that happened or didn't happen, as this case may be, in the past. But you know I have to report a threat. And I hope there won't be another one, or any attempt to harm Mr. Upshall. The Sheriff's Department knows you threatened him, and if anything happens to him I think you'll be their prime suspect. You or your husband."

"My husband? My husband is about as dangerous as my two year old!"

"That may be, but law enforcement doesn't know that."

Crystal looked stunned, then thoughtful. "We'd be suspects? Well, I guess I get that. It's not fair, but I get it."

Allie felt her mood soften as she noticed that Toby now reclined against his mother's body, eyes half closed in the complete comfort and security of ownership.

"Crystal, there's a wonderful book for survivors of childhood sexual abuse that I'd like us to work with. It has chapters about whether or not to confront the abuser, and about feelings of rage and wanting revenge and even about wanting to harm yourself. When you come next week, will you start it with me?"

An obviously more thoughtful Crystal said, "Sure."

"It looks like Toby is almost asleep, and our time is up. Next week, then."

Crystal disengaged her now limp toddler, settled him on the sofa and went to the tumbled pile of books but Allie was quick to say, "Don't. Leave it. I'll have time to do it before lunch. Just go home now and take care of your baby."

Allie smoothed the pages of her books and reordered them in the book case. She also tried to put her thoughts in order. The session had been good, as far as it went. She might have just prevented another attempt on Upshall's life with her warning to Crystal. Also good, Crystal had agreed to work on the molest issues. The best thing that could happen now would be for Crystal to file charges against Upshall and get him put in jail where he belonged.

But what if she found out that Allie had saved the life of this man she hated so much? Allie had a rule that she never counseled sex offenders. They repelled her. Her countertransference with such clients would be inappropriate anger or contempt.

Revenge fantasies were a normal part of healing when people began to confront memories of abuse, abuse of any kind. One question lingered. *If they tried to kill him, why the Well?*

She halted her automatic task with a book in her hand. *Kim and Crystal both called him "the blood sucker." Oh! They didn't throw him in the Well to drown. They threw him in the Well for the leeches.*

***

At lunch time, Allie worked to assimilate all that had happened in the past few days. The person or persons who had thrown Upshall in the Well, those she suspected or someone unknown to her, believed it a just end, a punishment suited to his crimes. But what strange quirk of fate had involved her in that, brought her there to save him, a person she would have been glad to consign to the tortures of Hell?

She remembered the eerie directive from years ago that had urged her to go 'up and over the Mogollon Rim.' Why, to rescue that miserable excuse for a human? She couldn't believe that. Then she considered the text of the *I Ching*, '*...a positive misfortune.*' Maybe it wasn't that she had saved a man who didn't deserve to be saved. Maybe she had saved a client from committing murder.

No matter who had tried to kill Upshall, Allie knew that if Crystal found out the part she had played in rescuing him, their therapeutic relationship might end.

She walked down the hall to Betty's office, hoping to find her there. Betty sat at her desk, going through handouts for a therapy group.

"Have a minute, Betty?"

"Sure. What's up?"

"Do you believe in karma?"

Betty pushed her chair away from the desk and turned to face Allie, who had seated herself on the clients' sofa.

"I'm not sure. That could mean anything from 'what goes around comes around' to the belief that souls begin in rocks and work their way upward, life after life, to angel status. It's called the transmigration of souls."

"Some people reduce the theory to the most simplistic ideas, like they did in that silly TV show a few years back. You know, like if you harm someone you're immediately beset by bad luck until you go back to the person and somehow undo it. Instant karma I'd call that, if it's karma at all."

"Hum. More like the workings of a Twelve Step program. More like 'making amends' than my idea of karma. I guess most people who believe in karma also believe in reincarnation, that the soul is on a learning curve and karma is just a natural part of it, a law of existence. It's not punishment or reward although people might feel that way about it."

"That's what I think, too. I think if someone sets out to be an instrument of karma, they're taking on more than the law allows, natural or spiritual law as well as human law.

"Maybe. Now would you share with me the reason we're having this deep philosophical discussion today?"

"Can't tell you much except that one of my clients believes she's an instrument of karma and I believe she may be looking for revenge."

"Not against you, I hope."

"I don't think so. I know you have group in just a few minutes, Betty. I won't bother you any more."

***

The session was going well.

"I'm glad you're writing down your dreams. If you stick with it, when you read them over in a few months or a year, you'll see how valuable they are."

Allie said, "I started reading that book you recommended and so far I like it. And I'm using dream analysis with some of my own clients. It's a revelation for some " She hesitated. "Um, speaking of dreams, what would you say if a man tells a woman he had an X-rated dream about her?"

"I'd say he has poor boundaries or he's deliberately being provocative."

"Oh. By the way, I had an interesting dream about my ex-husband the other night, and when I thought about it...I've been thinking about him a lot since I got that letter. Or maybe obsessing would be a better description. What came to me after the dream is, at last, over."

"Hasn't it been over for about five years now?"

"Technically speaking. But somehow, because he kept writing to me and talking about getting back together, it hadn't ended. What I realized is that because he hadn't accepted that it's over, I hadn't accepted it a hundred percent, either. So I hadn't grieved."

"That is an epiphany. But *you* left *him*, right?"

"I'm not questioning what I did. Still, the marriage wasn't all bad and *he* certainly wasn't all bad. It was a loss I hadn't admitted to myself."

"How so?"

"You know, when you're young and naive and you think about marriage, you build a pyramid of dreams with the power of hope. The cap stone of the pyramid is that it will last forever, 'til death do us part.' When the pyramid topples you look at the wreckage and if you're honest, you mourn. It's not just what you lost, it's that a failure like that weakens your capacity to hope and dream again."

"So you've been grieving?"

"Not too much." They exchanged smiles.

"Allie, it sounds to me as if you've been doing some real, honest introspection."

"I have to practice what I preach, don't I?"

"Which is why I'm glad you were finally able to talk to me about the sexual abuse by that neighbor of yours when you were a child. Working through that is something you needed to do for yourself but also for your clients. Unresolved issues can create real problems with counter-transference."

"If I'm honest, I have to say maybe they did."

The therapist cocked an eyebrow.

"Oh, nothing unethical or anything like that, maybe just over-involvement."

"Let's go back to the question you asked earlier. I'm a little confused. It wasn't your ex-husband who told you he had the x-rated dream about you, was it?"

"No. And this is something I've been struggling with that no amount of introspection seems to solve."

"Interesting. Let's have at it."

"Okay then." Allie had to coach herself silently to tell a story she was not proud of. "This guy...he's someone I'm attracted to but he's married. I'm not even sure why I'm attracted to him except that he's intelligent and interesting and it seems he's attracted to me."

"This isn't Bob you're talking about, is it? I thought you had a friendly relationship with him, not an intimate one."

"It isn't Bob. Besides, Bob's not married. I don't think I feel comfortable telling you who the person is."

"That's fine. I don't need to know."

"Honest, I don't know why I'm attracted to him when I'm not sure if I even like him."

"You know what they say. The most powerful sex organ in the body is the human brain. If it's not hormones, it's the cerebral cortex and the pheromones communicating with the limbic system." She smiled. "Knowing someone is attracted to you is an aphrodisiac for most people. Did he express this sexual interest in you before you became attracted to him?"

"Hum. Yes, as a matter of fact. But what has me freaked out is that his wife seems to be involved. I mean, she watches him say and do things that--that most wives wouldn't tolerate from their husbands. It makes me wonder what would happen if I said, 'yeah, let's get a room.' Do they have a ménage-a-trios in mind, or is she just pimping for him?"

The therapist slapped the arm of her chair hard, startling Allie When she spoke her voice held the coolness of contempt. "He wouldn't say either, Allie. He would say, 'I don't know what you're talking about. You're obviously projecting your own desire for me, and it's not going to happen.' And then he'd walk away with a snide smile on his bearded, obnoxious face."

Allie leaned forward in her chair. "You know who it is!"

"Do you think you're the first woman he's engaged in this little farce of his? Or that he's the first man to get a thrill from chase and conquest? Another variation is to let it progress to a sexual encounter and afterward cut the woman off cold, with no explanation. But the ones who do that are probably proficient in the sexual relm. Ralph never takes it that far. I'll bet I could guess which little ploys he used on you. He lacks imagination. He uses the same provocations over and over again."

Allie felt paralyzed by a memory flooding back in vivid detail, the look on Ralph VanDeusen's face when Wanda had insulted him by commenting about his crossed eye and she had inadvertently deepened his pain with a clumsy comment. The look had been one of deep resentment, then appraisal and then self confidence.

Now she understood. This whole episode was his way of getting revenge. But what a price he wanted as payback for his wounded ego! She felt small, deflated. When words finally came they were a whisper. "You know, in the movies the bad psychiatrist is a serial killer, a cannibal who eats his victims. In real life, he tries to eat your soul."

The therapist looked at her with an expression of deep compassion. "Allie, there are lots of ways that damaged people try to take control, or stay in control, or wield power."

Allie clenched her fists. "Damn him, damn him, damn him!" Then she opened her hands and lowered her face into her palms, knowing self pity was a bitter second away.

Blood rushed to her face with a sudden realization. She felt her cheeks burning, burning against her hands and when she looked up at the therapist her eyes were wide but unseeing.

Upshall and VanDeusen, she thought. *The same sick motivations drove them both. They are monsters vomited out of a common maw, narcissistic, pathologically selfish and willing to betray the most basic moral precepts in their attempts to gain control and dominance. In that struggle for primacy, sexuality is their weapon.*

The therapist saw her in deep reflection and waited for Allie to speak. Silence persisted. The therapist's voice was soft. "Anger and remorse are very appropriate emotions when you've been hurt or humiliated. But what are you going to do about it?"

Chapter 8

After her appointment with Allie, Crystal's sense of urgency grew while she drove home. By the time she braked to a stop in the driveway of her modest little starter home in Camp Verde, urgency had progressed to anxiety.

The time needed to get a drowsy and limp Toby unbuckled, un-entangled and lifted out of his car seat felt like an hour. He didn't protest when she put him down in his tiny youth bed for a nap, leaving her free to call Kim at the hardware store. When the store's other clerk put Kim on the line, relief flooded her. "Kim, you're there!" she said. "I was afraid…".

"Me too. I waited all the rest of last night and all morning for the police, the deputies, but when they didn't show I got ready and here I am at work, still waiting. I can only talk for a minute," she added, "or until the next customer comes in, anyway. So what happened, what have you heard?"

"She knows. Allie knows."

"Knows what?"

"She knows about Upshall in the Well last night."

"That's ridiculous. You're imagining it."

"No I'm not! She was talking about him and then she mentioned the Well and last night."

"Are you sure she meant him?"

"She said his name and she said if anyone tried to harm him, the police would come after me or Danny. Because of that stupid threat I made. I guess they know I couldn't have thrown him in the Well, so my husband is the logical suspect. A 'person of interest' they call it.

But that means she knows about last night, and it means he's still alive."

"How could she know?" Then Kim answered her own question. *Maybe it was Allie at the Well...or someone she knows.* She hesitated. If she revealed that suspicion to Crystal, her friend's tenuous relationship with the therapist might be compromised even more.

"Kim, I don't think he told them it was you."

"Why wouldn't he?" Before Crystal could answer, a thought flashed into Kim's mind that was infinitely more fearful than the prospect of arrest. He didn't tell because he planned revenge. He would come for her. Wary of sharing that alarming thought with Crystal , she blurted, "I have to go. I'll get off work early and come over there. Bye."

Kim felt lucky that her boss was in a good mood that day. He let her leave work two hours before the end of her shift. The six block drive to Crystal's house took less than five minutes. Crystal had unlocked the door for her. When she walked in without knocking, Crystal had just given the children a snack of milk and homemade cookies and they were watching TV in the living room.

Kaylee looked up from the frantic action on the screen, a roadrunner with coyote in hot pursuit, and saw Kim. She smiled, held out her arms and kicked her legs up and down on the sofa in anticipation. Kim picked up the little girl, spun around with her a few times just short of dizziness, then kissed her cheek and put her back down on the sofa. Then she reached over to tweak Toby's hair.

"Hi Toady," she said.

He looked up from his child sized rocking chair, stopped rocking, pursed his lips and glared at her in a mock scowl. "Not Toady. Toby!"

"Oh, that's right, I forgot. Toby. Hi, Toby." She high-fived his tiny hand. He rewarded her with a radiant, toothy grin. Then, having exhausted most of his speaking vocabulary, he resumed rocking with reckless vigor.

Kim's ritual greeting with the children gave her a minute of respite from the cold fear that had gripped her since her telephone conversation with Crystal. She went to join her friend at the table in the dining area, which afforded a full view of the children. It seemed to Kim that Crystal always had her eye on them.

Crystal placed a glass of cold milk in front of Kim and pushed the plate of cookies within her reach. Kim ignored them. "Thanks for picking me up last night. What did Danny say when I called and woke you up at one a.m.?"

"His exact words were 'Oh, crap!' Our phone never rings in the middle of the night so he was spooked. I'm glad I was the one who answered it. I told him it was Auntie, that she fell and she said she was okay, but I would go over to her house to make sure."

Kim rubbed her eyes with hands scored by dozens of scratches then asked, "So what happened out there last night after I left? Do the police even know? And where is Upshall?"

"After I talked to you today, on a hunch I called the hospital. That's where he is. He's in stable condition, whatever that means. Somehow he survived. That person you heard last night must have saved him. I can't figure out who or how or why."

"A mystery to me, " said Kim. She shook her head. "Maybe he didn't need to be saved."

"What?"

"Well, I guess he needed to be saved from me. I was within seconds of shooting him. That would have killed him. Hypothermia or drowning might have done him in, too, but the leeches wouldn't have killed him."

Crystal cocked her head in question. "Why not?"

"After I got home last night, I went on the internet. I found out the leeches are a different kind. They don't suck blood, they eat, like, water bugs. They're harmless to people."

Crystal stared at her friend in disbelief. Then, "Weren't we stupid?"

"Not stupid, Crystal. Just uninformed."

"It seemed so right for him to die that way." Glancing at the children, she lowered her voice to a fierce whisper. "I should have stayed there and killed him when I had the chance, that night in his garage."

"I don't think so. When you told me you wanted the gun for target practice I knew that was bullshit. I knew who the target would be, but I didn't believe you could actually do it. Then, when you told me your idea about the Well I knew I had to help. It's my karma."

Crystal put her elbows on the table, closed her eyes and put her face in her hands. "I'm exhausted," she said, "and you look like you've been in a cat fight, with real cats." She looked up sideways at Kim. "I thought karma was something that happens automatically, maybe in a next life time, if there is such a weird thing. You know, like reincarnation."

"Maybe. But what if there isn't any next lifetime? What if there's no reincarnation, no heaven or hell? There's no proof of any of that, is there?"

"I haven't thought about it much but I guess there isn't. They say it's faith that makes you believe in that kind of stuff."

"Some people don't have any faith. Or they just don't want to wait. They want justice now, right now, when and where they can see it, not after the person dies and goes to hell or on to some next lifetime."

"So is killing him your karma or not? You're confusing me."

Kim shook her head. "I guess I don't know any more. Maybe I don't have that faith people talk about. Maybe I'm unconvinced and impatient." She took several deep swallows of her milk while she considered it and then leaned back in the chair, wiping her upper lip with a pinch of thumb and forefinger. "Let's face it, after what he did to us we both wanted him dead. I still do."

Crystal closed her eyes. One tear slipped from under an eyelid and slid down her cheek.

Kim took one of the chocolate chip cookies from the plate and broke it in half. "What I do know is that taking him to the Well was a mistake. The Well is sacred. Generations of Indians like me, maybe even some of my own ancestors, lived and died there. They owned it for a thousand years and it's still special to us. It didn't deserve to be violated by him. I should have known better, but the Well knew. It's like--it spit him back out, knowing how evil he is."

When Crystal opened her eyes her brows drew together and her face contorted in an expression that could have been rage or anguish or both. "Kim, he knows you tried to kill him but I don't think he told the police. I don't think he will."

"Maybe the flaming coward is embarrassed to say a woman got the best of him."

"Or maybe the reason he didn't tell the police is that he's going to come looking for you. He's going to try to kill you, Kim."

"If he can spare the time from molesting little kids." Kim quickly put down the uneaten cookie and wiped melted chocolate from her finger tips with a paper napkin. "I have something that shows what he's still doing to kids."

"What? Pictures?"

"They're on a memory card from his phone."

"My God, Kim. You should give it to the police!"

In a reflex, Kim patted her breast pocket, as if to feel the memory card, although she knew this wasn't the shirt she wore last night and the card wasn't there.

"I'm not sure they could convict him on just the pictures, " she said. "He could deny the card is his. The kids look like they're from Vietnam or Thailand or somewhere like that. They could never find them and get them to testify in court." She looked directly into Crystal's eyes. "But we could always report him, like Allie told you."

And have some idiot judge let him out on bail, so he could run? And if he stayed, we'd have to testify. My family would know, the whole town would know and someday even my own kids would know. I can't do it, Kim, I can't." Silent tears slid down Crystal's face, wetting the strands of brown hair that fell across her cheeks.

"I need to find that darn memory card first and then figure out what to do with it."

"Kim, we're not talking about the important thing. What if he comes after you? He's got guns, rifles and handguns. You're my best friend, " she said, as if that summed up everything. "He's done enough to us already!"

Kaylee turned quickly to look at her mother with a question on her face, alarmed by her mother's voice. Crystal shook her head at the little girl and gave her a reassuring smile. Kaylee turned back to the TV.

Lowering her own voice, Kim said, "Don't worry, Crystal. He's not going to win. I want you to call the hospital every day to check on him. Then you call me. The minute you say he's about to be released, I'll take a little unplanned vacation from work and go someplace safe. Just until we figure out what to do."

***

Allie sat alone by the swimming pool on the evening she arrived at the hotel. The patio surrounding the pool held several small groups of travelers absorbed in their own concerns, which allowed her to enjoy the quiet and solitude undisturbed. The water was lit from below the surface. It gleamed like pale aqua cellophane, the play of shifting light and shadow across it hypnotic.

A soft breeze lifted her hair and stroked the surface of the heated water. In response, it rippled and undulated voluptuously, releasing a few small tendrils of mist here and there.

She loved the soothing display and mused to herself that it could be set to music, perhaps the strains of the 'Moonlight Sonata'.

The hotel hosting the seminar she would attend tomorrow made the best of Arizona sunshine and seventy-degree weather, an irresistible lure for hordes of tourists from northern climates.

The four-story hotel was set in a luxurious landscape of acres of lush green grass, pools and fountains, palm trees, hibiscus bushes covered with red flowers the size of saucers, and bird of paradise shrubs, shamelessly fecund, displaying arm-like fronds of orange and yellow blossoms.

Allie thought how different from the Well it looked. On that night just a few days ago the surface of the Well resembled a black mirror reflecting the stars, while mist conspired to obscure its victim. She felt relieved that the episode merited no more than a paragraph in the local paper, in which her name had not appeared. She had begun to doubt that Kim or Crystal were involved at all. She could almost forget it had ever happened.

A clanking sound recalled her to the present. The wrought iron gate to the fence that surrounded the pool swung open. A man in tennis shoes, shorts and a Hawaiian shirt entered and walked around the pool to the row of chairs and lounges where she sat. She thought that like her, he didn't plan to swim. He merely wanted to enjoy a leisurely evening comparable with life on a tropical isle.

"Do you mind if I sit here?" he said, indicating the lounge next to hers.

"No, not at all." The muted lighting showed a man in his late forties or early fifties with a muscular build, a receding hairline and blue eyes that were large and round like those of a baby. They lent a fresh and innocent quality to his otherwise mature, masculine appearance.

He settled back into the plastic lounge chair and took a deep breath. "Isn't this place the best?" he said. "I wish I were staying longer than two days. I'm here for the conference on ethics and the law."

"So am I. It's a good way to start the New Year. Now that all the holiday hullabaloo is over, I'm trying to refocus on my career."

"I'm focused on getting those CEUs," he said, smiling.

"Of course," she said, "me too." Allie had also come for the continuing education units that therapists needed to renew licensure every two years. Some of the CEUs had to cover specific topics such as professional ethics. This two-day seminar in Phoenix would complete her own requirement for re-licensure.

The man still smiled at her. "I'm Phil Wilson. I'm staying on the ground floor, right over there," he said, pointing to a room that overlooked the pool. Then he extended his hand for her to shake.

"Allie Davis," she said, as their hands touched. "I'm up on the fourth floor."

He was a nice looking man. It occurred to her that the Moonlight Sonata in her head might at any moment fade into the soft strains of a romantic refrain for violin. She told herself not to be silly and juvenile.

Phil was easy to talk with. He told her he lived in Tucson and worked at a shelter for homeless veterans. This same seminar would be offered in Tucson in another month, he said, but he needed his CEUs now, and his agency was willing to reimburse him for most of the cost of travel and tuition.

He said, "To be honest, I just needed to get away and decompress for a few days. "

"All of us doing this kind of work need that. The social work journals call it self care and say it's burnout prevention, as if we need to justify taking time off just like everyone else."

The chatter of female voices interrupted his response. A group of three women that Allie recognized from previous trainings entered the pool area. The women joined them and half an hour later they went to dinner together as a group, choosing the hotel's best restaurant, where silence and discreet lighting were the featured ambiance.

The hostess showed them to a cozy half-circle booth of plush red leather that embraced a circular table with snowy white table cloth and crisp white linen napkins.

Phil quickly slid into the booth next to Allie, sitting to her left. He insisted on buying a margarita, which she accepted reluctantly but sipped with relish. The others, too, had their favorite drinks as they waited for dinner. Phil took the role of host and raconteur, making them laugh with half a dozen jokes that began "Tucson is so hot...".

To Allie's relief, the conversation didn't require her to consider each statement with clinical judgment, structure questions to be non-threatening, or filter her comments through the sieve of empowering encouragements. She forgot everything but this moment and these people, reveling in the effortless exchanges, a stark contrast to the controlled therapy sessions that had comprised most of her communications lately.

The atmosphere of collegiality around the table refreshed her almost as much as her earlier reverie at the pool. A hand on her left thigh provided a brief reality check. Her head jerked to look at Phil's face. He removed his hand immediately and continued his story seamlessly, without a blink or a blush.

At around ten p.m. they found no more excuses to linger. They left the restaurant together and said good night in the lobby.

Allie had changed into a pair of silk pajamas, washed her face, brushed her teeth and was about to get into bed when her phone rang. She looked at it for a second. She doubted it was really for her. Who did she know who would call her here? She hadn't told Bob or Betty where she would be staying.

She picked up the phone expecting a wrong number but the male voice was familiar.

"Hi, it's Phil down here on the first floor."

"Oh. Hi, Phil."

"I enjoyed our dinner tonight Allie. Ah, I couldn't sleep and I was thinking you might be awake, too. Would you like to come down to my room for a while?"

"Oh. Well...actually I was about to...to go to bed. I want to get up early and be on time for the seminar. But--thanks anyway. Bye."

Her eyebrows shot up as she hung up the phone, then she laughed out loud. Phil wanted to hook up with her, and shocked by his directness, she had thanked him for it.

She wondered if that was proper hook-up etiquette, or if he was now thinking it over and considering her pathetic. Well, she had been taken off guard. Other men had approached her with the same carnal intent, but never so directly.

She sat on the bed, unmoving, then realized she was considering it. She pictured herself slipping into her robe and taking the elevator down to Phil's room, the knock on his door and... . No, she couldn't imagine it. But she wasn't above accepting and appreciating the little ego boost. In no time, sleep came to smooth the smile from her face.

The next day she felt invigorated rather than distracted by the tropical ambiance of the hotel and she enjoyed the course on ethics. She arrived at the conference room on time at the start of both days and returned on time after breaks and break-out sessions. She took notes diligently and while making copious notations about inappropriate relationships in the workplace she thought about her own workplace and then about Phil's straightforward and honest invitation to a sexual encounter.

They saw each other around the conference venue several times a day. He remained cordial and polite, showing no evidence that he felt insulted by her refusal to have sex with him or that he intended to pursue her further. It sparked an idea that she at first rejected then tried to ignore. It rose and increased like yeast bread in a warm oven, forcing her to consider it. If she followed it through to execution it might help her cope with an issue that troubled her.

The basis of the plan involved sharing what she had learned with other professionals. All licensed professionals were expected to informally support and mentor new, unlicensed colleagues. She had attended many informal, peer-taught trainings as well as trainings for licensure. She felt she had graduated from her newbie status by now. Presenting a training would confirm a more seasoned status in her own mind and in the minds of others.

On the last afternoon of the seminar she walked through the lobby pulling her suitcase and waved a combined hello/goodbye at other attendees who were also leaving. She was about to walk through the door when she saw Phil turn from the reservation desk and beckon to her.

"Hey, Allie," he said, "hold up a minute. Heading out, huh?" Without waiting for an answer he said, "Me, too. I've really enjoyed talking with you the past few days. Seems we have a lot in common. Here, take my card. Call me some time. Let's think about getting together again. Just for fun."

A rush of joy filled her. She looked at the printed information on the business card from his agency then turned it over. No home telephone number handwritten on the back. It was a dead giveaway that squelched her joyful hope. She had been taught to consider what her *clients* didn't say, or information they didn't give, as important as details they did reveal. It was wisdom that could be applied even here.

She looked from the card into his face. "Phil, are you married?"

He hesitated. She knew he contemplated a lie. Then he shrugged. "Busted."

"I enjoyed you too, Phil," she said. "But I won't be calling."

He turned to go and over his shoulder gave her a parting smile that crinkled the corners of his sweet, innocent blue eyes.

***

Back at her office in the Verde Valley she approached Betty with her proposal to give a training.

"I think it's a great idea," Betty told her, "and I think I know your audience. The Cottonwood social services networking group is looking for ways to learn skills and improve services. A lot of them would love to come and I think some of them need to." She added, "We meet twice a month, but there's a computer list serve, so I can e-mail everyone to announce the training. We have about thirty-five members. When are you doing it?"

"The sooner the better, before I forget everything and have to work to decipher the notes I took!"

They set the date for the middle of the following week. Allie made a few calls to other therapists in town, keeping track of the number who said they might attend. The list soon lengthened to a number beyond the capacity of the break room, so she reserved the largest meeting room at the local library.

At a little after five p.m. the following Monday, Heidi stopped by Allie's office to chat. "I think it's wonderful that you're doing this," she said. "You're brave! I'd rather work a month of Sundays than get up in front of an audience like that."

"I'm not looking forward to it, to tell you the truth. Public speaking isn't my forte either. But...". Allie hesitated, wondering whether confiding in Heidi was fair to the younger woman. Finally she said, "It's not all pro bono and benevolence. I have an ulterior motive."

Heidi said, "Most of us do at any given time. And now I'm intrigued. Can you give me the juicy details?"

"They're juicy, all right. Come over and have dinner with me this evening and I'll explain. But I don't know what I'll feed you. It may be something from the freezer nuked in the microwave."

"My own *spec-i-al-ity*. My sauce pan is rusting in the cupboard as we speak."

Chapter 9

On the same morning Allie would give her training, Crystal was unaware of how her day would go. She answered the phone to hear her aunt's thin, sweet voice.

The old woman's words were a little tremulous but clear. "Crystal honey, how are you? How is Danny?... Good, good... What about my darling little Toby?... That's good. He's turning into a real little character, isn't he?... And Kaylee? Is she still loving that pre-school?... She's a smart little girl... Well, good, that's good. Crystal, if you could, honey, I'd like you to come over to see me later this morning... What?... We have some things to talk about. No, nothing's wrong. Don't be upset. It's nothing but it would be better if you came while Kaylee is in school and Toby is with your neighbor, those morning play dates you told me about?"

Crystal said, "Yes, sure, of course," while trying to halt a thread of alarm stitching through her mind. A second after she ended the call with her aunt she called Kim at work. "Kim, I need you to meet me at my aunt's house during your lunch break."

"Why, what's up now?"

"She says she wants to talk to me and she asked me not to bring the kids."

"She loves the kids!"

"Yes, Kim!"

"She doesn't want any distractions, hum? Yeah, I'll be there."

Hours later Crystal mounted the steps of her aunt's house. Without her children in tow she felt alone and vulnerable. Other brief episodes of freedom from mothering usually involved window-shopping, a visit with a friend, or the simple pleasure of a bubble bath and a do-it-yourself pedicure. Today she had no such sense of freedom. It felt, as her aunt would say, like the chickens were coming home to roost.

The door to the little 1950's craftsman style house opened before Crystal could knock. "Come in, come in honey. I just made some coffee."

Aunt Iva wore one of her favorite dresses, a cotton print with sprigs of blue rose buds and lavender daisies on a field of dark blue. She had topped it with an ancient brown sweater that hung from her shoulders like a monk's robe.

Crystal hugged her aunt gently, aware of the woman's fragile skin and brittle bones. She grasped and patted her aunt's age-spotted, blue-veined hand with a rush of affection and tenderness. For the moment it overcame her anxiety. She followed the old woman's shuffling, arthritic steps past the living room where an antique Queen Anne sofa reigned, into the dining room.

The dining set stood over a worn rag rug and polished hardwood flooring. Late morning sunlight flooded from the window which was framed by white lace curtains that had been pulled back, the roller shade raised to welcome warmth and light. A coffee service sat ready on the table.

Crystal sat and stared at the shafts of light over the table. They swam with tiny particles of dust like microscopic fish in the sea of air. While her aunt settled, she followed the swirling motes with her eyes, willing to be hypnotized by her senses instead of think about the coming conversation. She noticed that in spite of tiny motes in the air, not a speck of dust or dirt marred the surface of the worn maple wood table and chairs, or anything else in the room that she could see.

She marveled again at her Aunt's determination and resolve to adapt but not surrender to the disabilities brought by age. To struggle with dwindling physical and material resources toward the single goal in sight, one's own mortal end, took a courage she could hardly fathom.

"So, what did you want to see me about, Aunt Iva?"

Aunt Iva smiled as she spooned two heaping teaspoons of powdered coffee into the strong black brew in her cup.

"Auntie! What are you doing?"

"Honey, how do you think I get going every morning at my age? You know, if you rest, you rust." Auntie sipped the potent black coffee with apparent relish. When she had carefully placed the cup back in its saucer with trembling hands, she looked up at Crystal.

"Danny came to see me on his way to work yesterday, Crystal. He wanted to find out how I was doing after my fall. You know, for a few minutes I wondered if I had fallen and then forgotten about it. But I'm not that far gone yet, honey, thank the Lord."

Crystal felt her face flush as she withstood her aunt's questioning eyes. She was struck dumb with guilt and anxiety.

"Then there's that charge on my credit card. For a stun gun, for heaven's sake, and no charge at all for my toaster oven. Honey, I know very little about guns. What is a stun gun?"

Crystal still couldn't speak. She felt her throat swell and eyes burn with incipient tears.

"Honey, just tell me what's going on. I can't be angry at you no matter what the trouble is, and if it's as bad as I think it is, maybe I can help."

"You wouldn't be angry, Aunt Iva? Even if I told you I tried to kill someone?"

"What?" Her aunt's faded blue eyes squinted and teared as if she'd been slapped.

Crystal wiped her own eyes and clenched her teeth to stem the tide of emotion. It was time to tell her aunt the poisonous secret she hadn't been able to confess as a child, the poisonous secret that had fueled a murder plot. Slowly, she choked out the sordid details.

Her aunt gasped several times and her face twisted in apparent anguish but she said nothing.

Crystal feared for the old woman's heart.

Finally Aunt Iva said, "He did that to you? You were only six or seven years old?"

Crystal nodded. The old woman brought both fists down on the table, rattling her cup in its saucer, making Crystal start in surprise.

"That immoral, unprincipled, miserable son-of-a-sea-cook! He...". She registered the look on her niece's face and stopped.

She placed one hand on the table to steady herself, rose and went to Crystal. "I am so sorry that happened to you, honey," she said, grasping and hugging the young woman to her as she would a child, as if the years had never passed.

Crystal accepted her aunt's understanding with a flood of relief, and with her head against her aunt's warm stomach, she was comforted.

When Aunt Iva released her and settled again in her chair she said, "I told your Aunt Evelyn there was something not right about him from the very start." She massaged the knuckles of her gnarled hands then rubbed her knees absent-mindedly, as if trying to banish the pain while she allowed memories to overtake her.

Crystal heard Kim's knock at the door before her aunt did. "It's just Kim," she said. "I asked her to come. I hope you don't mind. I'll let her in."

At the front door they remained silent but Kim's cocked eyebrow asked for an explanation. On their way to the dining room, Crystal whispered, "I told her. Everything!"

When they sat down at the table Aunt Iva just shook her head and looked at them as if still trying to assimilate what Crystal had confessed. Kim refused her offer of coffee and instead went to the kitchen and poured herself a glass of water. When she returned Aunt Iva fixed her with a look that suggested she saw Crystal's best friend with new understanding. "So he did that despicable thing to you, too?"

Kim glanced at Crystal. "Yes."

"Honey I am so sorry. I never even suspected such a thing could happen--was happening." She hesitated. "But I should have. Crystal, just after your Aunt Evelyn got sick, she told me she had found something of Frank's that shocked and upset her. It happened when she was looking for some tools to try to fix a leak in the kitchen faucet. That big tool box of his, the one as big as a refrigerator, there was a separate compartment in there, a false bottom to the thing. I don't know how she found it, but there were some photographs and some videotapes in there. She was so distraught by what was in them I think it made her sicker."

Kim and Crystal exchanged glances again. Crystal had hidden behind the tool chest that night in Upshall's garage. An almost imperceptible nod from Kim told her that she had seen the tool chest too when she had entered the garage to kidnap Upshall.

Auntie continued. "Your Aunt Evelyn said she put those horrible things right back where she found them. Didn't try to watch the movies after what she saw in the pictures. She wouldn't say what they were, but she said it was unnatural and it made her hate her own husband. She didn't talk to him about it. Said there was nothing he could say that would explain it. She would never let him come near her after that, not even when she got sicker and needed help taking care of herself. She went into the nursing home rather than let him help her. That's where she died, you know."

Auntie's hands gripped the edges of the dining room table and she looked both tired and sick.

Crystal said, "I'm sorry to bring all this trouble on you, Aunt Iva. I don't want to burden you. Maybe you should go lie down and rest."

"No, honey, I don't want to lie down. I just want to understand this. Were you really going to shoot him, Crystal honey?"

"With Kim's gun."

"But then you changed your mind and decided to throw him in that well?"

"That's why Kim bought the stun gun...on the computer, on the internet, Auntie. She put it on your credit card but paid for your toaster oven in cash. They were the same price, so it didn't cost you anything."

"Well that's very nice, honey. I'm happy about that." She waited for Kim to speak.

"I'm the one who...who threw him in the Well the other night. Then someone else showed up. I had to run. I couldn't drive his car back so I called Crystal to come and get me. Other than that, Crystal didn't do anything."

Auntie leaned back in her chair and clasped her hands in her lap. "It helps me to know what happened. For a while there, I thought I was slipping." She fell silent for a moment then said, "Crystal, honey, he needs to pay for the things he's done but you don't want the sin of his murder on your soul." She looked at Kim. "Or yours either, Kim."

"You're right. We don't," Kim said, glancing at Crystal, who nodded her agreement.

"You both have your whole lives ahead of you," Aunt Iva said. "And bright futures, too. You're a good mother, Crystal. You want to set a good example for your kids, see them grow up to be good people."

She turned to look at Kim, who had dressed in a flannel shirt and jeans and pulled her hair back in a pony tail. She wore not a speck of makeup. "And you, Kim, you are such a beautiful young woman. Didn't I hear, a few years back, that you were going to California? To make movies?"

"I…I had an offer. I did some modeling during my senior year in high school. The agency in Phoenix told my mom they had some inquiries from a casting director in Hollywood. An agent offered me a contract. He said he was sure he could get me some parts."

"Honey, why didn't you do it, an opportunity like that?"

"Because I guessed the kind of parts they had in mind for me. In grade B pictures, horror flicks, cheap westerns. Maybe they were even planning some X-rated stuff for me. I didn't want to do that."

"You don't know they wanted that, Kim," said Crystal.

"I think at best they'd want me to be a mannequin, like when I modeled, the beautiful Indian maiden who doesn't say anything, just struts and poses. A freaking caricature of myself, of all Natives. A cheap stereotype!"

"I've never understood that, Kim," Crystal said. Why not? Why not become rich and famous, stereotype or not?"

"Because I don't think I have a right to exploit what I haven't worked for or earned. I inherited this body and face." She looked at the small pitcher of milk on the table and said, "It's like being lactose intolerant."

Crystal shook her head, uncomprehending.

"We're not responsible for what we're given. Here's what I mean. For every generation until the last few, Native Americans didn't have access to milk after they stopped nursing from their mothers so their stomachs didn't evolve to digest milk when they were older. And mine doesn't digest it, either.

"It's a nuisance for me not to be able to eat and drink dairy products, but I don't judge and condemn myself for it. So why would I personalize and exploit my 'better' inherited traits? It's the same thing. It is what it is, the good with the bad and all of it what Mother Nature intended."

***

On the evening of the training Allie would give, the turnout surprised her. At least twenty therapists, including several from her office, and other social services professionals filled the room.

Most were locals but a few had come from as far away as Sedona and Flagstaff. About eighty percent were woman, the usual gender ratio for social service workers.

Heidi and Betty were there, as much to lend support as to gain information, she thought. Since she had confided in Heidi about the ulterior motive for the training, Heidi had become her supporter and accomplice for outing Dr. V and his wife.

She hadn't expected that he would attend, but she and Heidi had persuaded Sherry to come. She sat in a row near the back of the room, wearing a business suit with a frilly red blouse beneath the jacket, one leg crossed over the other swinging in a languid rhythm. Allie thought she looked bored.

The room filled, the audience settled in while Allie shuffled her three-by-five note cards, surprised at how nervous she felt. At four minutes after the scheduled start time she adjusted the microphone to greet the audience and introduce herself. The microphone gave a few squawks of feedback, then settled down to its job.

As she spoke she noticed her self-consciousness yielding to her own interest in the subject and desire to do it justice. By the time she reached the mid-point of the talk she felt confident and comfortable.

She said, "Another consideration in professional ethics is dual relationships. When I was in school, one student thought dual relationships meant dating more than one person at a time." She smiled and paused for laughter from the audience. "But that's okay. A good example of a 'not okay' dual relationship would be to try to counsel a relative.

"Dual relationships can be tricky because they often start with a desire to help people in as many ways as possible. For instance, suppose you have a client who is struggling financially, and who does housecleaning for a living. The thought naturally occurs that it would be of benefit to both of you if you hired her."

She smiled when she saw heads shaking 'no.' "That's right. It can open up a whole can of worms about the quality of the work, about the worth of the work, payment for the work and about your personal space and privacy. Or suppose the client is a man who does great carpentry work and your front steps need replacing. Same thing. One rule is, if money has to change hands, other than their payment for your professional services, don't even consider it. Instead, consider whether your boundaries or theirs will get tested or altered in any way. If so, just don't go there."

She pushed her hair back from her face and reminded herself to stand up straighter. It was going better than she had hoped. The audience seemed attentive and respectful, with the possible exception of a few younger women texting on their cell phones. Even they were respectful enough to do it surreptitiously.

"Now, some ethical and legal situations are cut and dried, like the ones I just mentioned. Other cases are more complex. A lot might depend on the rules in your agency, the ethical guidelines of your professional association, or just your own good judgment. Relationships between therapists and clients are the most clearly defined. Professional associations all say that a social or romantic relationship with a client is not appropriate until at least two years after the counseling is over. Preferably, never.

"It's the most obvious but also the most important part of any professional ethics training." She paused for emphasis, willing the audience to hear and assimilate what she had to say next.

"Don't have sex with your clients. Don't have romantic relationships with your clients. Don't drift into a friendship with a client while you're still their service provider or therapist. Maintain your boundaries.

"I know we've all heard it a hundred times, but as long as we continue to read about law suits and people losing their licenses it bears repeating. Some of our clients have a deep pathology that causes them to be seductive and they can be very subtle in that process.

"Drawing a firm boundary in relationships also applies to coworkers. It most certainly applies to relationships between supervisors and supervisees."

Heidi's hand shot into the air.

"Yes?"

Heidi asked, "What about sexual harassment in the work place, or just, say, intimate relationships that are brewing in the office? What are the ethical boundaries there?"

"Wow. That could be a whole different training. It's not always easy to know when you're starting to tread on dangerous ground in the office. I'm not saying that office romances are always out of bounds as long as both parties are willing and it's not against your agency's policy.

"But here are some warning signs that you may be sliding into the danger zone in a relationship with a coworker or with a client.

"First, never tell a client or coworker that he or she smells good. I know that sounds ridiculous, but body odor, whether it's good or bad, is a very personal thing, a sensual thing.

"Next, watch your PDA's, your public displays of affection, even if it's with your spouse. Glimpsing a bit of intimacy between you and another person can start a client or coworker thinking about you in a different way, maybe an inappropriate way.

"And speaking of intimacy--maybe I don't need to tell you to avoid romantic behaviors like touching coworkers or using terms of endearment when talking to them, even if you're a person who usually calls people 'honey, sweetie' or 'dear'."

She paused for a second. The ubiquitous hum of an audience, the sounds of whispers, bottoms shifting in chairs, someone getting up to go to the rest room or take an important phone call had all but ceased. Good. It meant an increased level of attentiveness. What she was saying needed to be heard for two reasons.

She continued, "If you don't want a personal relationship, don't give them your home telephone number. Oh, and very important--don't talk about nudity or nakedness, especially your own. Last, if you happen to have an erotic dream about a client or coworker, do not, I repeat *do not* tell them about it."

A grey haired man in the audience chuckled but an attractive young woman in the front row stared at Allie in horrified confusion or even embarrassment. Allie could read in her face the beginning suspicion that she had been manipulated by someone she trusted. She felt a rush of empathy for the woman. *This is downright painful,* she thought. *It's like reliving the experiences myself.*

She didn't speak, but watched as several audience members turned to whisper a comment to the person next to them. She had both expected and dreaded this reaction. During a twenty second pause the undercurrent in the room, the buzz, continued and grew louder.

One woman, then two, then three, turned to search out Sherry's face. She responded by planting her feet on the floor and tilting her chin upward to gaze at the ceiling, at the walls, anywhere but back at accusing eyes. Even from the front of the room, Allie could see her body language and expression speak discomfort. *Ha! Guilty as charged,* she thought.

"That's about it, folks. I hope this was helpful. Are there any questions?" Applause interrupted her and brought a smile of relief to her face. "I can answer questions now or if anyone would like to stay afterward and talk with me privately, I'd be glad to do that."

Sherry stood and made it out of the door before she had finished speaking. *Wow, what a hasty retreat,* she thought. Then some aphorism she had heard echoed in her mind, *When your hidden cage of shameful deeds opens, guilt springs out to pursue you like a wild beast.*

Allie put one hand on the podium and saw with surprise it was shaking. She turned back to her audience. The face of the pretty young woman in the front row had been transformed by fury as she looked where Sherry had exited the room.

A woman Allie recognized as a Child Protective Services worker walked toward Allie with her brows draw together in confusion. Another woman sat immobile in her chair, seemingly on the verge of tears, as most of the audience swept away around her in a tide of chatter.

Still at the podium, Allie leaned on it for support as she shared their grief, anger and confusion. Beneath those emotions, bolstered by it, she felt vindicated.

Chapter 10

Kim and Crystal left Aunt Iva's house together. They exchanged glances of mutual relief, then both drew their coats closer. A cold front was moving in. Lowering clouds had begun to dust the world with snow. Crystal put her hands into the sleeves of her coat and hunched her shoulders against the chill. "We've got to find out what's in that tool box."

"Maybe. If it's the same tool box, and if there's still something in it besides tools, after all these years. What I've got--what I think I've got-- is new and it shows his face."

"What do you mean, you think you've got?"

"Crystal, the memory card is tiny, smaller than one of the corn flakes you had for breakfast this morning. I can't find it but it could still be there, anywhere, stuck in a crack in the floor or something. I'm looking for it. We could send it anonymously, trust it would be enough to put him in with the rest of the perverts. It's our best bet."

A shudder shook Crystal's body, whether from the cold or thoughts of Upshall, Kim didn't know. She grabbed her friend in a hug then looked into her face. "I'll find it, Crystal. I'll keep looking until I find it."

Back at the store, Kim and had just rung up an order of plumbing supplies for a do-it-your-selfer when her phone rang. Crystal again. "Kim, he's out!"

"When?"

"I don't know for sure. I called a minute ago and they said he was on the discharge list for today. They weren't certain if he left already."

"If he comes looking for me on the res, he won't find any welcome there. My brother would as soon shoot him as say hello."

Kim's brother didn't know her history with Upshall but disliked him because he sensed the extremity of his sister's loathing for the man.

The 'res' in Camp Verde consisted of three separate tracts of reservation land separated by several miles. The one near the center of town was tiny, one dead-end road lined by single-family homes amid a jungle of shrubs, vines and rose gardens, an overgrown oasis in the otherwise spare landscape of the town. Its ingress was also its egress, where a large building, the Native Community Center, stood guard.

Any unfamiliar vehicle or stranger on foot coming in or out would not escape notice. This was the res where Kim had lived as a child, when Upshall knew her. Other tracts of tribal land to the north were larger and more rural. Kim now lived in the largest native community on the banks of the Verde River.

Crystal dismissed Kim's comment about her brother shooting Upshall while she considered the risk to her friend. "Maybe he doesn't know where you live, but you can't take that chance," she said.

"I know. I'll go up to Flagstaff, to the hunting camp. The shack isn't much, but I'll make do. I don't think anyone's there now; they got their limit, the freezers are full."

Crystal knew about the camp in the ponderosa pine forest eleven miles south of Flagstaff and two miles east of Oak Creek Canyon in the Coconino National Forest. It was the base from which Kim and her relatives hunted deer and where they dressed the venison after a successful hunt.

Crystal had gone there with Kim several times as a child. She had cried when she first saw what they did there, the open carcass of a large deer hanging from a tree, its spread-eagle cavity of naked, coral colored flesh and grey-white bone gaping obscenely.

Now Crystal said, "I don't like to think of you alone in that place, Kim." Her voice cracked. "How long can you hide there?"

"Damn!" was the answer, as the prospect of becoming a fugitive for the foreseeable future hit home for Kim.

"At least you can call me, Kim. Let me know you're still alive. Every day."

"Sure, Crystal, as long as my phone holds out. There's no electricity in the shack, but I have a charger in my car. I'll do my best."

She left work by pleading sudden illness, and drove home to grab staple food items and a change of clothing. She stuffed the items in plastic grocery bags at random. Her backpack, sleeping bag and other camping gear were already in the back of the SUV.

She took the fastest and most direct way to the camp, up I-17 to the exit at the small regional airport. Airport Road was a one mile stretch of blacktop that ended on the east at the tiny air field and on the west at the junction with 89-A toward Oak Creek Canyon.

Located a hundred yards before that junction, the dirt road to the camp was marked by nothing but a faint set of tire tracks through the ponderosa pine forest.

She turned the SUV left onto the track to the camp. Here at an elevation of seven thousand feet, the snow fell harder and faster, the air twenty degrees colder than in the valley. The tires of the SUV crackled on the track's cover of pine needles newly dusted with snow.

She slowed in caution, turned the windshield wipers on low and rolled the windows down an inch. No sounds but those she made. The roar and hum of the highway had faded to nothing and nothing was visible now but trees, walls and roof of trees. The floor was the narrow, needle and snow covered road in front of her. She entered silence and solitude that brought with it a semblance of peace antithetical to the sensory overload inflicted by the world she had left.

The cabin came into view. Seconds later she saw the round, black rump of a bear, distinct against the backdrop of snow and towering evergreens. No doubt it had been drawn by the lingering smell of deer blood. It appeared to be scavenging for any unburied remnants of that common prey of man and beast. She tapped the horn once, lightly. It turned to see her, the interloper, then ambled away with a rolling gait.

She stopped the car in front of the shack and watched for almost half an hour to be sure the bear didn't return and there were no others lurking in the area. She went to open the creaking door of the cabin.

Dim illumination from the open door and one south facing window showed two low and wide wooden shelves against the far wall that served as cots. Inset high in the north wall were shelves for food storage. A wood burning stove in the middle of the single room completed the furnishings. It was cold dark and desolate. She would be fine here.

She went back to the SUV, intending to unload and then settle into the cabin but instead she half turned the key in the ignition, hit the play button on the control panel and allowed the sounds of flute and drum to enfold her. The notes were a natural accompaniment to the soughing of the wind in the pines muffled by the soundless fall of snow. She might have been drifting off to sleep when the phone rang, startling her. Jarred, she turned off the CD player to answer it.

"Kim, he's on his way there! You have to leave!"

It shocked Kim into silence for a second. Then, "Crystal, I just got here. Besides, how could he know where I am?"

"I don't know, I really don't, but he stopped at the gas station where your boyfriend, uh, your ex-boyfriend Ted, works. Ted doesn't have your number any more, so he called me. He said Upshall asked about the weather in Flagstaff, road conditions. Then he asked if you were still driving the SUV that Ted fixed for you, with that white quarter panel that never got painted red. Why else would he want to know that?"

"I don't know Crystal. It could be coincidence. It could be for future reference or something. I just got here!"

"You already said that. Ted didn't like the way Upshall acted. He's worried about you, too."

"Crystal, I have to go." She pushed the off button of the phone and again the cool, forest-scented silence overtook her. Leaning back against the car's headrest, she felt the cold begin to penetrate the floor boards and seep through the soles of her boots. Other than that she felt comfortable here in the driver's seat of her car. Except for her thoughts.

From the time Crystal returned the borrowed gun it had all seemed so clear, her mandate to act and the outcome of that action. Until now. Now things had gotten so twisted. And wasn't Crystal just overreacting again? Crystal did tend to overreact. If she heeded Crystal's warning to leave the camp, she'd be running from a phantom, and with this weather... . It would be dark soon. Better to get into the cabin and start a fire for the night.

With all evidence and thought to the contrary, she turned the key in the ignition, backed up and turned around, heading back toward Airport Road.

When she reached the blacktop she prepared to turn right and then right again onto I-17 south, but an approaching truck brought her to a stop. It was a heavy-duty, late model Dodge Ram, one of those wide, squat monsters with a V8 engine and a payload of over two thousand pounds, nothing she'd want to go head to head with.

Her hands on the wheel were set to steer right but when the truck came closer she saw the driver's face. Upshall!

The truck accelerated and veered across the left lane toward her. Turning right wasn't an option. She gunned the SUV. The tires lost traction against the snow covered pine debris before they bit down and she shot onto the blacktop, swung left onto the road she knew ended at Highway 89A south, down Oak Creek Canyon.

He came up fast behind her even as she pushed the accelerator to the floor. In the rear view mirror she had a split second glimpse of his face, expressionless beneath a dark felt cowboy hat. When he was almost on her bumper he dropped back, anticipating, as she was, the hard left onto 89A where Airport Road dead ended.

She took the turn too fast. The two right tires rose off the road as his truck lunged forward to push her into the trees. He missed her rear bumper by inches. Before he could brake to a stop his truck plowed into the brush. She heard the roar of his engine as he backed up and turned to pursue her. When she turned the next curve she lost sight of him.

The road ahead would drop almost two thousand feet in twelve miles of switch-backs and hairpin turns. The buff colored Kaibab limestone cliff rose to implacable heights on her right and dropped in a sheer vertical fall of five hundred feet at the outside of the left lane. The creek at the bottom of the gorge appeared like a silver thread hiding at intervals among stands of pine. Closer to the bottom, in the ravine nearing Sedona, the limestone cliffs and the basalt lava flow of the east rim would give way to red sandstone and oaks would intersperse the pines and juniper. She wondered if she would make it that far.

She felt the wild beating of her heart pulse in her throat and temples. Her palms were slippery with sweat against the steering wheel. She took each hand off the wheel in turn and wiped it on her jeans. She had a few seconds lead, but he was after her and she knew his goal. When he had survived the Well, he planned to kill her any way he could. Now that way was to push her and her car off the cliff.

Visualizing her only escape route, she knew the stretch of road here at the top formed a narrow shelf on the cliff side but further down the floor of the canyon widened, making room for cabins, camp sites, shops and tucked-away bed and breakfast lodgings on the banks of the creek. If she got that far, she would turn onto one of the side roads to lose him.

She squinted through the windshield at the road ahead, willing the glare of the afternoon sun to dim, to hide her flight.

The most dangerous place would be the hairpin curve just a quarter mile away. In her mind's eye she saw the litter of wrecked cars at the bottom of the precipice, metallic glints of blue and red far below, vehicles that hadn't made it. Another image tried to insert itself into her panicked brain, her own SUV hurling into oblivion, joining them. She refused to let it in.

The next curve to the right slowed her to twenty miles an hour. In the short straight-away following, she saw the truck again in her mirror, less than thirty yards behind. A car approached, going up the canyon, then another. None came in sight on the south-bound slope ahead of her.

She neared the drop-off. She willed herself not to look down the embankment. A sign warned fifteen miles per hour but she took it at twenty, holding her breath. The SUV slid on the inch-thin coating of snow, veering into the left lane within inches of the precipice. Then back. Her breath exploded in relief. But she wasn't home free yet.

A glance behind showed his truck had fallen back. At the turns the empty rear end of the heavy truck lagged the front, threatening to slew in the opposite direction and cause him to spin out. Even her high profile SUV had better maneuverability. Maybe she would make it.

Under the best of conditions, the descent required heavy braking with just occasional taps on the accelerator. Now she kept her foot off the gas, letting the incline propel her. It took her into the next turn wide, into the left lane again, close enough for a hair-raising glimpse of another drop-off.

As she descended further, the glare of the setting sun struck its last, hostile beams through her windshield, seeking to confuse and distort her vision.

Halfway down, out of nowhere he was there, close on her bumper again, so close she could imagine his breath on the back of her neck. Closer. Then contact! He was trying to push her down a forty foot embankment into the creek. The tap of his front bumper against the SUV was a tentative thrust of the knife before the plunge over the abyss.

She stepped down hard with her left foot, heard a protesting squeal from her brakes as they locked. She fought with the steering wheel and pumped the brake as the car slid toward the brink. Another car approached in the left lane. He saw it too. The pressure on her bumper stopped as he backed off! He wanted no witnesses.

She gasped in relief and realized she had been holding her breath again. She inhaled deeply to renew her determination. She stepped on the accelerator. Fumes from scorched brake pads and the smell of rubber filtered through the vents. It filled the car with a stifling scent she forced herself to breathe while she squinted through the glare on her windshield.

Within seconds the glare relented as the setting sun surrendered to drop behind the red sandstone cliffs. Now the gathering darkness seemed to push her downward, inexorably, uncontrollably downward.

She reached for the headlight knob but resisted the habit of switching them on. In another half mile she would be at the entrance to Slide Rock State Park, where the road went over the creek. The creek would be on the left then, and just past that point a turnoff led through the creek and into the woods.

Headlights behind her! Instantly she realized they were too low-set and close together to be his truck. Her side view mirror gave her a brief impression of a Volkswagen Bug. How had it gotten between her and his truck? It must have come out of one of the roadside campgrounds. No matter how it got there it was between his vehicle and hers. Irrational as it might be, she mentally celebrated the sense of safety it gave her.

Minutes later she crossed the bridge. Half a minute after that, without signaling, she swung the steering wheel hard left. The SUV forded the creek raising a huge spray of water. It climbed a small slope then the road took her into a thick growth of trees and shrubs. Afraid he would see the red flash of her brake lights she allowed the SUV to coast to a stop.

In her peripheral vision to the right she saw the Volkswagen flash by and close behind it, what must have been the truck.

Breathless, she climbed out, prepared to strike out through the woods running if his truck doubled back. For long moments nothing, no headlights approached from either direction.

Trembling, she leaned back against the SUV, feeling her body arch back, spine and head against the metal. It felt like the only solid thing on earth. Her arms hung limp at her sides, fingers stiff from her death grip on the steering wheel. She waited, listening to the busy rush of the creek until at last she felt safe and conspired with time and full darkness to cover her return to Camp Verde.

***

Allie gasped and grabbed Bob's hand. They were headed southeast toward Sedona on Highway 89A in Bob's truck. The view was a spectacular composition of form and color. The storm last night had frosted the Verde Valley with a glistening veneer of white. The red peaks and spires in the distance formed a backdrop to juniper and pinon pine of deepest green edged with snow that dazzled the eye and returned light to the sun. The cool, scented air and sun-lit purity of the land were like the dawn of life itself, better than a Maxfield Parrish painting No words of appreciation were adequate. They rode in silence.

Ten miles out of Cottonwood a sign proclaimed, 'Welcome to Red Rock Country.' It validated Allie's appreciation of the panorama rising before them, the contrasting colors like a gulp of water on a scorching day. The intensity and contrast of red, green and white were exquisite. She could almost taste this beauty.

Bob glanced from the road and smiled at her, his tanned face a comfortable presence. "Never better than this," he said. Nodding in the direction they were headed, he said, "Those smaller spires of red rock are called hoodoos. Hiking today could be a little bit of a challenge because of the snow. It could be slippery. So where would you like to go?"

"I've been up to the area around Coffee Pot Rock and Steamboat Rock, and I hiked up on Airport Mesa once, but other than that, your choice. You know the area better than I do."

They had passed the turnoff to Red Rock State Park on the right and were heading down the hill into town when a buzzing noise came from the floor-boards of the truck.

Allie reached down to fish her phone out of a small purse she slung from her shoulder when hiking. She said, "It's my burner phone. It only goes off when it's one of my clients. They don't have my other phone numbers except my answering service. I give a few of them who might be in crisis this number so they can call me directly." Then, into the phone, "Hello. What's happening?"

Crystal's voice was calm. "I don't know about coming to see you this coming week."

Before Allie replied she asked herself if it would be a breach of confidentiality to say Crystal's name where Bob could hear. She decided it wouldn't. Bob didn't know Crystal and there could be any number of women with that first name in the area. She sighed. She knew what this call was about, what was troubling her client. She asked anyway, "What's worrying you, Crystal?"

"Was it you at the Well with my uncle last week?"

A direct question. No option but the truth. "Yes, it was."

"Why? Why would you want to save him? Who told you to go there?" Crystal's voice escalated in synch with her emotions. "What were you doing there? Were you watching us?"

"No, Crystal, I wasn't watching you. I just had a feeling I needed to go there. I can't explain it."

"Whose side are you on, anyway? Is he your client, too?"

"No, no he's not and I'm not on his side, never was and never could be. You're my client."

Silence, during which Allie felt a trace of desperation about losing a client who needed her. The words of a typical co-dependent therapist went through her mind, *I'm only trying to help you. Please trust me.* She chided herself for remembering the platitude and refused to say it.

Into the silence Crystal said, "Yeah, I'm your client but I don't know if I want to be anymore."

"I understand. You have a decision to make. Regardless, I hope you come to your next appointment even if it's just to say goodbye and get a referral to another therapist."

"Yeah, maybe." Then a dial tone.

"Big trouble?" Bob wanted to know.

"No. It'll work itself out." Allie put her disposable cell phone back in the hiking purse. Realizing while on the call they had driven down the hill and turned right onto the highway, she asked, "We're going to Bell Rock?"

"You got it. Not too many tourists around this time of year, so it should be pretty quiet."

The parking lot at the trail head was almost empty. The snow might have discouraged other hikers, but in her water proof boots and gore-tex jacket, Allie couldn't have been happier. The bottom part of the red sandstone 'bell' had a gentle upward slope that eons of wind and rain had washed smooth. The center apex

211

was several hundred feet in diameter and as tall as a two-story house. There was no pathway etched into the rock. Hikers chose their preferred route.

The going was a little slippery but the easy pace left more time to appreciate the transcendent beauty of the area. According to new age mystics, Bell Rock was a vortex of some form of energy. Allie felt only her own physical energy and well-being as she hiked with Bob.

At times Bob grabbed her hand or put an arm around her waist to steady her in a comfortable familiarity. Their pathway circled to the north side of the rock. They stopped before the hike became a vertical ascent that would require climbing gear. They chose a flat, wind-swept red rock as their table, and ate lunch in comfortable silence.

Finished with his sandwich, Bob said, "See over there? That's Back O' Beyond Road, leading up into those peaks. Look at the saddle between the two sections. They say if you hike up there with someone you're--someone you're interested in, and look this way, you'll know if that person is right for you and the right things will happen. Sort of a make it or break it deal."

"Odd. Why is that?"

"From there you get a great look at the top of the Bell here. From a distance, the two highest spires here look like a man and a woman standing back to back. There's a native legend about it."

Allie smiled. "There's a native legend about a lot of things around here."

"This one says the rocks were once a couple who lived in the valley. They were always fighting, arguing. I kind of picture those old TV shows, you know, Jackie Gleason as Ralph Cramden and his wife Alice. Bicker, bicker, bicker. 'Right to the moon, Alice.' But they loved each other. The native couple didn't or they just took it too far. They couldn't stop the arguing. So the Great Spirit told them they had to soften their hearts to each other and become a peaceful, loving couple. If they didn't, their hearts would turn to stone."

"Sounds about right."

"Yep. And that's what happened. Not just their hearts, but all of them turned to stone and there they are." He gestured upward to the top of the Bell and smiled at her. Usually a quiet man, he had just said more in an hour than he did in most entire days. Allie looked into his eyes and thought they were very beautiful.

"And here we are," he said, and bent to kiss her. It was a long kiss, their lips lingering, unwilling to separate.

When she caught her breath, Allie said, "Bob, I don't think we need to go over there to see the stone couple. We're not the arguing kind.

"Yeah, and my heart's already soft enough."

***

At the end of the next week, Wanda buzzed Allie's extension as she prepared to leave for the day. Most of the other therapists were already gone. Leaving early on Friday was something of a custom for those eager for the weekend.

"There's a man here to see you," Wanda said. "He called earlier and I told him the best time to catch you was right before you left for the day, while you were doing your notes."

"Who is it, Wanda?"

"He said his name is Smith, and he wants to talk to you about one of your clients. He's a relative."

"Did you tell him I can't talk to him about a client unless I have a signed authorization?" Allie wondered which of her clients this 'Smith' might be related to.

"Of course I told him about that HIPPA privacy crap. Should I send him back to your office or not?" Wanda had lost patience with her.

Allie grimaced and threw down her pen. "Sure, I'll figure it out when I see him." She put away her paperwork and when she went to the door she saw the man was already more than halfway down the hall to her office, using a cane to compensate for a limp. Other than that, he was unremarkable in appearance, average height and weight with brown hair, wearing blue jeans, shiny new cowboy boots and an open-neck shirt under a green sports jacket.

She held out her hand. "Mr. Smith? Hello, Allie Davis."

He didn't shake her hand or wait for an invitation. He brushed by her, limped to the sofa and sat down. She felt a vague irritation, but no presentiment of danger. Telling herself to ignore his rudeness and get to the point so she could get out of here for the day, she went to sit at her desk. "What can I do for you? Wanda tells me this is about one of my clients."

"Yes, maybe two of your clients."

The sound of his voice. It was somehow familiar but she couldn't place it. Then his face came into focus, a snapshot from recent memory. It was Frank Upshall, the man from the Well. A start of alarm, then revulsion went through her. She believed she was a practiced enough profession to hide it when she said casually, "I don't recall that I have an authorization to speak with you about any of my clients, Mr. Upshall."

He leaned further back against the sofa, stretched his legs out straight and slid his grip on the cane from handle to shaft. "You know who I am, then. You saved my life. You didn't think I'd neglect to come by to thank you did you?"

"You're welcome. Now I want you to leave. I'm busy."

He didn't move. "I expected you'd be a little more polite, seeing how you took such good care of me that night."

"I said you're welcome. We have nothing more to say to each other."

"Come to think of it, how is it you were at the Well that night? If you weren't with her?" He unbuttoned his sports coat and pushed it aside to reveal a large handgun in a leather holster.

She couldn't hide her alarm.

"Oh, it's legal in this state," he said, "I have a permit. Would you like to hold it?" He took the gun out of its holster and held it toward her, butt end first.

"No, I do not want to hold it," she said, feeling the blood rise to her face. "I want you to leave, now."

He replaced the gun. "Not before I find out what I came for. Where is she?"

"Where is who?"

"Kim Altaha. I've been asking around, and I know that both my niece Crystal and Kim Altaha are clients of yours."

"I wasn't with anyone at the Well that night, and I certainly don't know where Ki...where that person is."

He continued as if she hadn't spoken. "I spent a week in the hospital, had to be in a wheel chair for a few days after that little swim, what with injuries and infections in my feet. Made me sick, all that putrid water I swallowed. There's arsenic in it. Runoff from all the mining they did on the plateau, years back. Stuff seeped into the water table and it's still bubbling up in that sink hole."

Then louder, "Where is she?"

Allie was angrier after listening to his monologue. If he thought he was gaining any sympathy from her he was mistaken. She got to her feet, went to the door and stood holding it open.

Upshall unfolded his frame from the sofa and without using his cane ambled to the door with no trace of a limp. He grabbed the edge of the door. With one pull that jerked the door knob from her hand he swung the door closed. He moved in front of it to within inches of her, staring into her face.

She was trapped. An alchemical blend of anger and fear shot through her, a bolt of alarm that raised hairs on the back of her neck.

"All right, Mr. Upshall. Take it easy. Let's talk about this." It felt like she moved in slow motion when she walked back to her desk and sat down. "This is too much at the end of the day," she said, with a companionable smile. "I need some coffee before I can do this."

She picked up the phone, and motioned for him to return to the sofa. She breathed a silent prayer that the prearranged danger signal to her receptionist would bring help. "Wanda," she said, after dialing the extension, "Mr. Smith and I both need a cup of coffee. Oh, how do you take yours? Black. He says black, Wanda."

Wanda's strident voice sounded loud enough for Upshall to hear. "Coffee? Since when am I your go-fer? I do a lot of things around here, but I don't run and fetch."

"Wanda!" Allie's hand clenched hard enough to gouge her palm. *Damn. Doesn't she remember that's her signal to call nine-one-one? If I live through this I'm going to kill her!*

"Get your own coffee," Wanda continued. "And don't forget to turn off the machine. I'm leaving for the day, and everyone else is gone too, so you'll have to lock up." Then the dial tone.

Allie put the receiver back with a renewed sense of dread and turned to Upshall. She was alone in the office with this sadistic nut. No help would come so she would have to handle it.

"Wanda is feeling a little cranky today. I don't think she's going to bring us coffee, so I'll just tell you straight out, and save us both a lot of time. I don't know where Kim is. I haven't heard from her. And why do you need to know? Are you threatening to harm her? Are you threatening me, Mr. Upshall?"

He stared, un-answering.

"You need to remember that you're on law enforcement's radar now. Both the Sheriff's Department and the Cottonwood police and the Maguireville fire department, even most of the hospital staff know about you. If you even think about doing something illegal, they'll know and you won't get away with it. Now I'll ask again nicely. Please leave. I'm tired and I want to go home."

He looked at her without expression. A smothering silence filled the room for a long ten seconds. He motioned with his chin at the diplomas and license displayed behind her.

"Women like you think those papers on your wall make you something special, don't you? Well, they're not fit to wipe my ass on, you snotty little bitch. They're nothing. You're nothing! And I know what those stupid sluts have been whining to you about in here but they can't prove a word of it, and neither can you. Put that on a diploma!" He rose, grasped the cane in the middle of the shaft to hold it parallel to the floor, and walked out of the office.

Her muscles felt weak with relief but Allie managed to rise from the chair and follow to make sure he was actually leaving. She was startled to see that Upshall didn't walk toward the reception area to exit by the front entrance. Instead, he turned the other direction, walked the short distance to the other end of the hall and let himself out the employees' door.

The heavy door, equipped with a push-bar rather than a door knob, closed behind him and locked automatically with a reassuring thump.

Allie hurried to the door, rested her trembling hands against the metal bar and looked out the small window to see him climb into a pickup truck, where he jammed a cowboy hat on his head and started the motor.

When he pulled away she noticed a rifle displayed in a gun rack in the rear window. Dangling from the rear bumper two golf balls had been tied into a section of nylon hosiery--a facsimile of a scrotum, what Mike would call 'truck nuts.' A laugh of derision rose in her throat but was choked back by fear.

She rushed back down the hall to the front entrance to make sure the door was locked, then down the hallway of the other wing to the other employee door, which she found closed and locked. No one was in sight in that area of the rear parking lot.

Returning to her office she reached for the phone before she realized she needed to search her file for Kim's telephone number. Kim had completed her court-ordered counseling and Allie hadn't seen her in weeks.

She fumbled with the paper that had the number on it and then the telephone, feeling her adrenaline rush recede. In its wake exhaustion and feelings of defeat filled her. She should have known; she had been in denial but now she knew that Kim and maybe even Crystal had been involved in the attempt to kill Upshall.

She waited for Kim to answer her phone, wondering what she hadn't said or done, what could she have said or done, to prevent this horrible mess?

A business-like female voice in a recorded message told her the party she was trying to reach was either out of range or not available. The receiver clattered as she all but tossed it back into the receptacle. Then she grabbed it back to call Crystal. She would know how to reach Kim to warn her.

***

On Monday morning she almost ran into Wanda in the door way of the break room as Allie entered and Wanda left with her coffee. Wanda stopped so abruptly a few drops splashed to the floor. "Hey!" she said, with an indignant look at Allie.

"Speaking of coffee, Wanda, did you forget the safety plan? The prearranged signal that you were to call nine-one-one?"

"What safety plan? I don't know what you're talking about."

"That clinches it," Allie told her. "I don't like the work you've been doing here, Wanda, and I intend to talk to the office manager about it, today."

Wanda jerked her head at Allie in a dismissive gesture and walked back to her desk with her coffee.

Allie left the office and drove two blocks to the police station, where she talked to a very nice, uniformed police officer about concealed weapon laws and what did and did not constitute a threat of bodily harm. She left feeling both disgruntled and reassured. Nothing Upshall had said or done was against the law. They would do a courtesy 'welfare check' on Kim and get her perception of what interest Mr. Upshall might have in her. And Allie or Kim could get an order of protection or file harassment or stalking charges if he contacted them in spite of their warnings to stay away.

Chapter 11

In early morning of the same Monday Kim felt sunlight, weak as tepid water against her closed eyelids, something hard and cold on her face. She started, wary of danger, then remained motionless with eyes closed.

Awareness returned gradually. Her body prone but pain free and warm, no sound but that of her own breath and the tentative twitter of a bird. That cold thing? One of her hands resting on her cheek.

She opened one eye. She lay on her right side, her right eye and face buried in the soft folds of a sleeping bag. Her left hand lay curled against her nose, circling her left eye. She watched the morning light as it struggled to top the ridge, as if through a spy glass.

Yes, she remembered. The Black Hills above Cottonwood, the Silverbell Mine. She drew her right hand down into the warmth of the sleeping bag. It felt like a chunk of ice warming between her thighs. She had survived her sixth, or was it seventh night, here in the forest?

The pressure of her bladder announced its need for relief, telling her the number of days was irrelevant. She stirred and pulled her wool hat down further over her brow, but couldn't bring herself to desert the warmth of the 'freezing-to-ten-below-zero' sleeping bag.

Six mornings ago her brother had driven her up Highway 89 and stopped at the place where she knew a two mile hike cross-country would bring her to the mine. Her brother seemed curious but was cooperative about her latest camping jaunt, after he told her she was crazy to camp in cold weather.

Before she got out of the car with her backpack, she gave him instructions not to plan on picking her up. From here she would go to stay with friends and she might not see him for some time. She made him promise not to tell anyone where he had left her. It was unlikely he would give away her exact camping location since he had never been to the mine and might not even know it was here.

There had been plenty of time to think in the past few days as she lay in her sleeping bag or went about the daily tasks needed for survival.

Her mind returned to the past as if on an endless loop, as if an exhaustive review of her past life would reveal the twists of fate that had brought her here, how she had become a failed murderer and now a fugitive.

She remembered Northern Arizona University in Flagstaff, the red sandstone building the University called 'Old Main'. When she had refused to continue modeling and chose instead to pursue an education, she graduated from high school with honors and enrolled there.

The institution had some of the best programs in the country for Forestry, Geology and other Earth Sciences. With many good choices, she still wasn't able to settle on a major. She was turned off by the college social scene and by dorm life.

By her sophomore year she lost interest and dropped out. Now she was just a woman who worked in a hardware store, a woman without a family of her own or even a boyfriend, a woman who had cast herself in the role of 'instrument of karma', on a mission to right wrongs, defeat injustices and defend the weak.

As a Supergirl she decided she had been a failure. Was this her karma, then, to be a fugitive from a maniac who justifiably, or at least understandably, wanted to kill her?

She thought about Allie and told herself a superhero's cape wasn't required wardrobe in the helping professions. Allie had helped her, and she knew that even Crystal had become calmer and more reasonable of late.

Crystal's new antidepressant medication must be working, but a larger part of the change could be assigned to Allie's counseling.

For a moment she pictured herself in Allie's office, in Allie's chair, a counselor herself, perhaps talking with a wife whose husband had just assaulted her or with a survivor of childhood sexual abuse. Could she play that role? She waited for an inner response. It was 'no.'

Her thoughts turned, inevitably, to Upshall. She had heard that he and his Z were under repair now, on the mend, so to speak. Her panicked glimpses of him in his truck a week or so ago revealed they were both tricked out for a macho, cowboy image. How stereotyped and how absurd was that? She and Upshall were locked in a cowboy-against-Indian fight to the death.

She rolled her head from side to side, then rubbed her eyes trying to brush the sleep from her face with both hands, one warm, the other cool.

If only she had found the micro memory card from his phone. Those incriminating pictures were worth a thousand words of accusation. After searching her clothing and shoes a last time, she had concluded with a now familiar sinking sensation of defeat, that she had indeed lost it.

The pressure in her bladder won against the need to stay warm. She wormed her way out of the sleeping bag and crawled from the rough lean-to, much like her ancestors' wickiups. She had built it on a bed of pine needles in a grove just to the east of the mine entrance.

Kim had explored the Silverbell and numerous other mines in the area as a girl. She marveled at their natural mineral formations, the lichens and other microscopic growths, the insect life and swarms of bats. Those impressed her more than the detritus of human endeavor, metal rail car tracks, ladders and other implements.

At least a dozen of these abandoned mines dotted the mountains surrounding the Verde Valley. In them, dreamers and driven workers once dug for gold or silver or copper.

Some of the mines were now caved in or flooded with water and impassable. Others were deep, vertical shafts surrounded by vegetation in the otherwise natural terrain, perfect pitfalls for wildlife or the occasional human on two legs or four wheels.

The Silverbell had a more traditional, horizontal entry shaft framed by wooden beams. A dead tree with stiletto branches stood sentry beside the entrance, an open doorway to a deep unknown. Tacked to the ancient frame of silvered wood a metal sign proclaimed, 'NOTICE   Entering Silverbell Mining Claims   Please   No vandalism   No salvaging' and attached to that a smaller sign, 'Federal Mining Claim'. Its small print, complete with legal citations and other legalese, provided evidence that typical government bureaucracy had reached the wild west many decades ago.

Hugging herself against the cold, she made her way several yards downhill to the slit trench she had dug for sanitation. She had chosen a sheltered, private spot for her toilet, even though any human eyes had to be dozens of miles away. It was in a declivity fifteen feet from a south-facing outcropping of rock that overhung the leaf and needle-covered soil.

The stone of the outcropping was an unusual red color for this terrain due to the high iron content in the soil there. Its overhang formed a shallow, cave-like hollow. When she had relieved herself and filled in the last inches of the trench, she went down on her hands and knees and began to dig another with the help of a small, folding shovel.

Moist humus and leaves flew as she dug, until a sound froze her. An unmistakable rattle. It was a sound that bypassed the frontal lobe of the human brain to target the atavistic fear center at the brain stem. It turned her spine into a rod of ice.

Without moving her head, she searched the ground. There, under the overhang, a rattle tipped tail pointed to the sky and around it, diamond shaped patterns, colors of tan and black, a few lazy, sinuous movements beneath the ground cover. Rattlesnake! Many rattlesnakes!

She had aroused them from semi-hibernation and they were resentful. They would be fatally resentful if she wasn't careful. She dared to draw a breath. Her mind began to work again and she estimated she was not within striking range. Still unwilling to stake her life on it, she began a slow motion withdrawal, first her upper body leaning back, then a backward crawl on her knees until she was twenty feet away.

The rapid fire rattling slowed, its volume decreasing to a softer, more intermittent death knell. With her eyes glued to the spot and heart still pounding, she rose and returned to the relative safety of her camp site.

***

In the early evening of the Friday Upshall visited Allie at her office, Crystal waited until the agreed-upon time when Kim would hike to a place near enough to a tower for reception and turn on her phone. When Kim's number showed on her caller I.D., she didn't waste time with a greeting. "Kim, he's looking for you again! He asked Allie about you. Are you sure you're safe there?"

"Safe, yes, but comfortable, no. My Native blood isn't making this winter time camping any easier. How quickly we become civilized. Heck, I've been acculturated, assimilated, downright homogenized."

Crystal ignored the words she didn't understand. "You left in a hurry. I'll bet you don't have much to make you comfortable. Should I come and bring you something--another sleeping bag or some more food and water?"

"No. After what happened this morning, I decided to find friendlier accommodations. I have a Supai friend who's coming on Sunday to pick me up. She'll bring me down to Havasupai to stay with her. He'll never find me there."

"The Grand Canyon. How cool is that? Close as we are, I've never been there. But what happened this morning?"

Kim laughed, relief in her voice. "What happened this morning is that I disturbed a den of rattlesnakes."

"A den? I didn't know they lived in dens."

"A den, a pit, a nest. Most often they're solitary, but not in winter. In summer they hunt for for shade and coolness. In winter they come out to congregate under sunny rocks, for the warmth. I thought a spot near the abandoned mine was a perfect place to camp because if it rained or snowed I could shelter inside. I built my wickiup in a grove of pinon pines near the entrance."

"They were in there, in the mine?"

"Not in the mine. About twenty yards away, where I started to dig my sanitation trench. That south-facing overhang in the abutment of red rocks. It's a warm, sheltered place, all the pine needles and oak leaves."

"I know that place. You took me to the mine when we were teenagers, remember? That outcropping of red rocks is the only one around there. So your friend is coming Sunday, day after tomorrow? I don't like you being there with rattlesnakes."

"I won't bother them and they won't bother me. But it will be nice to stay in a house down in the Canyon for a while."

Neither spoke until Kim blurted, "You should come too, Crystal, with the kids. Down to stay with the Supai Indians. I know you couldn't stay forever like I could if I needed to. It's just...I know you won't feel safe for yourself or your kids, until he's either dead or in jail."

Crystal was silent.

Kim said, "I couldn't find the memory card, Crystal. Maybe I should report him, just me. You wouldn't have to be a part of it at all."

"No. Not now anyway. Just go, Kim, be safe, enjoy the canyon and the waterfalls and everything. I've heard it's beautiful down there. We'll both think it through and figure something out." She ended the call, "Love you, Kim."

By late afternoon on Saturday Crystal felt her mood lighten as she imagined Kim hiking or mule training to the bottom of the Grand Canyon tomorrow, safe at last. She spent the remainder of the weekend with her husband and children almost believing that things were normal; things were all right again.

On Monday morning Crystal got her husband off to work and then left the house, walking with one hand pushing Toby in his stroller and the other holding her daughter's hand, to see Kaylee off to pre-school.

Toby had just about outgrown the stroller. On the way back he squirmed and literally dragged his feet on the sidewalk until she yelled at him that he was driving her crazy. Then she felt bad and carried him the rest of the way.

At home housework waited, a busy week day, as usual. Doing laundry in the tiny room at the rear of the house, she heard the door bell ring. *Just one of the neighbor kids, or someone selling something*, she thought, and continued to stuff her husband's dirty work clothes into the washer.

She stopped and turned. *Where did Toby go?* The question sent her dashing down the hall, but too late. Toby had practiced his latest skill pulling a chair over to the front door to unlock and open it.

Toby stood in the open doorway backing away as a man walked in. Toby heard his mother's gasp and turned with a wrenchingly contrite look on his face, knowing he had done something very, very wrong. When he saw his mother's expression, contrition turned to fear and he burst into tears.

"Crystal, you're looking good," Upshall said, locking the door behind him.

Crystal rushed forward to scoop up her son in a fierce embrace that squeezed an even louder shriek of fear from him. "Get out! Get out of here!" she said to her uncle.

"What a way to greet family," he said with a dingy toothed smile. "Family by marriage, that is. As soon as you tell me where your redskin friend is, I'll leave."

"No, I don't know where she is and if I did I wouldn't tell you. My husband will be here in a minute and he'll kick your perverted ass! Get out!"

"You never were very good at lying to me. He's at work. I saw him leave." When he stepped toward her she turned away, putting her body between him and her son, who clung to her neck, his soft baby's body rigid with fear.

Upshall reached her in a split second. He pulled the screaming toddler from her arms, stepped to the nearest door, the entry way closet, opened it, dropped the boy inside, closed the door and leaned against it.

Crystal launched herself at him, kicking, screaming, biting and clawing. Then he had her by the throat and as her breath stopped, time also stopped. Curiously, she heard her own inner voice, soft but strong. *Wait, calm down. This isn't helping Toby.*

She forced her muscles to relax. Upshall's back was still against the closet door. He appeared to be unmoved by the heart-rending shrieks and sobs emerging from inside. She felt his grip on her throat loosen, one sweaty finger at a time.

"I'm not interested in your brat in there, Crystal. Your little daughter, now, that's another story. She is so pretty. But we won't talk about that now. Tell me where Kim is hiding."

As her breath returned, so did the warning voice. *You know what to do. Careful, not too soon.*

"No, please," she gasped, through her own sobs. She backed away from him and when there was enough distance between them she lashed out with a kick to his groin.

He pivoted. Her foot glance off his thigh. He lunged forward to slap her face, once, twice, again, until she lost count, tasted blood in her mouth, felt the room spinning.

The voice said, *"Now, tell him now."*

"Wait! I'll tell you," she gasped, holding palms toward him in a gesture of surrender. "Just let me get him," she said, pleading, with her eyes on the closet door.

He stepped away. She flung open the door to take the boy in her arms again. She went to the sofa and sat rocking him in her lap while she whispered soothing words to comfort him. Upshall stood over them, his knees almost touching hers.

She looked up into his face for a split second, then down at her son, and she began to talk as best she could through numb, bloody lips, her voice a bruised whisper. "She's at the old Silverbell Mine, camped there."

A satisfied smirk widened his lips. "Give me your cell phone."

She nodded toward her purse on the hall table.

He retrieved the phone and put it in the pocket of his jeans. He said, "I took care of the land line before I came in." From his jacket pocket he pulled a small pair of wire cutters to show her. "There are other phones, but if you call to tell her I'm on my way, I'll come back for your daughter."

"You will not touch my daughter! Even if you kill Kim, it won't do you any good, because we've got the proof on you. You're going to go to jail for the rest of your life."

She saw in his face that he knew what she was talking about.

"Where is it? The memory card from my phone."

"I told you, Kim took it. Isn't technology great? She's got you, Uncle." Then the calm and quiet inner voice returned. *Wait, don't! Don't make him angry.*"

"I'll ask you just one more time. Where is it?"

She didn't look at him. She wiped blood from her chin with the back of her hand. "She has it with her. I didn't want any part of your...". *Careful,* said the voice. *Don't make it worse. Think of the kids.* "She buried it where's she staying. She put it inside three plastic containers, one inside the other, like nesting boxes. She buried it by the big outcropping of red rock, below the overhang."

"If you're lying to me...".

Good time to cry, the voice said. "I'm not lying, I swear." Without effort, tears sprang to her eyes. "She told me she put it there."

While she lied, a triumphant thought reverberated so strongly she feared he might sense it, *She left yesterday, Bloodsucker. All you'll find there is the rattlesnakes!*

He hesitated. She knew he was wondering whether he had frightened the needed facts from her, whether she was intimidated enough for his purposes.

He stared at her for a long moment then said, "Tell your husband you fell down." He opened the door and walked out, leaving his threats behind to hover like a foul odor over her and her crying child.

Chapter 12

On Sunday Kim began to tear down her shelter, an act of faith that her Supai friend, Bernita, would arrive before dark and she would not have to spend one more night alone at the camp.

Then Bernita called. "Hi, Kim. Sorry I can't make it today. Tomorrow, Monday. We're on Indian time, remember?"

Kim laughed. "Yeah. I might be on *borrowed* time. Get your butt up here, Bernita."

"Tomorrow, I promise."

"Okay, okay. I guess one more night here won't kill me.

"You know there's no phone reception in the Canyon, don't you?" Bernita said. "In the Canyon you'll have to rely on e-mail."

"Then where are you calling from?"

"My sister's house in Flagstaff. I'm here half the time, hitch a ride up or down on the helicopter whenever I can. Almost never, actually. The walk down to the village can be rough."

"That's what I've heard. "

"When we go down it will be on foot or bust our backsides on the mules. I would do that for you and you alone, my friend."

"You don't know how much I appreciate it, Bernita. You're a life saver."

After the call Kim reconsidered demolishing her shelter. She spent another cold but not too uncomfortable night, warmed by thoughts of being in the Supai village with her friend.

The wickiup deconstruction began for real on Monday morning after she had eaten the last of her power bars and dry cereal. She removed another branch from the bee hive shaped shelter and threw it back into the brush, determined to leave little trace of her campsite.

In what happened next, she later understood that her perceptions didn't follow the actual sequence of events. Sounds were out of sync with what caused them, visual memories didn't match muscle memories, some seconds were totally blank. It didn't hang together in memory at all afterward, but that was a relief to her.

In mid-throw of another branch she was face down on the ground...a searing pain in her thigh...the sound of a gunshot. Pain in her side as she rolled over to look up. Upshall stood over her, a pearl handled revolver in his hand.

Before she could react he kicked her in the ribs again. The pointed toe of his boot slipped between her lower ribs, biting deep into the intercostal muscles that controlled breathing. Air rushed from her lungs in an explosion of pain.

Gasping, she rose on her elbows and tried to push away from him with the heel of one foot. The other foot and leg did not follow the urgent commands of her brain.

"Here we are again," he said. He stuffed the gun into the holster on his belt then reached down to grab her by the front of her jacket. He lifted her torso off the ground and punched her in the face. She felt the back of her head strike the ground and rebound. Blood from her nose flooded down her throat, threatening to choke her. She turned her face to the side, blinking away darkness and pin points of light, a prelude to unconsciousness.

She managed to rise on one elbow and turned her face to the ground. Gasping through her open mouth, she saw a bright stream of blood flow into the dirt then slow to a few drops. She raised her head, wiped her face on her sleeve and saw the red-rimmed hole in the fabric of her left thigh. He had shot her.

When she looked up again he was smiling at her. She saw an opportunity. She kicked hard with her right leg, connected with his shin.

Off balance he went down, heavy. She reached into her jacket for her gun, the little 32, but he was quicker. He leaped toward her, grabbed her jacket with both hands and slammed her to the ground, again and again. Then his hands were all over her, searching, pawing.

She screamed, fighting with fists, arms and one leg but on her back, stunned by his blows, her efforts were like those of a frantic child. He defeated her again, as he had when she was a child. He had her gun and cell phone.

He stood, panting, and backed away. He put her gun in his jacket pocket, threw the cell phone on the ground, drew his own gun and with one shot sent the phone flying into pieces. He stepped toward her, landed another kick into her ribs then backed off. "Now we're going to have a little talk, aren't we, Kim?"

When the pain receded enough she opened her eyes to see Upshall sitting on a nearby boulder, aiming his gun at her. His breathing was rapid but with one booted foot on the ground, the other ankle propped on his knee, he appeared completely at ease, relishing his victory over her. His speculative look told her he was contemplating what to do with her next.

"That was some race we had down Oak Creek Canyon, wasn't it?" he said, in the amiable tone he might use with a friend. "If I'd been in my Z, you wouldn't have stood a chance."

She struggled to sit up. "Your Z isn't what it used to be, though, is it?" She turned to spit blood.

He continued as if he hadn't heard. "You know that little Volkswagen that got between us? When I saw I'd lost you, I just ran on up his ass and pushed that little scrap of tin into the creek. He never knew what hit him."

"Just like you, Upshall," she said, "a freaking bully." When she tried to push herself to a standing position he fired a warning shot into the ground inches from her hand.

Both his feet were on the ground now, close to her. He leaned toward her with hatred in his eyes. "Stay down in the dirt where you belong, you dirty bitch."

When she fell back onto her elbows he regained an appearance of calm. "You know, you never were my favorite," he said. You never were my helpless, compliant girl, like your friend Crystal. I wish she could see you now. You know, she told me where to find you."

His face glistened in the mid-morning sunlight. He blinked as a rivulet of sweat trickled into his eye. He took a handkerchief from his jeans pocket with his left hand and wiped his face, keeping the gun in his right hand trained on her. Then he bent to retrieve his black Stetson hat, which had fallen off in the struggle. He backed toward the boulder again. Slowly, he placed the hat on the rock on its crown, to avoid flattening the curve of the brim.

He looked down at her. "Now tell me where you put it, you filthy Indian."

"Put what?"

His snarl brought a froth of spittle to the corners of his mouth. He stepped forward as if to kick her again but stopped. "Time for that later," he said, as if to himself. He looked at her, spread-eagle on the ground, his eyes focusing on the v of her thighs.

"No, you don't appeal to me any more," he said, as if to shock or insult her. "But...hum...". He picked up a branch that was as big around as her wrist. Approaching her, he pointed it at her crotch. She scooted backwards. No use. With both hands he brought the branch down on her unwounded leg.

She heard the crack as her thigh bone snapped. A searing pain shot up her leg through her body to the top of her head. It formed a cap of agony in the nerves of her scalp, then raced back to her thigh.

She collapsed again, limp, powerless, gasping, each breath a stab of pain. She did a puzzled self assessment. Two useless legs, no weapon and the demon from a child's worst nightmare staring down at her. How strange.

Slowly, it seemed, she became aware of the earth beneath her. Cold but firm and familiar, the sweet, supporting earth. Soon it would cover her, protect her. She would be in it, a part of it. Soon she would be dead.

Her death. With eyes closed, in a split second that she vaguely recognized as a life review, instead of herself and her own life she saw the generations preceding her, native hunters and braves, Apache raiders warring with the Whites, the defiant faces of Cochise and Geronimo, the desolate face of Chalipun surrendering his two thousand warriors to General Crook.

She saw the proud, tough, fire-keeping women, hearty children, horses and dogs. So many generations of life, of human triumph and human defeat. It was the glory of life itself, the struggle for existence she had inherited. What had she been given? What had she given back?

His voice came from Hell. "Now let's get to it." he said. "What did you do with it?"

"I...don't remember."

"You remember, all right. I remember too but we remember different, don't we? Maybe this will help." Without warning he struck her thigh with the branch. The spreading gore around the bullet hole spattered onto her face. She felt the explosion of pain, saw a burst of stars behind her eyes followed by a few seconds of merciful darkness. She opened her eyes again, blinked away pain-released tears to focus on the cool blue sky, visible through a fringe of pine branches.

"My phone card! Tell me now!"

Gasping with pain, she rolled onto her side then up on one arm. She extended the free arm, pointing.

"I buried it," she said. "Over there. Under the overhang, the red rocks." A tidal surge of pain swept over her again, weakening and bringing down her arm, but she stayed on her side, eyes open, looking toward the place she indicated.

She could feel his eyes staring down on her. Then the bloody tree branch he had struck her with landed near her face. Unable to raise her head any further, she saw his booted feet when he turned away, then his legs, then his whole body when he neared where she had pointed.

His pace quickened. When he reached the rocks he went down on his knees and began to tear at the fallen leaves and branches.

She heard no warning rattles. His head jerked back as the first strike hit him. The snake's jaws spread wide, its fangs sank into his eye. He stood, reached up to claw at. Six feet of thick, angry sinew dangled from his face. He fell, then struggled up, blood streaming from his eye socket. He drew his gun, shot down into what had become a writing mass. Again and again he shot, the sounds sharp and clear in the thin winter air. The rattler strikes that hit his hands and legs were deathly silent.

236

He went down again. Blood stained leaves, beautiful, diamond shaped, black and tan patterns roiled in a dance of agony and aggression. It was the last thing she saw.

***

The last session was going well.

"Have you had any more of those dreams lately, where you can't scream?"

Allie laughed. "As a matter of fact, I had one that started that way the other night. Someone was chasing me. I knew if I screamed for help someone would come. I turned and opened my mouth and...". She laughed again. "I woke myself up, screaming."

"Scary!"

"No, not this time. It felt good."

"Then I guess that's progress, isn't it? Do you think it had anything to do with that fact that you've worked through some of your own childhood issues while you were counseling those two clients?"

"Maybe. But I think it had more to do with speaking up about things that had confused or offended me, things I needed to say but didn't have the strength or courage to say before. Like about Doctor V, for example."

"Wow!" Then the therapist shook her head, smiling. "I'm not supposed to say that. I'm supposed to say, 'How do you feel about that'?"

"I'll answer, no problem. I feel good about it. Very good. We've talked before about reaching a stopping place in my therapy. Now I think we have. With my background, though, I may need a refresher course, a booster shot from time to time."

"Of course. You know I'll be here for you. It takes strength to ask for help when you need it. That's something I'm sure you tell your clients, too."

"It is. And thank you. Thank you so much. You've really helped me."

"I know. I'm glad for us both."

***

As detached as she tried to be, she got a sinking feeling when Crystal's soft voice on the phone told her, "I won't be able to make it to my appointment tomorrow."

"I hope nothing's wrong. Do you want to reschedule?"

"Let's just make it for next week, same day, same time. Kim is in the hospital so this week when I'm not with the kids I'll be with her."

"Oh, no. What happened?"

"Upshall tried to kill her. I don't know all the details but you can ask her yourself. They moved her out of intensive care after just one day."

When Allie entered the large, three story building she reminded herself that it was a waste of energy to hate hospitals. They were a necessary evil, like public toilets and graveyards.

This one shed fluorescent light on colorful walls and clean floors in an obvious attempt at cheerfulness. Colored lines on the floors of the corridors were coded for different destinations.

Follow the yellow brick road echoed nonsensically in her head as she followed her color to the general medical ward, then to the room number given to her at the nursing station.

The bed nearest the door was unoccupied. Kim lay in the one near the window. When she turned her head to see Allie enter, Allie swallowed a gasp. The beautiful Indian princess was now a bandaged wreck lying supine amid bandages, tubes and tangled sheets.

"Hi, Allie. Don't mind me. I'm just rehearsing for the next mummy movie."

Allie quickly put the ivy plant she had brought on the window sill, and went to grasp Kim's hand. "Thanks for letting me come to see you."

"I'm glad you didn't forget all about me since I'm not coming for counseling any longer."

"When we talked on the phone, you--I didn't know it was this bad, Kim." The eyes she looked into had been blackened. Now the tender flesh was healing, it had turned a sick shade of greenish yellow. The proud nose was swollen shapeless. The skin on Kim's high cheekbones had been bruised and cut. One leg encased in plaster lay atop the covers. The one beneath the bed clothes was thick with bandages. A catheter tube coiled over the mattress to drip urine into a plastic container placed discreetly under the bed. Another tube suspended from a metal stand dripped fluid into the patient's arm.

Kim said, "It looks worse than it is. The broken femur doesn't hurt much any more. The bullet wound in my other leg is healing. The concussion isn't making me dizzy or nauseous any more. The worst is the ribs. They're still telling me not to breathe, but it's hard to obey." She smiled then winced, emphasizing the reality of her pain. "Just don't make me laugh."

Allie sat down in the chair next to the bed. "I wouldn't think of it. Is there anything I can get you? Anything you need right now?"

"Just your company. The nurses take care of me but it's nice to be able to talk to someone about something besides my grosser bodily functions or my pain level. Numbers from one to ten will have a different connotation from now on."

Allie smiled at her, then sobered. "I heard Upshall is dead. Is it really all over now, Kim?"

"For sure. Revenge isn't all it's cracked up to be. All those Die Hard movies and television shows make it look like fun, don't they?"

"Worse, they imply it's a reasonable course of action, a logical next step after a tragedy. So…for you…no more instrument of karma?"

"How can I enforce a universal law, a spiritual law like karma when I don't understand it? I've had time to think about a more realistic plan for my life. I thought about going into counseling like you. What I really think I'm suited for is law enforcement. Or maybe something in the medical field."

"Like a police woman? Or a doctor?"

"Don't look so surprised. It could happen. I like helping people. I don't have a criminal record and if I get a degree in criminal justice I could…".

"Yes, of course. Why not? I know how determined you are, Kim. I believe anything you really want to do is a done deal."

"You know, things have a strange way of working out. Yesterday a lawyer called Crystal. Seems that thirty years ago, when Upshall was married he and his wife took out life insurance policies. He made his wife the beneficiary of his policy with Crystal the contingent beneficiary. Crystal was two years old at the time, but I guess he named her because he had no other relatives.

"That's strange."

"He never had children. When his wife died, he didn't change the beneficiary. So now Crystal gets the money. The attorney told her that since he died intestate, she'll get the bulk of his estate. I think Upshall forgot about the insurance policy. He probably didn't think he'd ever die, so why bother with a will?"

"That is a very strange turn of events. But wonderful for Crystal."

"At first she said she wouldn't accept a penny of his money, but her Aunt Iva and her husband talked some sense into her. Now they're talking about buying a bigger house so her aunt can move in with them. And she's going to see a dentist about getting her teeth straightened. She says she's going to help me with college tuition. I'm considering letting her do it."

***

On the following Saturday the phone rang as Allie carried an armful of clean sheets to the bedroom. It was Heidi, who said that she and Mike had the day off. They wanted Allie to bring Bob to have lunch with them in Old Town.

Allie and Heidi rarely found free time together and Allie loved Old Town. "I know Bob isn't working today," she said. "Give us an hour. We'll meet you there."

She turned back to make the bed. She enjoyed the scent of lavender linen spray on the sheets as well as the burst of color when the bright spread settled and she smoothed it into place. She piled on the four pillows, then arranged the stuffed rabbit against them, one 'arm' under its head in a jaunty pose.

She finished by tidying the room. Lining up her small library of books on top of the dresser, she remembered the message she had received from the *I Ching* about Doctor V. At the time it hadn't made sense, *'...innocent, without guile...ulterior designs will meet with the unintentional or unexpected.'*

Now she knew just how devious and ulterior Ralph VanDeusen had been and how unexpected the consequences for him.

Men, men, manly men. The theme song from a popular TV show floated through her mind, bringing thoughts of her new relationship with her ex-husband, and then thoughts about Bob.

Bob was quiet but so understanding and patient, so easy to talk with, to be with. When she found herself humming another popular song she realized she was happy today, but something more. She felt a sense of satisfaction, of completion.

She drove the familiar stretch of Highway 89 until it became Main Street. She met Bob, Heidi and Mike at the Dillydally Deli, which advertised kosher Mexican food and bagels in twenty flavors.

Like many of the shops and restaurants in this restored section of town, it had character. Little more than a hole in the wall, it had been built in the Prohibition era with a brick façade, now-ancient hardwood floors and a high ceiling lined with hammered tin. The décor smacked of Early Salvation Army, half a dozen small wooden tables served by twenty or so painted wooden chairs, not one of which matched any other.

"My kind of place except it's not real private," said Mike, as they started to enter.

"Let's get it to go."

"We'll take it to the park," Bob agreed. He and Mike had established a cordial relationship after the first double date with Heidi and Allie.

"I don't need to look at the menu," Heidi said. "The bagel specialty sandwiches are the best."

Mike opted for a Santa Fe bagel with beans, corn and shredded beef. Allie chose a Baja bagel with guacamole, tomato and sliced turkey. Bob wanted the kosher pastrami *con queso*. Heidi joked that she would flirt with danger by ordering a Mexicali bagel with shredded beef and jalapeno peppers.

While the owner/chief cook and bottle washer prepared and bagged the order, they chatted with him. He was a small, wiry man with a perpetual smile that said he felt inordinately pleased with his customers, himself and the whole world. He was an unmistakable transplant from the East, evidenced by a Brooklyn accent that offered, among other things, a "cwupp-a-cwafee," and that dairy spread, "buttah."

"Coffee, you ordered coffee?" said Allie, looking at Heidi in surprise.

"Yup. Lately my nerves have settled to a pleasant hum on work days, instead of a roar and a jangle."

They strolled with bagged lunch in hand toward the little pocket park nearby, the site for their impromptu picnic. It was a place to enjoy this cool but sunny, light jacket day when being out doors felt as natural as breathing. Allie was comfortable in her walking shoes, jeans and boiled wool sweater over a turtleneck jersey.

Heidi and Allie walked together looking into the shop windows, while the men followed. Heidi appeared fascinated by the art galleries, antique shops, and gift shops. They displayed an amazingly eclectic range of paintings, sculptures, tie-dyed clothing, incense and bric-a-brac.

Passing the old jail, built in 1929, Bob gave them a brief history report. It had once held bootleggers, obstreperous miners, drunks and the odd vagrant. It was now the Visitor's Center.

"Did you make it to the Chocolate Walk in December?" Heidi asked Allie.

"No, missed the Chocolate Walk. I'm putting it on my calendar for next year. The Old Town Association has wine tasting, salsa sampling, and a farmers' market on the calendar too."

"So that means you'll still be here next year, right?"

"I'm not positive yet. The offer from the National Health Service is a good one but there are probably other ways--legal ways I could pay off my college loans."

By unspoken agreement they were in no hurry to reach their park destination set on the banks of a stream that was one of many seasonally flowing waterways that fed the Verde River. The park featured one picnic bench in a lawn-sized plot of grass that was a rare luxury in this arid region.

They emptied their wrapped food to spread the bags as place mats on the table before they began to eat. After a few bites accompanied by 'uuummms' of appreciation, Heidi sipped her hot coffee. She looked at Allie with raised eyebrows. "Can I ask you a question?"

"Sure, I have a master's degree and a license. That must mean I have all the answers. Half of my clients think I do anyway. The other half are gravely disappointed that I don't."

"Well, then answer me this, oh Oracle. Did you have anything to do with that new receptionist? Because she's great, a drastic improvement over poor old Wanda."

"Yes, I suspect I did. I talked to the office manager about Wanda. A few days later she started interviewing for someone new. I also take credit for that new security system, the red number." She turned to Mike and Bob to explain, "It's a separate number with a red button on all the phones. If it rings, the receptionist knows it's an emergency. She can tell from the extension number which therapist it is so she can send help."

"Score two for you," said Heidi.

Mike put down his sandwich then wiped his mouth. "Sounds like a good system."

Bob said, "For a while there, I thought I'd have to lend you my gun, or maybe my watch dog, Allie."

Mike nodded. "Yeah, she told us about Upshall, too. I'll allow as how Cottonwood is a little safer and a lot happier now he's gone."

"I never did get any real details from the newspapers. What happened out there? " Heidi asked, lifting her chin toward the mountains.

Mike followed her eyes. He said, "As near as I can tell, he assaulted some woman up there. Shot her, beat her real bad. Then, somehow he managed to stumble into a nest of rattlesnakes. They got his face and hands, took out one of his eyes. Then I guess they went to work on his legs."

"Damn!"

"Yep. By the time they found him he was as dead and as puffed up as one of those inflatable knock-em-down toys. More venom in his veins than blood." He picked up his sandwich again, prepared to take the final few bites.

"How does a person get snake bites on their face?" Allie wondered.

"Figure he must have fallen down, or been on his hands and knees for some reason. Couldn't have been for prayin'. That was one bad old cuss. Did things I wouldn't even mention in polite company."

Heidi said, "I hear the woman he shot is in pretty bad shape. How did they find them both?"

"A friend of hers, a Bernita Something-or-other, was hiking to her camp site to pick her up when it happened. She heard the gun shots, and hustled. Danged if I would have hustled toward the sound of gunfire. Anyhow, when she found them she knew he was past help so she just about dragged her friend to the car, drove her down to the hospital. Beat up some, like you said, but she'll recover."

Bob turned to Mike. "He must have been a real coward, doing that to a woman." Mike just nodded.

Heidi said, "I'll bet there weren't many people paying their last respects when they buried him."

Mike's firm mouth took on a strange, grim line. "What they didn't put in the newspapers is what they have on him for his worse crimes. Some old lady kept calling the sheriffs department, telling them about some pictures and videos he hid. They didn't pay it a 'never mind'. But then someone sent in a memory card from a phone. Enough there to send him away for a good long time. Or to Hell, as it turns out. Sheriff's got the FBI and Interpol trying to get a handle on the network he hooked up with so they can bring down the other perverts."

They were all silent for a moment. Then Heidi glanced at Bob. "Can I have a private minute with Allie?"

"No problem." Obligingly, both Bob and Mike strolled away from the picnic table to inspect the nearly dry creek bed.

"I didn't want to say it in front of Mike, but I'm glad he's dead," Heidi told Allie. "I think he was a child molester from what Mike just said, and from other things I've heard about him."

Allie didn't answer immediately. She couldn't violate her client's confidentiality but then reasoned she could explain to Heidi without naming Crystal.

"When you try to counsel victims of sexual abuse, before they can start to heal they need to feel safe. That's something I learned the hard way. I have a client who was one of his victims. Now that she's starting to feel safe, she's beginning to deal with it."

"Well I'm glad for her and his other victims that he's gone. Enough about Upshall the Evil. So, have you heard the latest about Doctor V and his wife? They're closing their practices, moving away."

"I hadn't heard." Allie raised her eyebrows. "It's because of all the gossip, isn't it? The e-mail buzz from all the people on the social services network. They compared notes about his sleazy seductions."

"Doctor V and his wife are doing the walk of shame, right out of town. He'll be lucky if he doesn't get his license yanked." Her smile flashed. She held up her hand for a high-five. Allie's hand met hers with a loud slap.

When she stopped smiling, Allie said, "I don't think he stepped over the line with his patients. From what I've gathered, his efforts were never, let's say, consummated. They were just his way of showing his displeasure with someone, a little game of 'gotcha'. So...?"

"What? You mean did he ever try to run his little scam on me. No. He liked me!"

They burst into laughter at the same time. Mike turned to look their way, then winked at Heidi and turned back to talk with Bob.

Heidi was still not done. "What I can't figure out is why Sherry went along with that sick game of his. What did she get out of it?"

"Simple. She got to keep him. After all, he proved to her that he could seduce just about any woman he wanted. I'm sure she likes the prestige of being a doctor's wife, having an income three times yours and mine put together. A lot of women would consider him a trophy husband. Knowing that might make her a little insecure. Or maybe she's twisted enough to enjoy it as much as he does."

Allie motioned for Mike to rejoin them then turned to admire the Chinese 'tree of heaven' that grew on the bank of the stream. It was also known by the less imaginative name of Chinese sumac. Allie liked the first name best. She could fantasize a heaven whose streets of gold were lined with magnificent trees like this. It was at least seventy feet tall. In summer it bore fern-like branches with thin leaves among huge sprays of scarlet blossoms. It made a three-story-tall display of glorious color.

Indicating the tree, Allie said to the others, "You know, that tree is an invasive species that needs to be eradicated. At least that's what I read on-line."

Mike looked offended. "Dang. I've heard so much about invasive species in the past few years. Terrorist attacks by vegetation, for pity sake. You'd think we were under siege from land, sea and air."

"In a way we are," said Bob. "Boa constrictors and wild boars in Florida. New Zealand mud snails in California. Africanized honey bees in the South, Asian long horned beetles in Vermont. We're in a fight to maintain the status quo. What makes a place unique is its plants and animals, the climate, the terrain, things like that. All these non-native species are stirring the pot, creating havoc in the environment"

"Maybe it's a losing battle," Allie said. "Sure, I don't relish the fact that the salt cedar trees along the Verde are crowding out native cottonwood. The bufflegrass in southern Arizona is giving them fits, too. They say when there's a wild fire the bufflegrass burns hotter and causes more destruction of the habitat than the native plants. They say it shouldn't be there. But hasn't migration of species been going on since the beginning of time?"

"Humans, anyway, have managed to migrate to every corner of the globe," said Heidi. "Maybe ecological balance is an oxymoron."

Allie had to contribute something she'd learned from a show on public TV. "Botanists call China the 'mother of gardens' because so many trees, shrubs and flowers we consider ours, American, actually came from China. Like the magnolias in the South. Lots of other flowers too. Forsythia, peonies, primroses."

"Even the cherry trees in Washington DC that tourists love so much came from from Japan. They were a gift from the emperor almost a hundred years ago, I'm guessing," Heidi added.

It occurred to Allie during the conversation that the human race itself was not in ecological balance. Perhaps there was no such thing in a world where people of different races and nationalities inter-married in a myriad of combinations. They produced an infinite variety, a rainbow of skin colors in the human species.

Other aspects of the human condition were also being melded, national and racial customs and beliefs. There was still a wide disparity in available resources and consumption of resources between regions of the world, but even those were becoming more leveled in the new global economy.

Was that a travesty, a crime against the earth, or did globalization provide benefits to humankind as well as to the planet?

Allie shook her head to dismiss an unanswerable question. There was no consensus. The jury was out and might stay out. It occurred to her that in the end, Mother Nature would do what she had always done-- destroy life, give life, change life, in a dance of extinction and emergence, allowing new creations to rise for their place upon Terra and under Sol.

She looked around again at her friends as they talked and laughed, at the grass, the trees, the sky. Suddenly she knew she was a part of it all, under the sun and inside the circle. She belonged here in the West if she wanted to belong here. The place did not own her and she had no claim on it except for a growing bond of affection, but it would welcome her if she allowed it.

In unspoken agreement they rose, gathered the remnants of their meal to toss in the trash can then turned and headed back down Main Street.

####

A Note from the Author: If you enjoyed this novel, please take the time to write a short review on www.Amazon.com. Reviews are so important for authors. I thank you in advance for yours.

Would you like to read more about Allie Davis and Kim Altaha? Kim stars in a second mystery/thriller novel, *Fatal Refuge*, Book Two of the Arizona Thriller Trilogy, available now from Amazon, on all e-readers, and in libraries. Coming in late 2016, read the third and last of the series, *Apache Refuge*.

To connect with the author, go to her author page on Facebook or access her website and blog at **http://sharonsterling.net.**

Made in the USA
San Bernardino, CA
19 January 2020